# THE
# MONTE CARLO
# CONNECTION

## A Jemima Fox Mystery

**JOSIE GOODBODY**

For my father, Mark Goodbody

*"A life without earrings, is empty."* —Elizabeth Taylor

*"Dear Prince, I must leave you, but I will never forget you, and next spring I will bring you back two beautiful jewels in place of those you have given away. The ruby shall be redder than a red rose, and the sapphire shall be as blue as the great sea."*

—Oscar Wilde, The Happy Prince

# PROLOGUE

---

## Monaco
## April, 1956

Margo Peters heard the cacophony of ships' horns from her cabin. She was still piling the clothes, creams, and other paraphernalia that had been strewn over the small, two bunkbed compartment during the past week into her suitcase. Lastly, she took a blue cloth bag, hidden under a rather thin mattress, and gazed into it. Her mother had lent her a beautiful rivière diamond necklace, a matching pair of earrings, and a little diamond and emerald ring on the strictest instructions, that she keep them locked in a safe at the apartment where Margo would be staying for the next week. Mrs Henry Peters III had read stories of what the newspapers were dubbing 'The Snow Leopard', a cunning cat burglar who had come to the public's attention when jewellery went missing in a smart seaside resort in Montenegro in 1954. It was reported that he would be heading to Monte Carlo for the wedding of Grace Kelly and Prince Rainier of Monaco. And Patricia Peters did not want her diamonds being stolen. Margo couldn't help but think that if this thief was going to be out and about, there were sure to be much more important jewels to take than her mother's.

The potential presence of the jewel thief in Monaco actually rather excited her, particularly after rumours that the future Princess of Monaco had once wanted Alfred Hitchcock to make a sequel to his 1954 film To Catch a Thief, about this mysterious man who seemed to go after Imperial Romanov heirlooms. After all, he had been written about in the newspapers just after Grace Kelly had finished filming the famous movie with Cary Grant. The American press couldn't resist the connection between the 1954 Hitchcock film and the feline thief wreaking havoc on the same Riviera that the movie was set. Margo pushed the bag under the lining at the bottom of the case. Her bag would soon be taken by one of the porters on to the dock, along with all of the others belonging to the transatlantic passengers aboard SS Constitution II. She proceeded to pull the cabin door open and raced up to the see the arrival of the future Princess Grace of Monaco in her new home.

Ten minutes later, having taken a circular route to avoid one of the cabin boys who had been showing a keen interest in her, Margo was standing on the viewing deck next to her new friend and cabin companion, Liz, one of the journalists sent to cover the wedding. Margo knew that Liz was a bit disappointed not to have had an exclusive pre-wedding interview with Grace Kelly, despite them all being on the same boat for the past week. It was the wedding of the century – Hollywood meets European Royalty – but the Kelly wedding party coming over from America on the transatlantic liner was separated from the press, for this very reason.

"Late again?" said Liz, raising an immaculately arched eyebrow. "You'd better be more punctual for the official events. I can't imagine they'd be happy if you weren't where you should be."

Liz was older and wiser than her nineteen-year-old friend and didn't seem to hesitate in making Margo feel her inferior, albeit as kindly as possible.

The sea breeze smelt beautifully salty as they leant out as far as they could over the balcony of their huge transatlantic liner to watch the Royal Yacht, so tiny in its shadow, bob up alongside it. At the helm stood a clearly visible Prince Rainer – tanned and brown in a navy jacket against the April mist. Liz was already frantically writing notes in her neat shorthand, red nails clicking against her pen.

With her blonde hair whipping around her face, Margo looked through the mist beyond the flotilla of boats to the crowds covering every possible surface of the marina and to the large rocky promontory of Monaco harbour, topped with its famous pink palace jutting out into the azure sea.

A murmur ran through the crowd, who were taken out to sea with all the excitement, and Margo looked back quickly from the harbour side to the Royal Yacht. There she was, Grace Kelly herself, the world's most glamorous woman, boarding the smaller vessel. Immaculately poised in a dark dress coat, dark glasses, and a large white hat, she was carrying a little black poodle under her arm.

"Isn't her dog cute?" Margo said to Liz.

"He's called Oliver," Liz replied. "He was a present from Cary Grant and his wife, Betsy." Liz knew everything.

The noise from the shore became louder and louder when the yacht carried Grace Kelly back to the cheering crowds, and, as they sailed serenely through the harbour, red and white carnations began to fall like rain from a seaplane on to the water below. Delighted, Margo took her attention off the royal couple to try and reach out to grab one, and, in a moment, the decks on the boat were covered in flowers as the seaplane turned mid-air and headed back along the coast.

"Well Done to Mr Onassis," said Liz in her New York accent. "That was quite the spectacle." She explained to Margo that Aristotle Onassis had organised the confetti of carnations to be dropped from his private plane.

In the whirlwind excitement of their arrival in Monaco, Margo Peters could have easily forgotten that her all-expenses paid trip to the Riviera was strictly business only. As the personal assistant to Morgan Hudgins, Metro Goldwyn & Mayer's formidable Head of Press, she had been sent along to accompany Hudgins with the coverage of the Royal Wedding. This was an onerous task for a wide-eyed nineteen-year-old who'd never been to Europe, let alone the fabulously rich, fairy tale kingdom of Monaco. MGM had a particular interest in the Royal Wedding: they were the film studio to which Grace Kelly had been signed since filming Mogambo in 1952. Often on loan to other studios, she'd only made a few pictures for them, and their reluctance to release her from a seven-year contract – even to marry a prince – had taken a huge amount of negotiation. Eventually, after much wrangling, they struck a deal that caught the attention of the press the world over – MGM would cut short Grace Kelly's contract on condition that they had exclusive rights to film the entire event. It seemed a fair deal to Margo. After all, as Mr Hudgins had told Margo innumerable times, if the studio hadn't been so kind as to lend Grace Kelly out to Paramount, to film To Catch a Thief with Mr Hitchcock that summer in 1954, she'd never have caught the eye of the prince in the first place. Mr Hudgins was there to make sure MGM got what they needed, and Margo was there to help him.

That being said, Margo hadn't been without her reservations about the trip. The journey to Europe seemed a daunting voyage for a, still teenage, girl. Her mother had, predictably, wanted to come too – outwardly deeming it unseemly for a nineteen-year-old girl to be staying in Monaco alone – but secretly wanting a trip to the Riviera for the Royal Wedding. The studio said no but, luckily, one of her mother's old school friends had come to the rescue from across the Atlantic. Cecilia Burgoyne had written to explain that her own daughter, Henrietta, would also be attending to cover the wedding for an English society magazine, and the two girls would be welcome to stay in her Monaco pied-à-terre. The letter had ended: "I'm sure our two dear girls will have the best of times getting to know each other and will become as firm friends as we are!" Margo dearly hoped so. She had been given a photograph of Henrietta so that she could find her when she reached the busy harbour, and she'd never seen anyone who looked so glamorous. With her dark hair, full lips, dainty face, and big eyes, Henrietta looked a little like Katharine Hepburn. Margo patted her own hair nervously. She was blonde, blue-eyed, and full of cherubic sweetness, but since her week with the grown-up Liz, she was increasingly worried that she looked hopelessly young and naïve, with her slim figure and flyaway hair. She had learnt a few things on the voyage, however. Liz had taken her under her wing and brought her along to all of the parties put on for foreign journalists, lending her lipstick and hair rollers, teaching her how to do her eye makeup, and even lending her a gorgeous green clingy dress for the last-night-onboard party, which had made quite the impression with the male passengers.

An hour later, Margo was stepping down the gangway of the boat, wobbling slightly as her week-long sea legs hit the firm rock of the jetty. She looked up to see a pretty girl who was around her age pushing through the crowds.

"Are you Margo?" the girl said in an English accent. She was just as pretty as she had been in the photograph, but while she'd been sulky and mysterious in black and white there, in real life she had an enormous merry smile, dark almost black hair, and piercing violet eyes. She looked more like Elizabeth Taylor than Katherine Hepburn.

"Yes, are you Henrietta?" she enquired.

"Yes, I am – oh, how do you do? Oh! I am so pleased that you're staying!" She linked her arm through Margo's and led her over to where a little car was parked by the dockside. "We're going to have the most wonderful time! Let me find a porter to locate your luggage – we can take it back to the flat, if you like, and then have some coffee? I know the most wonderful place we can go for an aperitif this evening; I do hope you like martinis. This is going to be such fun!"

Margo beamed. Monaco was shaping up to be everything she'd hoped.

\* \* \*

A few days later, Pierina Pantera was waiting just outside the hotel's tradesman's door. It had been raining almost non-stop for three days and, at 8.30pm on Sunday 15th May, it was only just beginning to cease. Sheltered in the arch of the door, the young chambermaid knew that no one would be coming in or out at this hour. Except, of course, the young man, whom she had met only four days earlier.

Beautiful Pierina, with exquisite tanned skin, long dark hair, and the greenest of eyes, loved Grace Kelly. She had seen her in as many of her films as a chambermaid's meagre salary allowed a trip to the picture house in Nice. She had loved the latest film, The Swan, in which the actress played a princess. Pierina had been standing amidst the thousands of people who lined the streets, hills, and the port of Monaco, all in a frenzy: screaming, shouting, and waving at their soon-to-be princess. Painfully up on tiptoe, gazing out at the spectacle, she felt a tap on her shoulder and, turning around, saw a handsome, albeit mischievous-looking, young man. He was halfway through saying something to her in Italian but, as their eyes locked, he seemed to momentarily forget what it was. She blushed. After stuttering for a moment, the young man managed to ask her if she would like a cool drink. Pierina was torn, wanting to stay and catch another glimpse of Grace Kelly, but one of her more daring friends nudged her into going with the handsome stranger and, with all the joy in the air, she did.

They wandered through the crowd, soaking up the happiness and noise, unable to find anywhere to sit for a coffee and speak above the roar of the crowds. Suddenly, she was alone, only for him to reappear less than a minute later with a bottle of wine, two small glasses, and a shrug of his shoulders in explanation. They scrambled through the crowd to the little park behind the Casino and he opened the bottle with a penknife he'd pulled from his pocket. She couldn't help noticing the mother-of-pearl handle and thought he must be a wealthy wedding guest only wanting to play with her. But that afternoon had turned into evening as they talked and laughed, and he eventually planted a tender kiss on her lips.

"What is your name?" he had asked her when he gave her that first glass of wine.

"Pierina, Pierina Pantera," she had replied.

He laughed; it had seemed too much of a coincidence. "I have a special affinity for panthers," he'd said.

Between Thursday and Sunday, they had seen each other for almost every hour that she hadn't been working or sleeping. And she had to admit that she was smitten. He seemed to offer everything that she wanted – a life away from being a chambermaid – and wonderful dinners in romantic little spots, where he paid for her champagne and oysters with wads of cash. He told her that he was going to spend the rest of his life with her.

Then on Sunday morning he mentioned that he just needed to be able to get inside the Hotel de Paris and retrieve something from one of the suites. He eventually told her that he was a prince from Montenegro and his mother had stayed in the room a few nights before the McCloskeys arrived. She herself had cleaned the room the morning before the wedding party's arrival in Monaco and hadn't seen anything left over from previous guests – but then she had been more excited about finishing quickly and getting down to watch the boats. And of course, the new princess. She was sure that she shouldn't go in but feared that, should she say no, she'd never have the escape from servitude that he offered. And she could be a princess, too, like Grace Kelly.

"Ahh, you are here!" he whispered in his funny accent as he placed a kiss on her damp cheek, and she felt it blush crimson.

"Yes, of course I am here, Nicolai. We must be careful – although all of the guests are busy in the dining room with a big dinner."

"Careful is my middle name – and Lucky my moniker! Do not worry. But I was thinking that it might be best if you go in alone… you can say that you are doing a turndown or whatever it is called?"

Pierina started feeling that surge of panic that she hadn't felt in a while – the kind where her feet started tingling and her heart started palpitating.

"But I don't know what I am looking for or where they are."

"A pair of blue and white earrings. I think they fell under the bed. They were my mother's; she stayed there last week and wants me to collect them for her. They're sapphires and diamonds."

"I haven't seen any," she said, crossing her fingers behind her back.

She had seen an incredibly beautiful pair of very large earrings that were as blue as the sea and had white diamonds around the edge. She was sure that they were very special – she had tried them on only that morning when the McCloskeys were at Mass and she was doing their rooms. They were heavy and the clips pinched her ears, before one fell to the floor. The big blue stone at the top, surrounded by diamonds, came apart from the large piece below. She'd remembered panicking and putting them back in the bag on the dressing table before dashing out of the suite, hoping she wouldn't be reported.

"They are definitely in there," Lucky said with a sudden flash of anger, so she reluctantly agreed to go and find them. His angry eyes had indicated that she had better not refuse him.

Pierina went inside and, without looking back at him for the tears in her eyes, closed the door behind her. She made her way up the stone staff staircase to the floor that the American couple were staying on and crept along the thickly piled pink carpet, past the ubiquitous vases of red and white carnations and roses, to the door to their grand suite. Using her skeleton key, she unlocked it and went inside.

Pierina headed straight over to the ornate dressing table where she had dropped the earrings that morning. There were no jewels on the top, as there had been before. As there were no safes in the rooms, since no one would dream that a hotel in Monaco would be broken into, she began opening a couple of the drawers and eventually saw a Van Cleef & Arpels box. Undoing the silk ribbon, she took off the pale green lid, pulled out a matching coloured leather box, and opened the top. Inside were the earrings: the two 'broken' pieces back together, sparkling brighter than the blue glass in the windows of Monaco's Cathedral of our Lady Immaculate.

Pierina took a deep breath and removed them from the green leather box. Then, after closing it, she put it back into the larger cardboard box and pushed the drawer shut, not thinking about her fingerprints. She ran across the room and opened the door, checking that the corridor was clear before she exited the room. She closed the door and walked quickly but carefully back to the staircase that she had come up on. Just as she was about walk down the stairs, she heard the head housekeeper talking to someone and ascending the stairs. Pierina gasped and slipped back into the corridor before running as fast as she could back to the McCloskeys' room. She knew the old lady would take an age to get up the stone staircase and wanted to get back in the room to replace the earrings. Pierina knew that stealing the earrings was a dreadful idea, just as she knew the earrings did not belong to the mother of the Montenegrin prince. But how did Nicolai know that they were in the suite if they didn't belong to his mother? It was all very confusing, but she didn't want to be a part of it and end up in the infamous prison on the Rock.

"Pierina, what are you doing up here?" the housekeeper bellowed down the corridor.

"The turn down, Madame Portier."

"Very well. I knew I could entrust these important suites with you." She smiled and went through a door to another section of the floor, and Pierina felt immediate guilt at the thought of what she had been about to do. Her sudden decision to replace them, she knew, was the right one

Pierina was about to reopen the suite door when she heard another one open. In fear, she dropped the earrings into a vase that was sitting on a small wooden table between the McCloskeys' suite and the one next door. She hoped that Mrs McCloskey wouldn't check her jewellery that night, so she could put them back in the morning when she tidied the guests' rooms and changed the flowers – which was also her job.

Pierina made her way back to Lucky and told him that she couldn't find any earrings that matched his description. Had he got the wrong room number?

"No, I haven't!" he said, taking the key and going past her into the servants' quarters. "I'll go and have a look myself." She wanted to leave him to it, suddenly wishing that she hadn't met him, but she needed her keys back or she would be reprimanded for losing them. And Pierina knew Lucky wouldn't find what he was looking for.

Twenty minutes later, he came back and apologised to her with her a kiss. But she could see he had a bag of something in his jacket pocket that she was sure hadn't been there earlier. He was also wearing a pair of black silk gloves that he took off and put in a trouser pocket.

"Come on – let's go and get a drink down on the port," he said with a smile. "We can try again tomorrow." And, hooking her arm through his, he took Pierina off for another evening of champagne and oysters at Bertani's.

* * *

It was a warm, balmy evening two days later when Margo came half-walking, half-running through the reception of their apartment block, La Radieuse, and went storming up the stairs to the flat.

"Bonsoir, Mademoiselle Peters," the guardien called out as she passed his tiny office by the front door and waved at Monsieur Bisset.

"Henny! Henny! You'll never guess what's happened!" Margo called as she rushed through the door.

Their apartment was a large suite of rooms at the top of the building with huge windows to the sea and a long, wrought-iron balcony, on which Henrietta sat, hair in rollers, painting her toenails. As their mothers had predicted, the girls had become firm friends in only a few days, and today, after the civil wedding ceremony for the royal couple, they were dressing for their biggest party of the trip – a press and publicity dinner-dance.

"Oh! Henny – the Hotel de Paris has been burgled!"

"What? No! Where all the royal party is staying?" Henrietta paused, nail lacquer in hand, gazing up at Margo – her mouth an O of surprise. "What kind of burglaries? Money?"

"No, not a single note or coin was taken," said Margo, sitting down opposite her, kicking off her shoes. "It was all jewellery! I've just got the whole story from some friends I met on the boat over."

They made their way inside the bathroom. Margo turned the bath taps on and began to hurriedly wash and roller her hair, leaving the door open so she could shout her story to Henrietta who was now sitting in her mother's bedroom.

"So, on the way over here, I met this rich couple, Mr and Mrs McCloskey," she began. "They're close friends of Grace Kelly's parents, and Mrs McCloskey is her godmother. Mr McCloskey made his money publishing the Philadelphia Daily News." She took a deep breath before continuing. "So, they checked into the Hotel de Paris when they arrived and said everything was delightful. It happened on Sunday night when they were in the hotel's dining room for dinner with all of the other hotel guests."

Wrapping herself in a towel and stepping out of the bathroom, Margo found Henrietta looking stunned.

"But that's impossible!" she said. "No thief could have got around the security at the hotel! What did they take?"

"I know! The police said it must be a highly skilled cat burglar, who knew someone on the inside," said Margo, beginning to apply lipstick and rouge in the mirror. "As for what he took – well, it would almost be quicker to tell you what he didn't!" She reached over to her bag and flipped out her notebook. "Around $50,000 of jewellery was taken," she read from her careful handwriting. "Including two necklaces, one was coral and diamond and the other was turquoise and diamond, and a pair of diamond and sapphire pendant earrings by Van Cleef, which, apparently, McCloskey was going to give to Grace as a wedding present." She flipped the page. "Then another friend, a Mrs McLain – her husband is big in horseracing – had a white diamond bracelet taken, which she describes as being Cartier, a Pan… Panth… Panther…"

"Panthère de Cartier?" supplied Henrietta helpfully.

"Yes! Apparently, it had been designed by the original creator, Jeanne Toussaint. Mrs McLain said she'd seen the design on Wallis Simpson's wrist at a dinner in the Caribbean and asked for a replica. And then–" she flipped another page "–you know that nice girl we met on Friday, the one who's going to be Grace's bridesmaid?"

"Maree Frisby Pamp? Who was there for that photoshoot, and

took that snap of us all together in the harbour after?"

"Exactly! Well, she's had all of her jewellery taken, around $10,000 dollars' worth, including a special brooch her grandmother had given her. Grace had to lend her some of the jewellery that the Prince has given her for this evening!" Margo pulled her evening dress off the hanger in the wardrobe and threw it across the bed, before rummaging in the drawers for some fresh stockings.

"Gosh, how exciting! Have the police had any clues as to who it could be?" Henrietta swung around from the dressing table, pulling her hair out of the rollers, and watched Margo hop around the bedroom, wriggling into her girdle.

"Well, they were all taken on Sunday night at the same time as the big dinner, so it can't be any of the guests. However, there's a suspect under the spotlight already! Apparently, Prince Rainier's mother, Princess Charlotte, has a chauffeur called René la Canne!"

"René la Canne sounds like a ridiculous name," said Henrietta. "What's he got to do with it? He's in the employ of the Royal Family – he surely wouldn't risk it?"

"Well, apparently Princess Charlotte is a little… eccentric, and the chauffeur's real name is Rene Girier – he's already been convicted of jewellery theft and has done time in prison for it!"

"No!" gasped Henrietta. "So, it must be him!"

"Don't be so sure." Margo turned so Henrietta could zip up her dress while she undid her rollers. "Mr Hudgins took me along to the police press conference. Everyone seemed keen to blame René for it, but Grace and a Gustave Renault, the Chief of Police, think otherwise. My mother told me before I came that there had been a spate of robberies in Montenegro a couple of years ago, just after Grace Kelly and Cary Grant had finished filming To Catch a Thief. A huge ring was stolen from a Russian princess. It was a large, white diamond panther ring." She used the English term this time. "I heard via some girls at the studio that Grace was very interested in the case – she wanted Hitchcock to make a sequel using the story, but it never came to anything. They never even caught the thief!" She applied a dab of perfume. "They called him… the Snow Leopard."

"The Snow Leopard! Because of his stealing the Cartier Panthère jewellery. Well, they got the cat wrong!" laughed Henrietta. "Gosh, Margo this is so exciting!"

"Grace thinks it's him who stole the jewels, and he must have had help from a chamber maid, or maybe someone with access to the rooms. They're all being interrogated, poor things," she said, as she put her mother's diamonds around her neck and on her ears – hoping that they, too, wouldn't be stolen. She left the ring in the safe – it was too big for her thin fingers.

"So, everyone, except you, will be diamond-less at dinner this evening!" Henrietta looked at her watch, "Gosh, quick, look at the time – we can't be late for dinner. It's the party of the century!"

Applying the last few dabs of makeup, the two girls rushed out into the balmy night where, unbeknownst to them and the police, the Snow Leopard was back on the prowl at the Hotel de Paris for the elusive Romanov sapphires.

# Chapter 1

---

## London
## Thursday 5ᵗʰ May 2011.

O ver half a century later, in London, in an attic flat behind Sloane Square, the shrill trilling of a phone jolted Jemima Fox-Pearl out of her champagne-induced sleep and, not for the first time, she wished that she could remember to change the setting from announcing the caller.

"Withheld number," she groaned to James who was lying beside her. "I bet it's Vogel."

"Don't answer it," James answered, without opening his eyes, sliding one bronzed hand down her back onto the cleft of her bum. "You're still suspended, aren't you?"

"Hmmmfff, suspended," she muttered into his shoulder. "And I thought you were the responsible one." She rolled off him and reached for the phone, squinting at the brightness of the screen, and pressing the answer call button.

"Hello?" she mumbled nervously.

"Jemima. It's Anna," said a clipped voice on the line. "Alexa wants to see you in her office in an hour. And don't forget it's in the new boutique."

Anna, diamond magnate Sidney Vogel's Personal Assistant,

spoke with an acid sharp tone that was nothing new to Jemima. Anna had never looked upon her favourably and, if anything, her venom towards Jemima had only increased tenfold since Vogel's Head of PR had uncovered her office favourite and former Company Secretary, Paul Pratt, as being the co-thief of the world's most expensive necklace, The Vogel Vanderpless. Karma, thought Jemima. Paul was a bully and had it coming, but Anna clearly needed more convincing.

"Of course, thanks, Anna," she said sweetly, and, before she could add anything else, James had pulled the phone away from her, turned it off, and thrown it to the floor.

Alexa Vogel was not only Sidney Vogel's daughter and the heiress of the diamond fortune, but the Director of the diamond empire's sales departments and fifty-five global boutiques that stretched across the planet from San Francisco to Sydney. Jemima Fox was Vogel's Head of Global PR and she had an inkling about what her meeting with Alexa Vogel might be about.

Jemima had recently returned from South Africa where she had recovered The Vogel Vanderpless necklace – or, at least, part of it – from the clutches of Paul and his co-conspirator, the world-famous supermodel, Sahara Scott. This is something that had earned her Mr V's undying gratitude. The necklace had been stolen during a charity gala at Somerset House, only a month before, and, whilst in South Africa on suspension after a rather foolish act of spilling a story to a news reporter, Jemima had masterminded its discovery. But there was one rather major snag: the four largest diamonds, in what was the world's most expensive necklace, had been swapped for cubic zirconias – otherwise known as fake diamonds. Jemima, however, had managed to work out who had stolen the real diamonds: Petrina Lindberg – who, it was increasingly becoming clear, operated in the gang known as the Pink Panthers. When she had returned to the UK, Jemima had been summoned to a debrief meeting with the Vogels and DI Paige of the Met's Flying Squad. They had been so impressed with her detective skills that they had suggested she spend the summer based in Monaco, where the Pink Panthers were likely to be relieving more billionaires of their bejewelled heirlooms. She knew they wanted her to catch Petrina red-handed and retrieve the missing diamonds of the Vogel Vanderpless necklace. These rare gemstones comprised some 196-carats' worth of D-Flawless diamonds, valued at more than half the value of the whole piece, which had been bid at the gala's auction for £105 million. There was a great deal at stake here.

\* \* \*

Just under an hour after she had received the call, Jemima hopped off the number 22 bus at Green Park station. Relieved that the rain was lessening, she walked along Piccadilly towards Bond Street, London's smart diamond district, and saw, in the near distance, the grand fortress of Vogel with its gold-plated doors. It was Vogel's brand-new Bond Street flagship store, which commanded the corner of Piccadilly and Old Bond Street with a direct view of The Ritz, like a sort of diamond mothership. Side-stepping the remaining puddles as she passed the De Beers boutique, Jemima crossed the Old Bond Street junction with Piccadilly, and was greeted by what seemed to be the largest bodyguard she had ever seen, almost as tall and wide as the double door itself. He must be new, she thought, as she didn't recognise him and the grunted "Good morning" that came from his mouth in an Eastern European accent. Odd, as most of the security were Israeli ex-soldiers, who Jemima privately had to admit she found very easy on the eye. He didn't recognise her, and he clearly didn't believe her to be a client, so she quickly gave her name, and he had a brief word with someone inside through his microphone cufflinks. After a moment, he ushered her in.

The Vogel boutique, like most jewellery stores and banks, had airlock-like doors to prevent thieves escaping. Once Jemima was through the second door, the two sales staff at their desks jumped to attention, causing her to wonder if they were waiting for someone extra-important. The new store had swallowed up the two small shops either side to become a diamond palace, of sorts. The west end of Piccadilly had been going through a bit of an upheaval, getting rid of the tourist shops that were edging their way up from Piccadilly Circus and making way for the luxury brands that were increasingly opening their doors in London, thanks to the non-stop influx of foreign bankers and businessmen buying top-priced properties all over the city. Vogel was, undoubtedly, the pinnacle of luxury, and the new store was beginning to resemble a smaller version of Harrods with its regal green and gold signature colours. The theme carried through inside, with interiors so lavish that Jemima felt she could have been inside one of the state rooms of Buckingham Palace. Vogel-green silk carpets had the Vogel logo woven in, five tables had tops made from a pale serpentine marble and legs of gold lacquered wood, and pale gold walls were dressed in cabinets full of sparkling jewels. There was no natural light on the ground floor, for the windows housed even larger cabinets – double sided for both interior and exterior viewing – which also guaranteed privacy for those permitted entrance. A huge elliptical staircase swept up to the first floor where Anna had said Alexa's office was. She could see the VIP suite scintillating next to the

Vogel Gallery that had housed replicas of the company's most important pieces throughout the years. Although she hadn't been to the store, she had been involved with the architect's drawings since she had started at Vogel just over a year ago.

"Hello," she said, smiling at the familiar faces behind the desks. "I have an appointment with Alexa at 11.30."

"Good morning, Jemima," said Charles Fenwick crisply. "Welcome to Vogel's newest boutique," he added proudly.

Charles Fenwick, in his mid to late-fifties, was the Director of Sales and the epitome of Englishness. Today, he was dressed in an impeccably cut grey suit and silk shirt – probably from Drakes around the corner on Clifford Street. Jemima recognised the shirt's print detailing.

"Hello, Jemima!" trilled Lenka, Head of Russian Clients.

Her tiny frame appeared from behind the desk and she tiptoed like a ballerina towards Jemima to give her a peck on the cheek. Jemima was overwhelmed with a waft of Guerlain's Shalimar, which seemed to have been sprayed somewhere near the blond braids that crossed Lenka's head, rather like Princess Leia in Star Wars.

"I will let Ms Vogel know that you have arrived. Please wait here." Charles smiled before Lenka had a chance to speak further, and snapped up the desk's telephone as Jemima wandered over to one of the window cabinets that contained a collection of sparkling ruby and diamond jewellery. Everything Vogel created took Jemima's breath away.

As Jemima continued to look about her, a man walked in and she caught herself staring because he looked so unlike a typical Vogel client. He was a very unattractive, shaven headed, shortish man, wearing board shorts, trainers, and a T-shirt. Jemima's astonishment was only increased when Lenka greeted him with immense politeness and led him over to her desk where they began chatting rapidly in Russian.

The man sat down at Lenka's desk table, probably said a few short sentences about what he was looking for, and then started tapping away on his iPhone with stubby fingers while Lenka produced tray upon tray of stunning pieces of Vogel jewellery. After a few minutes of examining the jewels in careful silence, he barked some unintelligible orders into his phone, in what Jemima could only assume was one of the hundreds of Russian minority dialects. Less than a minute later, in walked a small man wearing a too large shiny grey suit and carrying a briefcase. As he clicked the case open, for who she presumed was his boss, Jemima caught a glimpse of piles and piles of £50 notes, most of which were then taken out and handed over to Lenka in exchange for an elegant green and gold ribbon-tied bag.

Jemima snapped back to attention as Charles announced that Alexa was ready for her and to follow him. It almost looked as though he ice-skated as he moved smoothly over the shiny new marble floor to the impressive staircase and floated up it, while Jemima went more carefully – the carpet was new and silky, so the last thing she needed was to slip down and land with a thud at the feet of, what appeared to be, a Russian mobster.

"This way," ushered Charles at the top of the stairs.

Passing the Vogel Gallery and VIP suite, they walked towards a lit cabinet holding some small examples of Vogel jewellery: little pendants and delicate earrings. Vogel had recently bucked tradition and launched a diffusion line called Vogelette, aimed at the children of their clientele who were too young to wear their show-stopping high jewellery pieces. This didn't stop the little girls from receiving Vogel gifts in their luxurious gold and green bags, or indeed buying their own small pieces of jewellery. Mr V had thoroughly approved – after all, it was important to tempt them away from Tiffany, who had managed to corner the teenage market. With all the celebrity babies and little Middle Eastern princesses giving their mothers a run for their money, Jemima thought it would no doubt be another triumph for Vogel.

Charles pressed an ornate switch and the cabinet slid to the side to reveal an inner office. It was huge, with a large carved oak table in the middle, which was bare apart from a sleek black Apple Mac Air. The walls were covered with frames of photographs of fashion shoots, magazines covers, celebrities, and socialites dressed in diamonds and other precious stones from the Vogel collections over the years. There were photographs of Alexa with various film stars on various red carpets – the Oscars, as chair of the Met Ball with Anna Wintour, movie premieres – and with her father and son at Buckingham Palace when Mr V received his MBE over a decade ago. The far wall was dominated by a huge nude of Alexa by Lucien Freud, which was rather difficult not to stare at.

"Ms Vogel." Charles spoke nervously to the back of Alexa's chair. She was sitting facing away from her desk, and Jemima thought that this was probably to intimidate her. "Jemima Fox-Pearl is here."

"Thank you, Charles," Alexa replied. Her voice was as sharp as the cut diamonds she sold. "You can leave us now."

# Chapter 2

---

## Vogel Boutique, Old Bond Street

As the door closed behind the store director, Alexa swung her green leather chair around in exactly the same manner her father did.

"How was your long weekend?" Alexa asked as she put down her phone on the glass desk in front of her. "Do sit down – you're making me nervous."

Jemima, who had opened her mouth to reply, sat quickly. She couldn't believe that was true but felt much better for sinking into a pale blue leather chair.

"It was lovely, thank you. What a wedding. Wasn't it an incredibly beautiful dress that Kate wore?" she asked semi-rhetorically, trying to calm her nerves. She wondered if something had happened between now and the meeting she'd attended on Friday with the Met police and the Vogel family.

"Very much so. Sarah Burton is an incredibly clever designer," Alexa said firmly, briefly looking down at her own outfit that was designed by the same woman. She smiled at Jemima, just as her Blackberry pinged. "Right, I have someone downstairs who I must see," she said, looking at the diamond encrusted Vogel watch, before tapping something on her phone, putting it down again, and continuing, "but we've got some time. Now, thanks to your revelation at Friday's meeting with my father and DI Paige, some new intelligence has come up in relation to Nicolai Poparic and his family."

With long pale pink nails, manicured like a Manhattan Upper East Sider, Alexa opened one of the Vogel embossed files that they kept on each client. As usual, the cover was marked 'Confidential' and she pulled out a stapled sheaf of printed A4 papers and pushed them across her glossy glass desk to Jemima, who apprehensively picked them up. On the front page was typed simply "TCAC".

"My father was going to brief you when you arrived in Monaco tomorrow," Alexa continued, "but there is an important Interpol meeting that he is attending, so he has asked that I do so instead." She raised her eyebrows. "He would also like you to attend the Interpol meeting with him as it might prove important to your other task."

"Another task?" Jemima asked.

"Yes." Alexa took a sip of water from the crystal glass on her desk. "Firstly, to recap, as we said on Friday, when you are in Monaco, not only do we want you to keep an eye on Petrina, we want her to lead you to the Vogel Vanderpless diamonds that she stole. We want these missing diamonds back for Mr Petrovich who bought them at the auction. We also want to make sure that Petrina and the Pink Panthers don't pilfer anymore precious pieces of ours."

Jemima wished that she knew what this Petrovich looked like, but her drink had been spiked during the April charity gala and she could still barely remember who anyone was.

"I need you to befriend her," Alexa continued. "Introduce her to the Vogel Boutique in Monaco. Ask if she'd like to borrow anything for her mother's premiere. But never let on about the Vogel Vanderpless necklace or the remaining stolen gemstones – don't bring it up at all. You're not to let on that we know she has them."

Jemima looked at Alexa with panic rising in her stomach. This was not going to be a walk in the park, but she already knew about this 'task', so what else was she being expected to do while down there?

"But there is something else that we want you to do. Equally as important." Alexa said.

Jemima wished she was recording the conversation; she knew Alexa was in a hurry, but she was speaking so quickly it was hard to keep up.

"As you know, my father had been an apprentice at Van Cleef & Arpels in New York in the mid-fifties. While he was there, Van Cleef was commissioned by a Mrs McCloskey to design a pair of earrings around two large sapphires that had apparently come from a Russian tsarina. Although," she added wryly, "a great deal of jewellery is said to have been Russian at that time, particularly in America. The earrings were to be a wedding present from her godmother to Princess Grace, but they were stolen just days before the ceremony."

Jemima's ears pricked up at this. The theft of a pair of earrings that had a link with Princess Grace of Monaco sounded vaguely familiar, but she couldn't for the life of her remember why. She made a mental note to Google it when she could.

"Do they know who stole them?"

Alexa smiled. "It was believed to be the Snow Leopard."

"Petrina's grandfather!" Jemima exclaimed. After all, they had been talking about him only in the meeting on Friday.

"Precisely. It is rumoured that he was responsible for a spate of burglaries across Europe in those years – but the earrings were never found. Anyway, my father got to know Princess Grace in the late Seventies when he opened the Monte Carlo boutique. He said that he would create a replica pair of the pendant earrings that he had helped make as an apprentice. Sadly, the Princess died before he was able to find the right coloured sapphires. The original Romanov ones were a beautiful pale blue from Ceylon that were very rare."

Jemima knew quite a bit about sapphires since starting at Vogel. For example, she knew that 'Ceylon Sapphires', from Sri Lanka, are generally thought of as being the highest quality sapphires, along with those from Burma and Kashmir. However, the gemstone can be found in many places on the planet, and she remembered the ancient and romantic story of how King Solomon and the Queen of Sheba wooed each with 'coloured stones' from this magical island off the tip of India. It was thought that these would have been sapphires, as the gem comes in many more colours than the traditional hues of blue, and occurs in Sri Lanka in abundance. In fact, as she'd learnt, if someone is talking about 'a sapphire', they are referring to the blue variety – the best of which is Royal Blue. Other Ceylon sapphires can be pink, green, or yellow. Sapphires also come in orange, violet, and even black. Jemima thought about Sri Lanka, and how she'd love to visit the sapphire mines, particularly the deposits of the very rare Padparadscha sapphire that has a pinky-orange, almost peachy hue. It is important to differentiate that a red sapphire is, in fact, a ruby. Rubies and sapphires are formed of the same mineral: corundum. The particular coloured sapphire that Mr Vogel had finally found, after thirty years of searching, was an unusually pale cerulean colour – almost azure, as opposed to the traditional darker blues that sapphires are often seen in.

"Now, as you know, it is the premiere of the movie *To Catch a Thief* next week in Monte Carlo," Alexa continued. "It is the first screening of this year's Cannes Film Festival."

"Oh, yes – it was before I started, but you lent the jewellery that's in the movie." Jemima had seen lots of the movie stills; she had been working on a big article in Vanity Fair's September issue to coincide with the movie's worldwide premiere, after it had been shown at Cannes.

"Exactly, my father was approached by Chuck Chaffinch to lend jewellery to be used in the remake of the original Grace Kelly and Cary Grant movie. Chuck is a friend of mine and although we have never been involved in lending our jewellery for red carpet events, let alone film shoots, my mother wanted us to be involved. Plus, the gala premiere next week is in aid for the Princess Grace Foundation, with tickets selling for €10,000 a seat."

Jemima gasped, then, in order to cover herself, she slipped in, "I met the director at Christmas in Dorset."

"Donald Jones Jr." She was pleased to get an impressed nod from the glamorous woman in front of her.

"Well," said Alexa, shuffling the papers. "Don is a great guy. The movie should be fantastic, and I am pleased that we will get great coverage in a way we don't normally do. Well done on the Vanity Fair piece, by the way. Graydon Carter sent it to me a draft for approval. I told him that you would send the journalist information to be added about the Princess Grace Sapphire Earrings, now that they've reshot the cover with Evie Talbot wearing them."

Evie Talbot was the movie's leading lady, taking on the role of

Francie Stevens, that Grace Kelly had played in the original 1954 Hitchcock film. The September issue was now going to have a cover of Evie wearing a priceless pair of Vogel diamond and sapphire pendant earrings, called the Princess Grace Sapphires, with the story behind the movie's remake and the jewellery that Vogel had lent being the lead piece of that issue. Jemima hadn't yet seen these mysterious earrings, and she didn't know why they were 'priceless'. Everything Vogel sold was priceless, or rather overpriced. It was really hard being the Head of PR for a brand that didn't share many secrets.

"When the movie was being filmed back in 2009," Alexa continued, "we knew nothing of the its connection with Nicolai Poparic, aka the Snow Leopard. You bringing it to light has, in fact, unearthed a potential problem."

"What is the connection?" Jemima asked. "And the problem?" she added nervously, wondering what on earth she could have done now to have caused it!

"The movie's producer is Fortunata Lindberg."

"Petrina's mother!" Jemima exclaimed. "So, the Snow Leopard's daughter!"

"Precisely. I've met Fortunata. She's divine and we became friendly during production. Although I've not seen her since the Vanderpless auction when she was having dinner at Annabel's, there is absolutely nothing to hint that she has anything to do with jewellery heists. Goodness, if so, she could have easily stolen some jewellery two years ago on the set in Monaco!"

Jemima's mind was busy making two and two equal four; she felt that she had missed something and looked at Alexa, trying to seem on the ball, but, despite her calm outward composure, she was internally struggling.

"So, we are not unduly concerned that there will be a heist on Monday night during the premiere. Of course, Interpol, the Monaco police, and our security are going to be on the ground before and during the event. As the movie's official jewellers, we are lending several of the pieces – initially borrowed for the film – to be worn by the actresses Glenn Close and Evie Talbot that evening. And Jane Fonda, Jessica Chastain, and several other actresses who will be attending the gala, will be borrowing Vogel jewels." Alexa paused and Jemima realised that while she was away in South Africa, a lot of exciting work had been going on. "However, what concerns you is the close connection between Petrina and the Pink Panthers, the bunch of Balkan jewel thieves. On paper, she is a beautiful American lawyer, with a movie producer mother and a father who is incredibly highly thought of in Manhattan."

"However, as we know, her grandfather was once the world's biggest jewel thief. And she has proven to be taking on his mantle. She will be at the event with the perfect insider's opportunity to organise a jewel heist." Jemima interrupted, and sighed – she had got there.

"Exactly." She gave Jemima a frozen smile. "We have, since Friday's meeting, received intelligence from both a Private Detective and Interpol that there are increasingly more similarities between the Pink Panthers and the old work of the Snow Leopard. Not least, they are also targeting very valuable estate pieces of jewellery as opposed to *only* modern jewellery. Of course, it is the season for the thieves down on the Riviera, and we believe that the event we are sponsoring – which is being held on The Rock of Monaco – is a principle target. Petrina's grandfather managed to steal for several decades in Monaco, so I don't think Petrina will have much of a problem sauntering in and out of a venue she has a legitimate excuse for being at." She took a sip of water. "Why Petrina is now doing the work her grandfather was put in prison for, as opposed to sticking to her seemingly successful career as a lawyer at Nortakers, is anyone's guess. But it is also increasingly possible that her grandfather isn't dead and is actually behind this whole Panther operation. As I said, there are several traits that the Private Detective has said are similar to those of the old Montenegrin. Namely, the theft of former Romanov jewellery.

Interpol has been trying to track down whoever is running the gangs since it started in the late nineties. They don't believe it is *the* Nicolai Poparic, despite us presenting our own findings. In fact, officially, they won't even entertain it. Except one man, Charles Renault, who is the Head of Police in Monaco and runs the Interpol international jewel thefts division from the principality."

"And you are entrusting me to safeguard these special Princess Grace Sapphire Earrings, as well as track down the remaining Vogel Vanderpless diamonds?" Jemima asked.

"Well, yes, I suppose so." Alexa smiled as much as her Botox allowed, and Jemima was thrilled. Her favourite job was back – and now she was being sent to Monte Carlo for the film festival! But she was sure there was a catch.

"But what is so special about the sapphires? I guess I should know if I am putting my life on the line for them?" Jemima semi-joked still not knowing what the big deal with them was.

"I hardly think Petrina is likely to start a shoot-out on a red carpet, is she?" Alexa admonished. "The original sapphires that my father worked with at Van Cleef in the fifties were set with a pair of very rare sapphires that were supposed to have been part of a brooch worn by the Romanov Tsarina Maria Feodorovna..."

"They were stolen by the Snow Leopard and never seen again…" Jemima interrupted.

"Yes. They were called the Romanov Sapphires, and were originally set in the brooch alongside a much larger sapphire that Cartier once had," Alexa said with a sniff – the Vogels weren't overly friendly with the other fine jewellery houses. "These are of an equally high quality and are a beautiful cornflower blue, from Sri Lanka. They are extremely rare and took my father decades to find, finally having been mined in 2009, we bought them and created the earrings later that year."

"I wonder if Petrina saw some of the designs when she was dating Danny, after all I know that she was up in his office before the gala in April?" Jemima said. "Maybe she told her grandfather that somehow the earrings that he stole decades earlier had resurfaced?"

Alexa looked at Jemima with an unusual stare of respect. "She might very well have done. After all, they appear identical to the originals." Then she changed tack, "But I would like you not to mention that she was in Danny's office." Danny was her son and in charge of the buying and selling of diamonds and fine gemstones. He and Petrina had dated for a few weeks and she had been his date at the charity gala in April when the Vogel Vanderpless was stolen.

Jemima nodded, but it was useful information to have she acknowledged to herself.

"Read through the notes and call me if you have any questions, but everything is in the file, including a new company credit card." Alexa had moved on. "Please use it sparingly, but, if you're going to Monaco, you'll need more than a PR's salary."

"Yes, thank you." Jemima hesitated, amazed that Alexa was

actually sort of admitting that she wasn't paid enough. "Where will I stay?"

"We have rented you an apartment for a couple of weeks. It's all in there." She pointed to the file on the table. "I know that Fortunata is staying at The Fairmont Hotel, so Petrina might well be too. I think that she will have Vogel Vanderpless diamonds with her if she is carrying them for her boss, to hand over down on the Riviera. If she invites you back to her room, go with her and try to find out the code to her room safe."

Jemima nodded.

Alexa pushed her chair back and stood up. "Right, Jemima, you will be meeting my father tomorrow at the Hotel de Paris in Monaco for the Interpol meeting. The officers in charge of the investigations into the Pink Panthers will be there – they'll give you any more information you need and go through the details with you, I'm sure."

"Yes, right, okay. Thank you, Alexa." Jemima picked up her bag from the floor and stood up. "I'll keep you posted." she said confidently, although she was quite apprehensive.

"Jemima, you will do fine. Just catch the cat!" she said with a wink, pointing to the acronym, TCAC, on the file before picking it up and handing it to Jemima who placed it inside carefully inside her bag.

For a second, Jemima was confused. A cat? Oh, yes! Panthers and Leopards – clever. She was going to catch the cat, get back The Vogel Vanderpless, and look after Evie Talbot, or rather the priceless pendant earrings, at the premiere. TCAC – To Catch a Cat, she repeated, as she turned towards the door with the file in her bag.

Then, just as Alexa opened the door with a pressure point on the floor, she added, "Oh, and Jemima, one last thing. . ."

Jemima turned, midway to the door.

"Try to be less Bridget Jones and more Bond Girl this time. If you want to catch this girl, then think like her, be like her." Alexa looked up, scrutinising her. "I want you to go to my hair stylist at The Dorchester. Tell them I sent you and that you need a good cut and colour. It's the Carol Joy Salon in the spa. Ask for Valerie. She's been looking after my hair for as long as I can remember. In fact, they've a branch at The Fairmont Hotel in Monaco which I use when I'm there. You can put it on my account. Afterwards, use that card to update your wardrobe," she said in a voice that Jemima couldn't decide was kind or condescending.

And with that, Jemima was dismissed.

# Chapter 3

---

## Cecconi's, Mayfair

As Jemima left Alexa's office and walked carefully down the silk-carpeted stairs, she was pleased to see that the coarse Russians had gone. The smile of satisfaction on Lenka's face meant the briefcase of banknotes must have bought a lot of diamonds and made the tiny lady an impressive amount of commission. With the file Alexa had given her burning a hole inside her Dior tote, she gripped the bag tightly and headed directly for the door. Just as Jemima reached the bottom of the sweeping staircase, however, she noticed someone vaguely familiar out of the corner of her eye. He quickly crossed the marble floor and slipped up the stairs behind her. Alexa's mystery man, perhaps? Alexa was famously single, despite being seen in tabloids both sides of the Atlantic with prospective new suitors at least once a week. Stepping onto the street, she clocked the large guard pulling out his mobile and sending a furtive text message. Not very professional, she thought, but it was probably pretty boring standing outside a shop all day long.

Jemima walked up Old Bond Street, thinking how she would love to go over the road to the office behind The Ritz, say hello to the team, and find out all the office gossip on Paul Pratt and Sahara.

She wondered if they were still held up in a third-world prison in South Africa for stealing the Vogel Vanderpless. She had forgotten to ask Alexa for an update, and there had been nothing in the papers over the weekend – whether this was due to Prince William's Wedding or Mr Vogel's influence, she didn't know. She'd also forgotten to ask about whether there was any news on whether the Vanderpless and the Cullinan were, in fact, originally part of the same stone. Jemima was sure they were, which would make the Vogel Vanderpless diamonds almost as valuable as the various Cullinans belonging to the Royal Family and locked in the Tower of London.

Jemima checked her phone to see if James had called. Just as momentary disappointment fluttered in her stomach that he hadn't, a text came through to say that he hoped the meeting had gone well and that he was going to head out to Royal Berkshire Club for a game of polo with the owner.

So, thought Jemima, a free day in London. Perfect. She could go to the salon at The Dorchester and then update her wardrobe at Selfridges or Harvey Nichols, but first she needed to read the file and have something to eat: she was starving after a long night with James. Without needing to think, she continued a few feet up the street, before taking a right at Ralph Lauren. Within minutes she had walked through the door of one of her favourite restaurants, Cecconi's.

The mid-morning warmth and buzz of the restaurant was especially welcoming after the rain outside. She had barely taken two steps when she heard a shout of, "Jemima! Where have you beeeeen?" from Giacomo, the manager, who welcomed her like a long-lost friend and ushered her into her favourite seat at the far side of the marble-topped bar. It was the best position to see everyone. As Jemima sat, she spotted and waved at a friend, the restaurant critic for The Daily Telegraph, who was having a coffee with his wife. The sight of them sitting together made her think of James for the hundredth time since she kissed him goodbye only a couple of hours earlier. Her mind drifted to all the things they had done during their two-night stay at the country house hotel Cliveden earlier that week. They'd barely left the room, exploring each other's bodies, instead of the luxurious establishment next to the Thames. She couldn't wait to tell her flatmate Flora every detail, and decided to text her. Flora only worked on Bruton Street and, like Jemima, was a firm fan of Cecconi's signature passion fruit martinis. But probably not at that hour.

"What would you like? Eeet's on the 'ouse!" sang Giacomo, as Jemima reached for a copy of The Times left on the bar, which was next to a man who had just sat down. Without waiting for her to reply, he said, "Ah, but I think what you would like is juice of half an orange and half a grapefruit, a long super-hot soya cappuccino in a latte glass, and Eggs Florentine with the Hollandaise sauce on the side – I know you Jemima! You've been up late again." He winked at her.

Jemima smiled, impressed he could remember her breakfast order. "Grazie, Giacomo." A cappuccino appeared moments later.

Wanting to read the file, Jemima put the unopened copy of The Times onto the empty green leather stool next to her and immediately noticed as the man picked it up and swapped it for the paper he was reading.

"Sorry, was that yours?" she asked him, and he looked up at her.

"No, no, it wasn't. I was actually reading *The New York Times*. But I prefer the UK version!"

"Oh, right – I've not heard many Americans meriting some of ours over theirs,' she said, recognising the sharp East Coast New Yorker accent.

"Except for your history.

"Exactly! We do go back a little further than you in terms of that."

"Colt Bond," he said, sticking out his hand.

"Jemima Fox-Pearl," she replied, wondering if she was being chatted up.

"You live around here?"

"No one lives around here!" Jemima laughed. "Unless they're Russian or Arab. Mayfair is far too expensive. I live in Chelsea," she said, thinking that, actually, that was also pretty expensive – if you didn't live in a tiny attic flat with a six-flight staircase to climb first.

"That's nice, I am just here on vacation," he continued, and she wondered why he was being so friendly. Was he flirting? She decided to put him off.

"Great, I am more of a beach holiday kind of girl. So, I am off to Monaco and The Riviera tomorrow with my boyfriend for a few weeks." She hoped she hadn't said 'boyfriend' too obviously.

"How cool," he said.

Satisfied that he had now turned to read the paper and didn't want to talk any further, Jemima pulled out the file and opened it up. The report gave a brief overview of Nicolai Poparic, his wife, and their life of crime in Monaco between 1956 and the early 1980s. Nothing was mentioned of their daughter or indeed their granddaughter, Petrina. It then listed all the thefts of the Pink Panthers since the gang began in the late 1990s, including how they got their moniker, which was in 2003 following a heist at Graff

Diamonds just around the corner from where she was sitting, and some reports from Interpol.

Jemima guessed that she would learn more the following day when she arrived in Monaco for the meeting with Mr Vogel and Interpol. Suddenly, she felt excited. After all, James had said he'd be down for work for a week, plus it was the Cannes Film Festival next week and the Monaco Grand Prix in ten days. Maybe they would be able to get tickets to watch it? James said that he normally stayed at The Fairmont, which was renowned to have the best viewing of the famous hairpin bend on the track, as well as the most incredible rooftop swimming pool.

Jemima was just about to turn over the page to read a report on the Pink Panthers from The New Yorker when both her brunch and her flatmate arrived at the same time.

"Jemima! Is that work? Put it away and tell me what's going on! I didn't know you had a job at the moment, or have they reinstated you? And tell me all about Cliveden! I'm so jealous. Benjy wouldn't know how to book a bed and breakfast if you left him step-by-step instructions! Although he is meeting me at Aubaine on Dover Street for lunch in a bit." The Honourable Flora Fairfax slid into the seat next to Jemima and stole a sip of the now tepid frothy coffee from her abandoned cup.

Jemima quickly described just a few of the best parts of her romantic getaway, before dropping her voice and telling Flora she was being sent to Monaco.

"Lucky you going to Monaco!" gasped Flora. "Are you staying with Delfine?" Delfine was a Dutch friend of Jemima's who she'd stayed with the previous year for the Monaco Grand Prix.

"No! Vogel have rented me an apartment for a month!"

"How exciting! I am going to miss you though, darling. The

flat's been so lonely this past month, and now, just as you're back, you're off again!"

"You can come and stay." Jemima hugged her friend. "Don't forget, we've got Alice's marriage in Gassin in ten days. It's an only an hour or so down the coast. You can come down earlier and we can hang out on the beaches to get a tan in time for the wedding weekend," she giggled. "The sooner you arrive in Monaco, the sooner you can help me catch the cat and then we can have fun!"

"The what?"

Jemima explained in a whisper what she was really going to be doing on her trip.

Flora's mouth, now full of her friend's Eggs Florentine, fell open.

"Stolen Russian jewels! Grace Kelly! Jemima, don't forget the envelope that Granny Tinkerbell gave you after Christmas! Wasn't it full of notes with just those phrases scribbled on?"

"Yes!" Jemima said, making a mental note not to forget the Fairfax Park embossed envelope that the Dowager Viscountess Fairfax had given her on Boxing Day, just after she had solved the mystery of the Duchess of Windsor's stolen jewels. It had 'For your next mystery' written on the front. Maybe the answer to where Princess Grace's sapphire and diamond pendant earrings were, would be amongst the newspaper cuttings and notes enclosed in the envelope that she had tucked safely away in her bedside table.

## Chapter 4

---

## The French Riviera
## Friday May 6<sup>th</sup>

Amidst the azure blue of the Mediterranean, with nothing to be heard but the gentle splash of waves and the call of the occasional gull, the old man reflected that he really should be feeling much calmer. Despite the quiet and the dozy rays of sunlight spilling across the deck, he was alert and listening to the slightest noise, though he was pretending to slump in his chair, eyes half shut, the perfect pastiche of an old man enjoying a sunbathe.

The enormous yacht he was sitting on belonged to his boss, a Russian several decades younger than him. During their backgammon game after lunch, his boss had delighted in telling him every detail of the design. Made in Livorno by his favourite yacht maker, Benetti, it had been delivered the week before and as the butler was ordered to bring them both a vodka, the Russian joked that it was the first 'property' he'd had that a wife or girlfriend hadn't insisted on overseeing the interiors. Now, at 5pm, the old man, who had too many years of experience under his belt working for the Russian's grandmother, felt he needed another, and signalled the butler again. He'd worked for the family for over fifty years and could remember his current boss taking his first steps as a child. By all accounts, he was practically family. They said that, for Russian Jews, family was everything, but after a long and busy lifetime, the old man knew there were a few rogue ones in that mix. Blood was not thicker than the blue Mediterranean waters that bound this coast of wealth and deceit.

Floating a few kilometres off the French Riviera, the mega-yacht barely moved up and down in the mid-morning sun. It was called The Romanov Sapphire. The old man thought the yacht was sailing a little close to the wind in view of their forthcoming task, but he did have to admit it was beautiful. The huge boat could sleep nearly thirty guests, and the same number of crew. There were four floors, plus three sun decks and an infinity pool, tiled in gold, that swept off the stern into the ocean, plus a helicopter sitting on the top, in case of any unexpected and unwanted arrivals. Or, indeed, to get the Russian's prized belongings off and away as quickly as possible. The interior was a bit too sumptuous for his taste: a bit too nouveau riche. But what would he know – he had come from a poor Montenegrin village and, unlike most oligarchs, this Russian was descended from Royalty.

The old man puffed idly on his cigar, his louche manner not betraying his nerves, and prodded a set of heavy gold and diamond-dust backgammon pieces around a mahogany board. The Russian had left him to sweat on the deck while he completed his daily twenty laps around the floating vodka palace. Already the sun was ferociously hot: he could feel the diamond and gold locket that hung around his neck singe what was left of the white hair on his chest. He wondered if perhaps the Russian was waiting for him to spontaneously combust. That would get rid of a few dirty family secrets, he thought.

The press knew him under his feline alias, the Snow Leopard, but to his friends – associates might have been a better description – Nicolai Poparic was better known as Lucky. For most of his life, Lucky had been the most skilful cat burglar on the Continent. His nickname had arisen at the start of his career, due to his uncanny ability to elude the police – admittedly, not quite the feat it could have been; back in the Fifties, policemen had been much thinner on the ground, often distracted in the fight for independence against the Yugoslav dictator, Tito. Early on in Lucky's career, however, he had not lived up to his moniker. Back in the early 1950s, when Montenegro, particularly the smart sea-resort of Sveti Stefan, was a haven for film stars, such as Sofia Loren and Elizabeth Taylor, he'd been less than careful on a job, stealing jewels from an exiled Russian Royal – a Duchess he'd been arrogant enough to assume was like all the other members of the Royal families who'd fled to the area during the Revolution: inbred, stupid, careless, and filthy rich. But Grand Duchess Tatiana Romanov was a formidable woman: cunning, clever, and utterly ruthless. He'd been emptying her safe by moonlight when she had caught him, and, whilst threatening him with a sabre, she informed Lucky that her grandfather used to behead servants who displeased him. Intrigued by his skill, she struck a deal with him. She had told him that many of her family's heirlooms had been stolen and disappeared in the Revolution, and how she'd been furious to see them appear on the necks, wrists, and fingers of the 'five-a-penny' film stars, as she called them, who'd risen from the slums to have money beyond their wildest dreams. She wanted him to get them back for her and her descendants. Naively, he'd thought he'd make a run for it, and he tried to. He'd booked a last-minute ticket under an assumed name on the next boat to America, had boarded the ship, and collapsed in relief on the narrow bed in his cabin, only to jump back up again almost immediately. On the pillow of the bed, someone had left a photograph of his mother and sister outside their family home, a bullet, and a note:

*Больше нет шансов.* (No more chances.)

Lucky had never questioned his loyalty to the Grand Duchess again.

In March 1956, Lucky had been sent by the Duchess to spend the spring and summer on the Riviera, where she said there would be more jewels than sweets in a sweetshop. He had several commissions to retrieve the Romanov's invaluable heirlooms for the old lady, but, just to keep his hand in, he liberated a black onyx and white diamond Cartier Panthère bracelet on his first evening from an unsuspecting English Countess at the casino when he was helping her put on her Musquash fur coat during his work as a cloakroom attendant. He felt a particular affinity with Cartier's Panthère line. His penchant for white diamond Panthère pieces was the reason he had been dubbed the Snow Leopard by the international press. The publicity encouraged owners to keep a better eye on their Cartier collections, but to Lucky this was all part of the fun: he couldn't resist a challenge.

That evening, the casino had been searched, but the bracelet was never found. Lucky had awoken the next morning, in the Duchess's apartment on Avenue Grande Bretagne, while she spent the season elsewhere. He stopped for a black coffee and a cigarette at his local café where he caught up with the owner – a tiny old lady with a huge bouffant coiffure, who remembered Lucky from his previous summer's visit and soon started, unknowingly, to fill him in on all the comings and goings of the monied in Monaco. Lucky was exceptionally charming with the ladies. As it was a Sunday that particular morning, he walked to the Gare de Monaco, down by the port, and took a train along the coast to visit the presbyter at the Russian Orthodox Church in San Remo. He went ostensibly on behalf of one of the church's most generous benefactors, the Grand Duchess Tatiana, who was widely believed to be too frail to leave her home but wished prayers to be said for her there. She was in fact staying with her royal relatives in Montenegro. After lighting a candle and discussing the Grand Duchess's health with some of the regulars who knew of her and asked after her wellbeing, Lucky had deposited the stolen jewels with the priest to be kept in the church's safe, and sold the non-Romanov jewels to a fence he met in a nearby café. There was very little risk associated with either of these activities. Lucky was a charming, well-known, and well-liked man amongst the attendants of the church, and the priest had been in the employ of the Grand Duchess's family for decades. Even the fence knew enough about the Grand Duchess that he understood the need for utter discretion. In fact, the most hazardous part of Lucky's Sunday trips to church was avoiding the mothers of the congregation, who seemed to have produced broods of daughters of a marriageable age they wanted to introduce him to, and who couldn't understand how charming Mr Nicolai didn't already have a wife.

In contrast to the previous years Lucky had been sent to the Riviera, however, the pace of spring and summer in 1956 were far from sedate. The wedding of the century loomed, with Hollywood, the American East Coast, and European society all gathering in the tiny seaside principality of Monaco. There would be as many diamonds for the taking as any jewel thief could wish for, and Lucky and the Grand Duchess had planned their next heists down to the letter. The most prized of all these was a pair of sapphire earrings sold by the "poor little rich girl" millionaire heiress

Barbara Hutton to the McCloskeys, who had then taken them to Van Cleef & Arpels, where the sapphire and diamond surmounts had been added to with extra gemstones and diamonds before they were to be gifted by Grace Kelly's godmother as a present for the bride for her wedding day. For some reason, the Grand Duchess was utterly obsessed with them. And they had cost him a great deal, he admitted with a pang in his heart, as he thought of his beloved wife and estranged daughter. At least he was now in communication with his granddaughter, Petrina.

A splashing noise made old Lucky look up from his reverie. The Russian was passing by on his latest lap of the yacht and looked up and waved as he passed. Lucky raised his cigar in greeting and took another puff. Pyotr was the Grand Duchess's great grandson. He shared her high forehead, snub nose, and rapidly changing temper. He might have just turned fifty-five years old, but with his youthful physique, blond hair, grey eyes, and a little help from the Botox needles of the world's best surgeons, he could easily pass for a man in his early forties. He made Lucky feel like the old man he was, swimming strongly while Lucky sat on the deck in the sun. Pyotr didn't scare Lucky, though, not in the way the Grand Duchess had. These days, the Grand Duchess occupied a marble crypt at the Russian Orthodox Church in San Remo. The butler returned with a bottle of gold flaked vodka and poured a good amount into a tumbler glass full of ice, before putting it on the table in front of the old man. One of the best things about getting old, he thought, was that the fear of death had lost some of its sting – should his next drink be poisoned, he wasn't missing out on much. He reached for his glass to take a glug, while tapping the cigar on the side of the crystal ashtray, and gazed for a moment at the sunlight glinting off the flecks in the liquid. He had drunk vodka at his wedding, he remembered, and kissed the last icy sting of it off the lips of his beautiful wife as they'd celebrated their union. That was one thing he had to thank the Grand Duchess for – without her, he never would have met Pierina. The love of his life.

Lucky had never returned to Montenegro. Over the fifteen years since they had met, he and Pierina settled on the Riviera and he continued to receive orders from the Grand Duchess, whose requests soon became more and more erratic. The jewellery was piling up in the safe in the San Romano church and the priest confided in Lucky that the Grand Duchess was no longer sending anyone to pick it up and return it to Montenegro, so Lucky began to skim a little more off the top of each hoard. After all, he had a wife and soon a baby to support. While rising higher in Monaco society, Lucky cleverly picked the pockets, purses, and palaces of the wealthy elite. He would then innocently drive over the border to the sumptuous food markets in Italy where he met his fence, Freddo, and came back with increasingly more money buried amongst the vegetables each time. On days like these, Pierina would have their cook make delicious meals from the produce, and they would drink rosé wine and eat on their terrace overlooking the sea, and Lucky would tell his wife he was the happiest and luckiest man alive.

After the old Russian Duchess died, there were no weekly prayers to be said at the church. But all this coming and going was easily masked with the delicious Italian produce for La Pantera, the Italian restaurant-cum-night club he'd opened in 1960 with the proceeds of his thieving. La Pantera quickly became the chicest and most popular restaurant in Monaco, if not the Riviera. On a par with the famous Tetou a few kilometres down the coast in Golfe

Juan. The same crowd would alternate between the two restaurants depending on where they were. To the outside world, Lucky was now a respectable man; behind closed doors, he masterminded fewer, bigger heists with his group of henchmen: his Panthers. His own daughter grew up, got married, and had a child of her own. Life was simple, happy, and easy.

There was a catch, however. In the glorious haze of the Summer that was 1956, and in the early stirrings of the Grand Duchess's eccentricity, Lucky never admitted to her that he had not managed to steal the Romanov sapphire earrings destined for Princess Grace of Monaco. He had no idea what happened to them; they were apparently stolen by someone else the night he'd attempted to take them. Lucky couldn't help but wonder if he had a rival thief in her employment. Of course, he should have done, but after the initial plan had been made, the Duchess had kept changing her mind, coming up with unworkable theories and, frankly, strange ideas. Lucky had decided to take his chances and enter Hotel de Paris one night with the help of Pierina, but hadn't managed to find the jewels that old lady wanted – although he'd still managed to take $50,000 dollars of other jewellery. He'd been frustrated by the failure, but had been planning a second attempt and was as surprised as anyone else to read the reports in the papers that the Romanov sapphire earrings had been stolen. The Grand Duchess had wired him her congratulations, instructed him to leave them in the church safe, and then promptly forgotten all about. He later found out from a maid that the old lady had fallen very ill very quickly and had spent much of the ensuing time on her sickbed raving about sapphires and Panthers and bad luck. Lucky didn't attempt to contact her again.

Lucky thought he might have gotten away with it, but here he was, decades later, back in Russian control. Before she died, in a rare moment of lucidity, it seemed that the Grand Duchess had told her ten-year-old great-grandson of the sapphire and diamond earrings that were amongst his family heirlooms, stolen by the Communist Government from her Aunt Maria and then sold with all the other Romanov jewels. Ten years ago, in what it seemed to be a definite mid-life crisis, the Russian had developed an interest in the family jewellery collection once again. He had unearthed Lucky and he expected him to unearth all the remaining Romanov gems while running the much more complicated operations of the Pink Panther jewel thieves. The Russian had initially been content to keep Lucky on his island off Cannes, Ile Sainte Marguerite, planning the Pinks' movements. But then, the previous month, he had spotted a photograph on the New York Post's Page Six of Lucky and Pierina's estranged daughter, Fortunata, wearing what he believed was part of his great-grandmother's missing jewels: a large sapphire and diamond double pear brooch pinned into the woman's thick dark brown hair. The coincidence seemed too close for the Russian to believe and in a storm of temper he came to the conclusion that Lucky must have been lying to his family for sixty years, and kept what was now rightfully his. When he was shown the photo, Lucky had to admit that his estranged daughter was wearing what looked very much like a part of the sapphire and diamond earrings which had been stolen in the days leading up to Monaco's wedding of the century, and his stomach churned as he tried to think of how on earth his daughter could ever have got hold of such a thing. Pierina must have given them to her somehow.

Lucky drained the last of his gold-flecked vodka and remembered the call to his granddaughter when he had asked her what she knew of the jewellery her mother had. They had only been acquainted the previous November, and he loved how Petrina, the apple of his eye who had inherited her grandmother's looks and her grandfather's cunning, had, without any persuasion, gone into the 'family business' from that moment. While Fortunata had distanced herself from the family, engrossed in making her movies and living her Upper East Side Manhattan lifestyle, Petrina liked nothing more than the thrill of danger. Now Petrina was meant to be bringing the diamonds from the recently stolen Vogel Vanderpless necklace to meet him in Monaco, to be handed over to the Russian, who seemed incensed at both grandfather and granddaughter. Lucky knew that the only way to placate him was to make a success of the multiple heists that they had planned for that afternoon, as well as to take advantage of the fabulous jewellery that appeared in the fine jewellery stores along the coast during the film festival. He glanced down at a magazine which had been pointedly left open on the table, and reread:

### Remake Of To Catch A Thief Features Ten Times More Fine Jewellery Than The Original

The biggest collection of Fine Jewellery from one of the world's most prestigious jewellery houses will be seen in the remake by Panther Studios, which has Glenn Close leading the cast, while Evie Talbot takes on Grace Kelly's original role, and Richard Wakefield takes that of Cary Grant. The premiere, on Monday 9th May, will take place at the exclusive outdoor cinema just below the famous palace of Monaco, and will be a charity viewing in aid of the Princess Grace Foundation. Many of the pieces will no doubt be seen that night and security will be stringent. It is only part of the huge collections of High Jewellery that appear in the jewellery boutiques in Monaco at the start of each summer season.

The article caused excited butterflies to beat frantically in Lucky's stomach. He remembered his granddaughter telling him about the movie when they were first back in touch. How ironic it was that Fortunata had produced it. After all, it had been Pierina's favourite film. She supposed his wife had seen him in Cary Grant, or was it the other way around? It did seem odd to host the premiere near to where her mother had died, and, had she known the terrible truth, it would have destroyed her. However, Petrina had told him that they all thought he was dead, and he told his granddaughter when he initially made contact not to tell her mother of his existence. It was just easier.

Lucky's mind was brought back to reality when the Russian, back on deck and having a glass of the vodka that the butler had left at the principle deck's bar, said it was time. He watched the younger man walk slowly to the side of the mega-yacht and lift a pair of binoculars to his eyes to watch the four sets of panthers – always in pairs, always in disguise – walk towards their targets, each within only a few hundred metres of the other. Van Cleef, Vogel, Cartier, and Chopard. Of course, the old man had orchestrated the heists, and was happy to be allowed off the island, where he had been held virtually a prisoner for the past decade, to watch them. He prayed that it went according to plan, probably because one of Panthers was his granddaughter. He had been plotting the raids on the Casino Square stores for months and had some of the best cats in play, but, more importantly, he needed the breathing space to come up with a solution to the dilemma concerning the sapphire and diamond earrings.

## Chapter 5

---

# The Hotel de Paris, Monte Carlo

"*Et voilà… mademoiselle, l'Hotel de Paris!*"

Jemima's taxi driver announced their arrival to her reflection in the rear-view mirror, whilst screeching his brakes to a halt outside one of the world's most luxurious hotels.

"*Merci, monsieur, et combien je vous dois?*" Jemima asked for the fare in as perfect French as she could, having managed not to vomit during the hell-raising half hour trip from Nice airport.

Next time she did this, she told herself, she would take the ten minute helicopter ride from Nice airport to Monaco. After all, it couldn't possibly cost more than the amount the meter was totalling.

"*Ça fait 128 euros, merci.*"

"*On dira 130 alors… je vous remercie et peut–être vous pourriez m'aider avec mes valises?*" Jemima gave him a meagre two-euro tip and asked if he'd help with her suitcases.

She had to get out of this smoke-smelling taxi before her tummy finally revolted against her will, or indeed against the driver's seat in front of her.

"Bien sur, mademoiselle." He pushed open his door, which screeched almost as much as the brakes, before semi-rolling out of the vehicle to open the boot for Jemima, who was leaning against the car with one hand, while the other poured the now-warm contents of an Evian bottle into her mouth.

Fortunately, before the driver could drop her three heavy bags to the floor, an elegantly clad doorman sprang forward, pushing a 1940s style brass suitcase trolley to catch them. The cases weren't Louis Vuitton, needless to say, but they weren't as shabby as they could have been, had her mother not given her a better set for Christmas before she went off to Cape Town and met James. Jemima remembered yet again the weekend at Cliveden and, though she felt nauseas, her heart leapt as she thought of spending the next week with him on the romantic French Riviera. Looking up at the grand façade in front her, she rather wished she was checking in with him now. The Hotel de Paris! When she first watched the Monaco Grand Prix last summer, she and her Dutch friend Delfine had stood just above where she was now, next to Ivana Trump, who had told them about how her ex-boyfriend had given her an old 80's Formula 1 Ferrari. She hoped that this year she'd be watching the Grand Prix from The Fairmont Hotel, overlooking the hairpin. If she was still alive, a dark little voice in the back of her head added.

Following the porter in through the huge doors, Jemima felt relieved that she had taken up Alexa's offer of an appointment at the Carol Joy Salon and her shopping spree at Selfridges and Harvey Nichols. The people in the foyer seemed as glamorous as any she'd seen at any Vogel boutique.

"Ah, Miss Fox-Pearl," she heard a familiar voice behind her say as she made her way to the concierge to leave her bags. She had also just realised that she had no idea where the apartment that she was supposed to be staying in for the next few weeks was.

Jemima turned around to see DI Paige, who she first met after the Somerset House heist, still in his Columbo-style raincoat. It might rain in London in May, but the temperature in Monaco certainly seemed to have caught him by surprise. Poor Paige, he did seem terribly out of place amongst the couture-clad clientele checking in and out.

"Detective Inspector Paige! What are you doing here?" she exclaimed, purposefully shaking his hand and congratulating herself on getting his title right. She hoped that he hadn't noticed she was shaking all over.

"I'm here for the big Interpol conference."

"What conference? I thought I was here to see Mr Vogel and some guy from Interpol? You haven't been transferred to Interpol have you, Inspector?" she asked teasingly. After all, he really had been no use whatsoever in tracking down the diamond necklace.

"Detective…!"

"Sorry, Detective Inspector. You know, in surroundings like these, I can't help but think about these Pink Panthers and Peter Sellers and the movies." She stopped, suddenly realising that it wasn't Columbo that Paige reminded her of, but rather Peter Sellars as Inspector Clouseau from the old Pink Panther movies.

"Mmm," said Paige, who was clearly aware of his resemblance. "We are here for the meeting of The Pink Panther Working Group," he continued after a brief, awkward pause.

"The what? I thought it was an Interpol conference," Jemima said, stifling a giggle at the aptness. She was starting to wonder if she was in some sort of live improvised remake of the movies and had to stop herself turning around to see if Steve Martin was about to walk through the door. Finally, her motion sickness from the tiny plane and the car journey from Nice was starting to subside. It must be due to the calming effect of the hotel lobby and her 5-star surroundings.

Before DI Paige could explain, Mr Vogel appeared suddenly like a vision in front of her, tall and immaculate in a beautifully cut Savile Row suit and John Lobb shoes, with his shock of white hair combed neatly back.

"Jemima, you're here. Good. And Paige, well done," Mr Vogel said in the Liverpudlian accent that occasionally arose, despite his years of elocution lessons to sound more like his clients. He leant forward to peck her on the cheek and, shaking the DI's hand, continued, "We've only just arrived. I've left my wife shopping until this Interpol briefing is over and then we'll be heading out to the villa in Cap Ferrat, leaving Jemima here with you."

"So, Mr V. What is this all about?" said Jemima, using the name for him that everyone else used behind his back. "The Pink Panther Working Group – sounds more like a movie than a meeting."

"Interpol have an annual briefing where the director of this division updates the jewellery industry on where they are with–" he paused to think of the words "–tracking down the Pink Panthers, I suppose." He got there with a resigned shrug.

Jemima knew that this was not a light subject for any jeweller. She had read in Anna's file on the Panthers that, so far, no one had been killed in any of their raids, but being held up at a gunpoint is not an easy experience for anyone to forget.

"It is a very serious matter, Jemima; these men are dangerous." Mr Vogel turned on his heel and motioned for them to follow him across the lobby. "This is not a game. The panthers are not domesticated."

Jemima wondered if she would be around for her next birthday as she and Paige followed the diamond tycoon along corridors both carpeted and wallpapered in pink silk.

* * *

"Welcome to the sixth annual meeting of The Pink Panther Working Group, or Project Pink Panther. I am Charles Renault – Head of Interpol's National Central Bureau in Monaco and Director of Project Pink Panther since its inception in 2007." The French Interpol officer addressed the highly-charged group from the front of the room. "Yesterday, the eighty investigators here, who are present from twenty-three different countries, were able to exchange and review information about the transnational crime gang. Today, I update you, the jewellery industry, on these discoveries and enable you to best protect your businesses against the Pink Panthers who have spent the past thirteen years targeting high-end jewellery stores in Europe, the Middle East, Asia, and the United States. As you know, this coastline is their prime target at this time of year."

They were congregated in what was normally the Alain Ducasse Restaurant, a sumptuously decorated room, as large as a ballroom, in which, according to the papers on her chair, were sixty investigators from twenty-three different countries, as well as members of the international fine jewellery industry. It had to be possibly one of the most exquisite meeting rooms Jemima had ever been in, and one of the strangest meetings.

Before sitting down, Jemima searched amongst the rows of people to see if she could spot anyone she knew, but it was hard, for they had come in late and were right at the back. She was also absolutely starving and wondered if it was appropriate to sneak over to the table just behind her, where she could both smell and see a delicious-looking spread of pastries and coffee. She thought perhaps not.

"Many of you will know all of this from our previous annual meetings in Berne, Vienna, and Paris. But, for those who are new to this, I'm going to give you a bit of background."

Jemima shifted in her seat; she was excited to learn more about this fictitious sounding gang – Anna's notes were good, but even Mr Vogel's PA didn't know as much as Interpol.

"But, firstly, a bit of history for anyone new to these meetings. The Pink Panther jewel thieves are from the Balkans. They are primarily Montenegrin and Serbian and mostly ex-military. They are the most successful thieving gang in history, and are known for their meticulous planning, life-like disguises, and their working in a nebulous network of cells. We now believe that their first strike was back in the early eighties – 1984, to be precise – when they stole around $60 million worth of jewellery from a boutique inside Cannes' Carlton Hotel. But this gang properly came to our attention in 1999 during the fall of Slobodan Milosevic at the end of the Kosovan war. By then, thanks to UN sanctions in Yugoslavia, they had established significant smuggling routes for basic items, with diamonds, drugs, and guns being the icing on the cake, as the British might say," he added, whilst appearing to smile at the British contingent in the room. "Since 1999, we believe there are over six hundred thieves operating who have carried out around three hundred armed robberies to date, targeting high-end jewellery stores and events where jewels feature. The value of these thefts is around $346 million euros. They work in their cells, not knowing the members of other cells, for a 'big boss' who places orders through intermediaries – these are often ex-Panthers, too old now to be doing the crimes themselves. Sometimes, the full piece of jewellery is ordered, but, more often than not, the Panthers remove the gemstones from their settings and get rid of the platinum or gold in the getaway car. It's easier to move loose stones."

The audience let out a murmur.

"So far," Monsieur Renault continued, "they have successfully targeted the most exclusive jewellers – mainly across Europe and the Middle East, and recently in Japan. Graff, Vogel, Van Cleef and Arpels, Chopard, Cartier, Harry Winston, de Grisogono, and Damiani, to name just a few."

There was a shuffle in the room as those he was talking to unconsciously identified themselves and began looking around at each other. Jemima glanced at Mr V, before noticing that Paige had disappeared from beside her.

"So, in 2007," Monsieur Renault said, "at Monaco's insistence, Interpol started this." He gestured around himself. "Project Pink Panther. Since 2007, over 200 have been caught!" he said proudly. "Up until now, there has been a minimal amount of violence, but they are becoming more dangerous and technologically advanced, which we will see after a short break. So, thank you for your attendance for the first part of this afternoon's session. Are there any questions?"

"I am presuming that the festival is on high alert after last year's two big heists?" an Italian male voice asked.

"I am sure that you are all aware that Signor Robbini is talking about the million euros' worth of jewels belonging to Chopard that were stolen from the safe of an employee's hotel bedroom, only a few days before two million euros' worth was taken from a de Grisogono party, both during the Cannes festival. And yes, we have the highest level of security at every event this year." He smiled confidently. "We are particularly cautious for the Vogel-sponsored premiere of To Catch a Thief on Monday evening at the Open-Air Cinema and Palais de Monaco not far from here." The detective looked across the audience at Mr Vogel.

"What about our boutiques? Are they to be targeted?" Another question came from someone in the 150-person strong audience.

"Very good question, and yes, we have intelligence suggesting that they will. Most of the jewellery boutiques, as you all know, have their best collections here during the summer season. The thieves know that," the Detective replied. "We have ensured that it is going to be very difficult to penetrate any of the boutiques and tonight we have a new CCTV surveillance system being installed across your boutiques."

A few more questions were asked and answered, and a few more murmurs were heard between jewellery brands, before Monsieur Renault closed the morning session.

"Thank you, everyone, and I look forward to seeing you here again after tea, which is now being served out on the terrace now," he said, looking at his watch.

There was a murmur in the room as delegates prepared to head out through the large French windows for tea overlooking the Place du Casino.

"Well, this is interesting," Jemima said to Mr Vogel. "Shall we go and have some tea?" she added hopefully, feeling her stomach growl.

"No, we are now having a private meeting with Monsieur Renault before the next session. You too, Paige." He nodded to the Detective Inspector. "Jemima, Renault will be giving you all the support you need to find these diamonds. I also have news for you, too, which I know you will be pleased to hear."

"What?" Jemima asked excitedly.

"You were right. There is a 99.9% possibility that the Vogel Vanderpless is the other half of the Cullinan Diamond. This means that it is even more important for you to get the girl to lead you to them."

"But," interjected Paige, "do you think that she, or they, might have cut the stones up into other pieces? Isn't that what they always do with large gemstones?"

"Yes, they may well do, but I have an inkling they won't."

"Jemima, may I call you that?" Paige turned to her.

"Yes, yes, of course!" she said, inwardly laughing at his formality.

"Thank you. Okay, so…"

"Good Morning, Messieurs, Mademoiselle." The man who had given the talk was now standing next to them. "I am sorry to have interrupted you, Monsieur?"

"Paige, Detective Inspector Paige," Paige said pointedly.

"Ah, Inspector, we have been looking forward to meeting you. You did such good work catching the thieves of the Vogel Vanderpless. Charles Renault," he said, holding out his hand to Paige, before turning towards Mr Vogel.

Jemima couldn't believe it – is that what everyone thought? With an angry frown, she looked to Mr V who subtly shook his head, so she didn't make a fuss.

"Actually, Monsieur Renault. I'd like to introduce you to Miss Jemima Fox-Pearl… we spoke on the telephone about her," Paige said, also seeing Jemima's look.

*"Oui, oui, bien sur,"* he said again, looking her up and down admiringly. "Let's find somewhere else where we can talk more discreetly."

"Thank you, we'll follow you."

* * *

After following the Monegasque Interpol director through corridors as ornate as the ones that Jemima imagined were in Monaco's Palace, Mr Vogel, Jemima, Paige, and Charles Renault sat in the dining room of what was an equally extravagantly decorated penthouse suite on the hotel's top floor. Heavy silk brocade curtains were partially pulled back to reveal the most incredible view of the whole of Monaco that stretched as far as the eye could see.

"Monsieur Renault," Paige began. "It was Miss Fox-Pearl here who was instrumental in finding the necklace and catching the two main culprits, as I explained." Jemima was sure he hadn't explained that at all. "However, there is a third one on the loose – a Petrina Lindberg. It was her grandfather who was, between the 1950s and 70s, known as the Snow Leopard, and who we believe created the Pink Panthers."

"Ah, yes, I know what you are about to tell me. Poparic, aka The Snow Leopard. My father has spent the last five decades chasing that villain," he said in disgust, spitting out the word villain.

"Yes."

"And you believe that they, or rather he, is still around?"

"Yes!" Jemima said in exclamation, determined to make her mark here. "So, this Petrina Lindberg... I first came across Petrina at the auction at Bothebie's in December when Mr V bought..." she was gabbling so fast that Renault was lost.

"Mr V?" Monsieur Renault asked, confused.

"Oh, sorry," Jemima said, looking at her boss apologetically. "When Mr Vogel bought the Vanderpless diamond."

"Miss Scott was also there, I believe."

"Yes, yes, she was," Jemima said, smiling; she was getting into the swing of things and finally getting some recognition. "So, to cut a long story short, I kept on coming across Petrina in South Africa, then she started going out with Danny Vogel, who is Mr Vogel's grandson. Slowly, she was getting closer to this diamond. It appears, however, that she double-bluffed everyone and it was purely chance that this famous diamond was, in fact, connected to her through her father's side. He knew Martha Vanderpless in New York in the 1960s."

"I have been told a little of this," Renault said. "I spoke with my father, Gustave, who was Head of the Monaco Police during the sixties and seventies. He spent years trying to catch whoever it was stealing priceless pieces of jewellery from our residents in Monaco, but to no avail. He always suspected Nicolai Poparic but it was impossible to catch him red-handed – plus, he owned the most popular restaurant in Monte Carlo, La Pantera. It was situated in what is now Sass Café. There would have been a public outcry if Nicolai had been imprisoned, despite the fact that he had probably stolen most of his clientele's jewels. I remember that he had a beautiful daughter who left to marry an American. Suddenly, old Nicolai disappeared, and so did Mrs Livanos's jewels. The restaurant went bankrupt and his poor wife died – they say of a broken heart. But it was suicide. She threw herself off the Rock." He was talking of the Rock of Monaco, on which sits the Prince's Palace amidst the oldest part of Monaco.

"What a story!" Jemima said, enthralled. "I wonder if he is still alive? Nicolai Poparic."

"I doubt it. These people are often murdered by their own. They get too complacent and make mistakes. However, if he is, he will be living in splendour somewhere where no one can catch him, possibly South America, protected by the very people who might otherwise have killed him. Rich Russians or South Americans."

"Very well," Mr Vogel said, looking at his bespoke Vacheron Constantin watch and standing up. "Mr Renault, can I entrust you with my best PR girl?" He looked fondly at Jemima. "Good luck, my dear. Please keep in touch. I know that you will find the diamonds that Petrina stole, and of course prevent her taking any more of our precious pieces of jewellery."

With that, their meeting was finished.

# Chapter 6

## Place du Casino, Monte Carlo

Before anyone else could get up from the table, they heard two gunshots from outside. One of the Interpol officers from the talk walked into the salon without knocking. It was clearly an emergency: his face did not display the cool collectedness of an hour earlier. The officer whispered in Renault's ear whilst Mr V's Blackberry starting vibrating on the oak table. She watched her boss, keeping an eye on the two Frenchmen. Renault glanced over to the diamond king as the other man whispered in his ear, and Jemima immediately knew that the diamond boutiques in the Place de Casino, maybe even Vogel in the Casino itself, had been burgled.

Pushing her Louis XV chair back, Jemima got up, raced over to the windows, and peered from behind the half opened pale blue curtains for the best view possible. Jemima had always been good at getting her bearings, so she guessed that, despite the size of the hotel and the corridors through which she'd followed the men, the room had a good view of the Vogel boutique at the Casino. If only the evening sun wasn't reflecting off the windows, she might have been able to see through. Jemima saw smoke billowing out of the front door of the world-famous Casino building, down the wide carpeted steps, and into the crowd that was already forming. The gendarmes were trying to keep everyone back, and didn't seem to care that the smoke was billowing around them like in an 80s nightclub, or that phones were being held up, waiting to capture the thieves on video. Jemima stepped back, retrieved her phone, and hurried to one of the suite's bedrooms, hoping to get a better view without the blinding sun. Jemima kept her phone focused on the commotion outside. It was only about twenty metres down from where she was.

"Mr Vogel," she heard Paige utter nervously, "can I do anything to help?"

"Where is Jemima?" Mr Vogel replied, surprising her, since he normally didn't miss a trick.

"I'm here," she called back from next door, determined not to miss what everyone down below was waiting for.

"Come here, away from the window," he said, knowing that was where she would be standing.

"They're bulletproof, and I am videoing it," Jemima called.

She had read in Architectural Digest that, since the Mumbai terrorist attacks in 2008, most of the top hotels in the world now had bulletproof windows.

"I am not worried about you being shot. I need you to come here now."

Embarrassed, but slightly perturbed that her safety was not important, Jemima went back to the big dining room table.

"You want us to go down there?" she asked nervously.

"No, the police won't want us there. I will go down and see how Diane and her team are shortly," he explained, talking about Diane la Comtesse de Ré, the boutique's director.

"I need you to get hold of Alexa. I want to keep my line open."

"I don't have her mobile number, I'm afraid." Her boss stared up at Jemima in confusion and, without a word, texted the number to her.

Before she could make the call, there was another gunshot, louder than before, and Jemima dashed back behind the curtain to see five men and a woman, who were holding a bag each, running through the now very thick smoke to a dark blue Mercedes parked outside the Van Cleef boutique, next to Vogel.

"Mr V, they're escaping!" Jemima shouted, before going back to where he was sitting. She couldn't help but notice that the two Frenchmen were no longer in the room.

"Paige, Jemima, come here and look at this."

Jemima pulled up the chair next to Mr Vogel and sat down as Paige made his way over from the other side of the beautifully polished oak table. They both stared at the small screen as her boss pressed play a video on his phone. It wasn't long before she noticed that it was the security camera from the boutique showing the heist. It was slightly scratchy and flicked between several CCTV cameras, but it was still obvious what had happened. Whoever had sent them was quicker than the thieves, Jemima thought, as she peered over Mr Vogel's shoulder at the screen.

A beautiful woman walked in through the first door. She smiled at the first bodyguard who, unlike when she herself went into the store on Bond Street, didn't ask who she was. Although Jemima felt briefly affronted, she knew this was the norm: any overt security made wealthy clients uncomfortable. The blonde woman looked wealthy, dressed elegantly for jewellery shopping in a dark-coloured, knee-length dress, and a pair of fairly high, dark-coloured heels, but not so high that it would make escaping hard. She held a large tote bag, with a Gucci emblem on the side. The bag seemed rather too big for her outfit, but considering what she was about to do, it made sense.

The woman was quickly approached by a female sales assistant and no doubt asked if she could be of help. It looked as though the woman had been in the boutique before and perhaps knew the layout well. They could see her point to a table cabinet beside the two windows at the front of the boutique. Jemima knew this particular cabinet: it held a new collection of diamond, aquamarine, and Paraiba tourmaline jewellery called The Caribbean Collection. She had been working on the launch of it before her suspension, and had come up with the name – it looked just like the Caribbean Sea and was high jewellery aimed at the Riviera crowd, who knew that sea as well as the Mediterranean. It had only come out a couple of weeks previously in Paris and Monte Carlo, and in their small jewellery store in a hotel Vogel owned on Harbour Island in the Bahamas.

Just as the assistant opened the glass cabinet, in walked a well-dressed man in what could have been a dark blue suit and a shock of silvery white hair. Although it was hard to tell from the scratchy video, it looked as though his face was not that of someone with white hair. The moment the second security door closed, the woman suddenly pulled a gun out of her tote bag and pointed it at the girl helping her. The man also slipped one out of his suit jacket and aimed it at the other three staff, the obvious waving of the gun telling them to get down. They slumped to the floor, as though already shot, and lay with their faces down, their hands behind their heads. Jemima had a lump in her throat – she worked with these people and cared for them. The man walked up to a male sales assistant and put the gun to his head, before his mouth showed that he was shouting something. The assistant shook his head. The gunman lifted his gun, pointed it at a cabinet standing in the middle of the room, and shot the glass, causing it to shatter all over the marble floor. He then pushed the gun to the man's neck and must have asked the same thing again. Without waiting for an answer, he aimed and shot the other freestanding cabinet. In the meantime, the woman had cleared the Caribbean Collection cabinet, putting it all in her bag. With the gun still aimed at the young assistant, she walked towards her accomplice and handed him what looked like a drawstring bag. They each emptied more than a million pounds' worth of necklaces and chandelier earrings from the smashed glass cabinets. Without sound, it seemed almost eerie. The woman grabbed the first assistant by the arm and, digging the pistol against her spine, told her to open the inner door of the boutique. Once this was done, she pushed the girl through to the secure chamber, passed a dumbfounded guard with his hands in the air, and went through the outer door on to the cobbled street that was filling up with smoke. The video finished as the man fired another bullet into the air, and Jemima could just about see the Mercedes that she had only just seen in person pulling up, before it sped through the smoke and crowds towards the sea. The heist had taken under five minutes.

"There we have it," Mr Vogel said sadly. As he cleared the video from his screen, Jemima's phone rang, an unknown number flashing on the screen. Hesitantly, she answered.

"Hello?" she asked.

"Jemima, pass me over to my father," came Alexa's distinctive voice.

She passed the phone to Mr Vogel and then got up to sit in her seat on the other side of the table. Paige was on his phone speaking to God only knew who.

Moments later, Mr Vogel's call with his daughter ended, and he handed back Jemima's phone.

"It seems that these two have stolen around €25 million worth of jewellery. The new Caribbean and Riviera Collections and a few pieces that were on display from the movie," he said with a cracked voice. "Fortunately," he added with a sigh of relief, "they did not take Princess Grace sapphires." He was talking about the pendant earrings, the replicas of those stolen before Princess Grace's wedding, that were to be donated to the new Jewel Museum of Monaco.

Mr Vogel's face was white – even his year-round tan had disappeared, ageing him a good few years. Jemima knew that he had been hit before; Vogel and Graff were the main jewellery targets. Graff on Bond Street in London had suffered a £40 million heist only two years previously, but this was the most Vogel had ever lost.

"It is the Panthers." Renault had come back into the room and announced what they all thought. "We believe that they have just stolen almost a €100 million of jewellery from you, Van Cleef, Cartier, and Chopard."

"I wonder if they knew about the meeting here today, and that all their targets would be in attendance?" Jemima exclaimed angrily, wondering if she would be expected to find this jewellery, as well as the missing Vogel Vanderpless stones.

## Chapter 7

# Port de Fontvieille, Monaco

After the relief that the priceless Princess Grace earrings were still locked up in the huge safe at the back of the store's office, Mr Vogel said that Jemima could go back to her apartment and they would reconvene the next day. He would call her if he needed anything, but there was nothing more she could do, and it was best she had the evening off to get to know her new home for the next few weeks. Jemima didn't add that she hadn't even been there yet. She said goodbye to Mr Vogel and the various detectives who were still in the room talking to her boss, noticing that poor Paige looked pretty spare. With the help of a hotel bellboy, she collected her three suitcases from the cloakroom and then made her way through the busy atrium to the front doors of the hotel. The square was in lockdown, but she managed to persuade a policeman to let her leave in a minicab that had dropped someone off before the incident happened. One of the thieves? She couldn't help but wonder as she got inside the air-conditioned car and sat on the worn leather seats, while the driver and bellboy piled her bags in beside her and into the boot.

Arriving at the apartment building, a mere ten minutes later, Jemima was happy to see it was in the Belle Époque style, not the mid-20th century style that many of the older Monaco buildings were fashioned in. It was a yellow painted building on Boulevard d'Italie and, like everything else in Monaco, not far from where she had just come. The quaint glass and black metal doors creaked a bit when she was buzzed in, and a small, rather rotund old lady stood at the top of two steps just inside the doors. It was clear that Jemima wasn't going any further in, and she fervently hoped that this *gardienne* had her key.

"Hi!" Jemima gasped, while dragging her three heavy suitcases in from where the driver had dumped them on the pavement, since he was keen to move his car from the traffic jam he was causing. How different this was from the bellboy and gold trunk trolley at the hotel!

"*Bonsoir,*" was the grunted response.

"*Oh, sorry. Bonsoir,*" Jemima replied now that herself and her bags were safely inside.

She hoped that she was on the ground floor, or at least that there was a lift nearby, because she could see a steep winding staircase to the right of the marble floored hall.

"*Vous devriez etre l'Anglaise, Madame Fox-Purrll?*" the French woman said, though she was clearly expecting 'the English woman', since she had her hands on her hips and was looking like she had seen many a foreign girl traipse into her beloved building. These women, the *gardiennes* of apartment buildings throughout metropolitan France who had replaced servants after World War II, were possessive and proud of their 'manors'. They commanded respect, even if they didn't dish it back.

"*Oui, Madame, c'est moi. En fait, je suis une Mademoiselle. Comment allez-vous?*" Jemima explained, probably unnecessarily, that she was still a 'Miss', and politely asked how the old lady was in what was the normal greeting in France.

*"Bien,"* was all that came back. And then, *"Voici votre clé. Vous etes au quatrieme etage, numero 1C."*

Jemima thanked her, took the key for her rented apartment, and was about to ask for some help with her cases up to the fourth floor when the woman pointed at an ancient-looking lift and scuttled back to her 'loge' – the ground floor *gardienne's* apartment often found in older style buildings and normally adjacent to the entrance foyer.

So, Jemima pulled them up the two steps and called the rackety lift. When it arrived, she realised it was one of those old grille, scissor gates that could chop off a hand or a head if attention was not paid. Using her handbag to prop it open, Jemima managed to squeeze the suitcases in, piling them on top of each other. Once at her floor, she unlocked and opened the plain brown door to her new home with a sense of excitement.

Inside was a large, high-ceilinged room barely visible in the low light. Jemima dragged the bags inside, closed the door, and walked quickly over to the French windows to open the glass windows and the shutters. She took a quick breath; the view was amazing. It was almost six pm, but the sun was still blazing hot, reflecting off the sea and making the boats, both big and small, sparkle. She could hear the traffic and the familiar sound of car horns that were typical of any French town. The cafes on the Larvotto Beach promenade, that she could just about see below, were full of people. Jemima wanted to unpack, but she also wanted to explore. She turned back to the room, which was painted in a pale green and had a polished wooden floor that led throughout the apartment. Jemima walked over to the pile of suitcases and opened one to rummage through until she found her running shoes and the one outfit she had that would be appropriate to run in. Pulling off her clothes, she got changed, and, remembering to put the keys into a small pocket, dug out her headphones. She checked her iPhone to plot her route, put it in the arm band she just put on her upper arm and left the apartment. It was only when she was downstairs, about to step on to the busy street, that she realised she hadn't eaten anything and running on an empty stomach probably wasn't a good idea. She'd find something along the route, Jemima decided.

Jemima ran down to the beach to where the people were sitting out drinking rosé, along the coastline, around the famous Monaco Port Hercule with its million-pound superboats bobbing up and down on their moorings, past the famous Rascasse restaurant, and around the back of Fontvieille, until, finally, she reached a little restaurant at Pointe des Douaniers – a piece of land jutting out into the greeny-blue sea. She took her time to have a lemonade and a small plate of pasta at the idyllic Le Cabanon restaurant before turning around to run back. It was just after 7pm and, if she kept up the pace, she'd be home by 8pm, maybe before now she had some food inside her. With music pumping in her ears, Jemima ran back along the coastal path towards Monaco. She could still hear the faint noise of police sirens, although she wondered why. The Panthers would be long gone by now, in any number of boats speeding away from the principality as quickly as possible. Jemima decided to run a different way back, through Fontvieille: Monaco's newest district. A little less expensive and tucked away on the other side of The Rock from the main part of Monaco, it was more private.

Just as Jemima was about to run along the back of the marina, she spotted a black Mercedes jeep stop and watched two people quickly get out. Although they were on the other side of the harbour, Jemima instantly recognised Petrina. Her male companion looked familiar in some way, but she couldn't work out why. They seemed to be in a hurry and, whilst carrying a few bags between them, rushed from the blacked-window Mercedes along the concrete of the marina to the dock nearest the sea entrance, and then to a long black speedboat that Jemima knew, from a *Tatler* jewellery photo shoot, was an Arno Leopard, probably worth several million euros. Curiosity getting the better of her, Jemima waited until they were out of view and then walked in the shadows of one of the buildings and then along the dock until she was only a few berths away from the boat they dashed onto. She could hear them speaking in a mixture of an Eastern European language, not dissimilar to the bodyguard outside Vogel on Bond Street, and English. Then Petrina's voice said something more clearly than before and, for a moment, Jemima thought that her nemesis would appear on the deck and spot her, but, fortunately, she slammed the cabin door shut, abruptly cutting off the voices. Carefully, Jemima crouched down and moved along until she could see through one of the tiny porthole windows. She couldn't bear to think what people would imagine if they could see her. Would she be arrested for trespassing? The prospect of being caught by Petrina and her co-conspirator was definitely more terrifying. It suddenly occurred to her that the marina seemed quiet for 7.30pm – maybe superyacht people had evening 'siestas' before hitting the Monte Carlo nightlife?

One of the porthole windows was open, so, without thinking, Jemima climbed on to the deck of the neighbouring small Sunseeker that bobbed close to the open window. Fortunately, it wasn't alarmed, and, with her better vantage point, she could now see the name of the Leopard: Milos od Montenegro. She couldn't really see much else; the angle was impossible, and, of course, the window wasn't to the cabin they were in. But she could hear them again as clearly as before the door was slammed shut, and they were talking only in English this time.

"I am going to take a shower. I'm all hot and sticky from the latex mask and that blonde wig," said Petrina.

"Okay, you go and run it. You'll need something to wear in the shower," said a male voice.

Jemima couldn't think what the man meant but she realised the window she was listening through belonged to the bathroom. The light flicked on and she could just about see it was exactly what she imagined the bathroom of a superyacht to be. And what a bathroom it was. White marble from floor to ceiling, tile to tile. She saw Petrina walk into the shower and, despite doing a lot of exercise, she felt a pang of jealousy at the naked figure that now stood under cascades of water. Jemima was relieved when the glass started to steam up; it felt uncomfortable perving at her nemesis, and although she wanted to leave, she had an inkling that there was going to be more than just naked bodies. And she was right. The guy whose face she still couldn't see opened the door and the steam rushed out to fill up the room – just before her view was ruined, she glimpsed him putting a large Paraiba tourmaline, aquamarine, and diamond necklace around Petrina's long neck and fastening it. It was part of Vogel's Caribbean Collection. She could imagine what was going to happen next. Before she let her mind momentarily drift to James and their nightly antics, the steam fortunately blocked her view, and the noise of the water muffled any talking.

As Petrina and the man were occupied, Jemima thought she should take the opportunity to see what else was in the boat. She nervously stepped off the older vessel on to the concrete dock. Her heart was palpitating and she felt sick, but, two steps later, she was carefully climbing up the steps of the Milos od Montenegro. She stepped up on to the main deck, with its black marble-looking table top surrounded by matching leather banquettes, and saw that the windows of the cabin were blacked-out, presumably to keep out the sun's glare. She tried the door, her heart still pounding, expecting to be caught by Petrina or even the port police at any moment. The door was unlocked, so she pushed it open and stepped inside to where she could hear the shower still pumping out water on the cabin level below.

It was then that she saw, sitting on a tan-coloured leather seat, a dark black rucksack. The zips had been pulled down a little, so the flap lay open to reveal a pile of brightly-coloured and very expensive jewellery that hadn't yet been broken up. Jemima tiptoed over, terrified of the floor creaking or knocking something off the table. Immediately, she recognised that the pieces were a mix of Cartier and Van Cleef, both stores positioned on the Casino square outside Hotel de Paris where she'd been when the heists had happened.

Jemima only looked at the pieces of jewellery sitting on the top and didn't dare delve deeper into the bag. There was a brand new 2011 Haute Couture example of Van Cleef's iconic zip necklace, the style of which she knew had been created for the Duchess of Windsor. The 'zip' was created from diamonds with turquoise and green chrysoprase either side, and a tassel of the green gem cut into briolette beads. A Cartier dress watch with huge pear and marquise shaped diamonds, and a large ruby to cover the face and turn the timepiece into a bracelet, was also slung inside the bag, jumbled up with a pair of opulent emerald and diamond earrings.

A large, oval-shaped Paparadscha sapphire, surrounded by smaller oval-shaped yellow sapphires and set into a cocktail ring, was also poking out from under a wide, white diamond bracelet. Jemima noticed a suite of yellow sapphire and white diamond necklace and earrings until she looked closer and suddenly wondered if it was a yellow diamond. Perhaps this was a piece from Graff, so famous for its yellow diamonds that only Laurence Graff knew how to cut. But they couldn't have stolen from Graff, hidden securely inside Hotel de Paris itself, could they? Jemima turned the piece over but couldn't see a Graff signage. Likewise, she couldn't see anything in the bag from Vogel – maybe Petrina only had the necklace that she was now wearing? One of the other six Panthers had the rest? She then noticed a huge sapphire cabochon, surrounded by smaller sapphires and diamonds, and set as a ring that was part of Vogel's new Royal Riviera Collection.

As Jemima gazed at the pile, agonising over whether to take the bag and hand it in, she heard the water turn off.

"Come on, you'd better hurry up. I've just heard from Piotur." The man's voice said a name that Jemima couldn't recognise and presumed it was a Balkan name – another Pink Panther from the earlier heists no doubt. "I've got to meet him in under an hour in Cap Ferrat, so I need to get the boat up and running. You wanna come along? We can have dinner at that little seafood restaurant on Paloma Beach?"

Jemima didn't wait to hear what Petrina's answer would be; she needed to take a photo of this, she pulled the phone out of the armband on her left arm but silently swore to herself, the battery was dead as she had forgotten to recharge it before leaving. She couldn't believe it: here was proof, but there was no way of showing it to Interpol. She crept as quietly as possible out of the boat, back down the steps to the platform, and hopped on to the deck. Her heart was pounding with a mixture of frustration, nerves, and excitement.

The next door owner was back on the boat that she had trespassed on only minutes before. She smiled at him confidently so as not to raise suspicion.

"You a friend of that nasty piece of work?" said an unmistakably English accent from a rather large red-faced man, sitting on the deck of his boat.

"Not really," she replied, wondering why the English rarely bother to speak in a foreign language when they are abroad. She might well have been a local.

"My wife says he's bad news. Too good-looking for his own good. With no manners."

Jemima laughed as though in agreement and wished him a good evening.

# Chapter 8

## Later that evening

Jemima had to find or call Renault and tell him where the boat was before they left for Cap Ferrat. This was a lesson for her to never leave without charging her phone.

She left Fontvieille by jogging under the tunnel, above which was the Rock of Monaco, where the Princely Palace and outdoor cinema would be hosting the gala premiere and party for To Catch a Thief in a few days' time. Jemima hadn't run like this in months but loved it when she did. When they first moved into Culford Gardens, she'd get up early with Flora and go for a run over Chelsea Bridge, through Battersea Park, and back over Albert Bridge to get home, then shower, change, and leave for work by 8am. That hadn't happened for a few months and Jemima was starting to feel it in her legs. But what she'd seen in the boat gave her the adrenaline to keep going, so, turning up Lady Gaga's Edge of Glory, she ran as fast as she could along the main boulevard, Albert 1er, along the port, where the Grand Prix started and finished. She remembered where the police station was from passing it the year before and took a left up Rue Suffren Reymond. Once Jemima got to the building with the white flag outside, she ran through the double doors and up to the officer on duty at the front desk to ask for Inspector Renault.

*"Bonsoir. J'ai besoin de parler avec Monsieur Renault – il est là?"* she said fairly abruptly, but she didn't have time to make pleasantries with the police at this time – she needed their help.

*"Non, Madame, je suis désolé – il n'est pas au bureau non plus."* The policeman said with regret that he wasn't there any longer.

Jemima thanked him before running back down the street to the marina, where she dashed between Grand Prix barriers that were already around Port Hercule, until she reached the pretty little chapel of Sainte Devote, the 4th century patron saint of Monaco. Unable by now to run up the hill towards the Casino Square, she walked as fast as she could, knowing that she would never make it back to her apartment before the Milo od Montenegro left for Cap Ferrat, but at least she was doing her best.

As Jemima powerwalked up the steep pavement of Avenue Ostende, she looked over at the port and the row of bars that sprang up every summer to lure people off their boats. The summer before she had spent a fun night there with Define, before heading to the famous Jimmy'z Club. She wondered if she would get the opportunity for some nightlife this summer, but inwardly knew it wouldn't happen; she needed to be on the ball and couldn't risk drunken disasters. She thought back to the Vogel gala she'd organised at Somerset House when the Vogel Vanderpless necklace had been stolen. Paul Pratt had spiked her drink and, consequently, she had missed Petrina stealing the main diamonds from the huge necklace. Maybe she should have an alcohol-free summer?

When Jemima reached the top of the hill, she looked up ahead at the Vogel and Van Cleef boutiques by the Casino. It was now almost 8pm and, despite the police presence, the usual Friday evening excitement was in full flow. Glamorous hotel guests were filing out of Hotel de Paris, people were making their way into the Casino to play roulette and blackjack, and the engines of fleets of Ferraris, Lamborghinis, and Maseratis were revving as the cars' owners drove them at no more than 5mph around the Disney-esque playground for the very rich.

"I'll call Renault from the store!" Jemima said aloud to herself, as she saw the lights were still on through Vogel's windows.

She made her way towards the same steps that, three hours earlier, had smoke billowing down, and was greeted by one of the security personnel at the entrance to the world-famous Casino.

"Madame, you are not allowed in here in sports clothes."

"But I desperately need to speak with the Comtesse de Ré! I know that she is still in there. I work for Mr Vogel," she pleaded.

"I am sorry, but I cannot allow you to enter," he said, shaking his head without even looking at her.

There was no point; Jemima knew she wouldn't get in, so she left, frustrated tears pricking her eyes. She wasn't much of a diamond detective if she couldn't even alert the Interpol Detective. She ran around the throng of mostly tourists sitting at the Cafe de Paris's outdoor tables and spotted Yves, an old colleague who used to work for Vogel in Paris but was now at Graff in Monaco, sitting next to a very good-looking man.

"Jemima, you look like you're on a mission to get somewhere fast!" he teased, seeing her purposeful pace amongst the crowded terrace of tables.

"Ah, Yves, I am. How are…" Jemima didn't have time for pleasantries, particularly as she didn't want to be spotted speaking to a rival brand, which was something that Vogel didn't like at all. "Actually, can I borrow your phone? Do you know Detective

Renault?"

"Bien sur, you can use my phone, here you go. And yes, I know Charles. Very well, in fact," he added in a whisper, with a twinkle in his eye. The man who was clearly his boyfriend turned away to light a cigarette. "Why do you need to call him?"

"I don't want to be rude, but can you call him quickly, and then I'll explain?"

Yves found the number and dialled. "It's gone straight to voicemail, *ma chérie*," he said, raising his shoulders in that typical French way before the phone started to ring again. "*Ahh, mais voila* – he is calling me back!"

Jemima pulled it from him and explained everything to Renault as calmly as she could, which she knew wasn't very calmly at all, since she was breathless from racing across from Fontvieille. She nodded and gave Yves back his phone.

"He's going to call me back." Jemima nodded again and sat down.

"Well, you have just arrived, and you have already caught the Pink Panthers!" Yves said, patting her on her back, having overheard the conversation. "Champagne?" She smiled at him gratefully.

"No, thank you, Yves. Let's find out whether the police do actually catch them!"

Yves's phone rang again, and he handed it directly to Jemima.

"Monsieur Renault?" she spoke into the phone.

"Thank you for your message, Miss Fox-Pearl. However, I cannot just send out a police boat on a whim without any evidence."

"What – but can't you just go and search the boat? They've gone to Cap Ferrat for dinner! The jewels will be on the boat.

They're in a dark blue or black rucksack!"

"I am sorry, but without photos or anything substantial… well, it is just impossible."

"Seriously?" She handed the phone back to Yves when it was clear that Renault had hung up.

"Apparently, he can't send the sea police after the boat without any proof and without any photos – but I don't have any." She could hardly believe it, but soon remembered how Renault hadn't regarded her much earlier, except for her appearance. She was deflated.

"I guess he is busy this evening, what, with the Interpol meeting and then this huge heist. They can't go chasing boats without any evidence. We lost nothing at the hotel." He nodded towards Hotel de Paris. "But you and all the others did."

"Yes, I know. I've got to go!" She couldn't think of who else to alert, but she needed to get her phone charged, so she sprinted the several hundred metres back along Boulevards des Moulins and d'Italie to La Radieuse. By the time she got there, it was almost dark and all she wanted to do was go to bed, but she hadn't even seen her bedroom properly yet.

Jemima went to retrieve the phone charger from her handbag and as soon as she plugged it in, the screen lit up with the big white apple and started to power up. A text from James popped up, saying he'd seen the news about the heists and hoped that she wasn't involved. Jemima couldn't help but laugh – it could almost be read as though she might have been part of an inside job. After she'd replied that all was fine and she couldn't wait to see him, she pulled her bags into the bedroom and then turned the lights on. She smiled when she saw the beautiful, big, four-poster bed that took centre stage in the large, high-ceilinged room that was identical to the sitting room next door, with the addition of some beautiful, antique bedroom furniture. The bed cover was the same 1980s Laura Ashley washed out cornflower blue and white that her mother had in the spare room in Dorset.

Jemima kicked off her running shoes, left her phone charging, then climbed up on to the high bed with her iPad and collapsed into the deep covers and pillows. It was pointless trying to persuade Renault again, she mused, and now it would be too late to catch them red-handed. She thought about Petrina, the guy, and all the jewellery they had. She remembered the name that sounded like *Piotur*.

Jemima proceeded to Google 'Piotur Pink Panthers'. There were endless articles about the police hunting the famous gang, how they got their name, and, of course, YouTube videos from the heist a few hours earlier, but nothing about a Piotur.

It was now 9pm. As Mr V had told Jemima to go home and unpack, she decided to shower and sort out her clothes before going to sleep. She wouldn't tell anyone else about seeing the boat with all the jewels and Petrina shagging in the shower, bedecked in diamonds and emeralds. She didn't want to look like an idiot and be told off for letting them go. But she would keep an eye out for the super-slick speed boat. Maybe she should go back and ask the red-faced Brit to keep her informed? But then, she might put her foot in it: she knew that she had a habit of doing that from time to time. Quickly hanging up only half of the clothes in her suitcases, she took a shower and climbed into bed. Before five minutes were up, she was fast asleep.

# Chapter 9

---

# La Radieuse, Boulevard d'Italie
# Saturday 7<sup>th</sup> May

Jemima woke up and looked at the clock on the bedside table. It was only 7.00am but she had left the shutters and windows open, and, although the sun was shining brightly, there was a cold breeze. She shivered as she realised she was lying naked with the duvet and covers kicked to one side. She must have had a restless sleep, but couldn't remember her dream.

There were three hours before she needed to be at the meeting with the premiere event planners and, unlike in London, the office was a mere ten-minute walk from her apartment. So, she stretched herself out in her huge four-poster bed in her large apartment with its beautifully high ceilings. It only had two rooms, but it seemed enormous for her, and it was the first time in her whole life that she'd ever lived alone. From the age of eight until eighteen, she'd shared a bedroom with up to ten girls at boarding school, and since then she'd always had flatmates at both university and in London. Jemima smiled contently to herself and opened her eyes again. She felt like a proper grown-up in this grand flat all on her own.

Then the events of the day before caught up on her and she wondered if the police had managed to track down the Milos od

Montenegro, full of stolen jewels. Jemima shifted herself up, so she was propped up on a cushion against the elaborate headboard, and turned to take her iPad from the bedside to see any news updates; as she did, she looked out of the large French windows that led from her room to the little balcony. She could see nothing but the blue – no, aquamarine – sea and a few ochre-coloured tiled rooftops. The sun was beaming through the high window on to the shiny wooden floor, and she could hear that seaside sound of seagulls squawking. Bliss.

Jemima thought of waking up in this bed, with this view, with James next to her, and felt her heart jump with excitement, something it tended to do more frequently than normal. She decided to get up and enjoy this beautiful morning. So, Jemima threw down the iPad, pulled back the incredibly soft white duvet, and jumped off the high bed on to the Laura Ashley bedspread that had slipped to the floor. She walked across to the balcony, pulling her thin cotton robe around her before she exposed herself – not that there would be anyone up this early on a Saturday, she imagined. Except, perhaps, a few fishermen along the coast.

Jemima stepped out on to the little balcony and was surprised to see people swimming at Larvotto Beach below and dogs running around. How she'd love to bring her small Jacksund terrier, Milo, here to keep her company: he would love the beach, although he could get in the way if she was diamond hunting! Milo had been staying with her parents in Dorset since she went off to South Africa after the gala in April, and she missed him so much. Breathing in the sea air, Jemima stepped away, crossed the bedroom to the bathroom, splashed her face with water, and dabbed on some Elizabeth Arden face cream.

Suddenly, Jemima felt incredibly hungry and decided to run

down to the small bakery a few doors up the street and get a coffee and a croissant, but, as she walked back into her bedroom, and once again saw the sea sparkling out of the window, she mentally changed her plan and decided to start the day with a swim. Jemima had packed a few bikinis from Harvey Nichols, so she dug around in her bags and chose a blue and white striped Melissa Odabash one. She put it on under a white linen dress, slipped into a pair of espadrilles, and checked herself in the mirror before putting a towel, her purse, phone, and keys into a wicker bag she found in one of the huge wardrobes which lined a wall of her bedroom.

Jemima was grateful that her temporary posting to Monaco provided an apartment that was furnished so beautifully. She wondered whose apartment it was that the Vogels had rented. Glancing back into the large sitting room, Jemima noticed, for the first time, that there were a few antique-looking pictures that clearly belonged to the owner. Maybe they lived there in the winter months and rented it out each summer? She walked to the windows and opened the glass doors and the white wooden shutters of the sitting room that she had closed last night before bed. As Jemima did so, she couldn't help but notice that they could do with a lick of paint, though she could see the sea even more clearly than from her bedroom. She couldn't stop smiling, but realised that, if she wanted a swim, she had better hurry up. So, grabbing the bag, she ran out of her apartment, down the few flights of stairs to the bottom, and out of the heavy glass door with iron bars.

Monaco is very easy to navigate, so Jemima knew the way down to the beach from her friend's apartment on Place des Moulins. She walked at almost a run up the street, grabbed a coffee and two croissants from Bar Tabac, then took one of the seven principle lifts down. Five minutes later, having devoured one of the croissants, Jemima crossed the road outside the Grimaldi Forum and walked quickly towards the shingle beach, still sipping her coffee. She noticed a tall, elegant-looking lady in a large sunhat, with two Jack Russell terriers at her feet, buying a copy of The Daily Mail at the kiosk on the promenade. She must be English, she assumed. As she walked past, she smiled at the beautiful lady who had turned to leave and threw her empty coffee cup in a bin and stepped onto the tiny pebbles.

The beach was pretty empty. After all, it was only 7.45am. So, she lay her towel down between the several cafes that lined the shore and the sea, thinking that she was probably the only person under fifty here. Hoping that she would, at some point, make some friends, Jemima remembered that she was there for work – and the sooner she caught Petrina Lindberg, the sooner she would be back in her flat in Sloane Square. In order to make the most of it, Jemima ran to the water, shallow dived in, and sprint swum out to the pontoon about ten minutes from the shore. Heaving herself out of the water, rather than using the ladder, she lay on it, gasping to get her breath back, and gazed back at the shore. The packed-in apartment buildings rose high against the grass and heather-covered mountains, behind which was the glorious blue sky.

Since she had awoken, Jemima had felt like she was on holiday but then with a shiver remembered why she was here. She thought back to the mess of the last evening, having been unable to get the proof she needed to catch Petrina red-handed, and started to wonder if she was actually equipped to catch her and find the Vogel Vanderpless diamonds. And what about the heist yesterday? Was she going to be involved in that too? Jemima wished she had taken that Vogel ring from the rucksack – it would have been the proof she needed, and she could have taken it to Mr V. Suddenly, she could feel that familiar flicker of butterflies starting in her stomach as the sun went behind a cloud. Shivering again from the cold and her nerves, she dived back into the water and front-crawled her way back to shore.

When Jemima let herself back into the apartment, she found that a smart Smythson of Bond Street envelope had been slipped under her door. Putting down the wicker basket, she picked up the envelope, took the fresh coffee she bought on her way back, and walked over to the little white metal table on the balcony. Putting everything down, she sat and used an arm of her sunglasses to open the thick blue paper of the envelope.

Dear Jemima,

I do hope you have settled in well and that you had a comfortable first night.

The apartment belongs to me and, should you need anything, please do knock on my door – I am on the sixth floor.

If you would like to join me for supper this evening, Saturday, please let me know by return.

Sincerely yours,

Henrietta Burgoyne de Bourbon

"Gosh, how lovely," Jemima said to the large fat seagull sitting on the balcony railing, before wondering how she would 'reply by return'. The only notepaper that she had was the pad she had pinched from Hotel de Paris and a few old Vogel business cards.

Jemima went into her bedroom, dug out the notepaper, and replied saying how she'd be delighted to have supper with Mrs Burgoyne de Bourbon that evening. Feeling refreshed from her morning swim, she threw the newspaper on the low coffee table in the sitting room, took her takeout coffee cup into the kitchen, and walked to the bathroom. As she stood under the power shower's hot water, she wondered who this lady was. 'De Bourbon' was a French aristocratic name affixed on to the end of a very English one.

* * *

Over an hour later and after unpacking, Jemima walked up the pavement, reluctantly passed the coffee shop – she really didn't need another one, although the smell of coffee and croissants was so tempting – walked down Boulevard des Moulins, and called James.

"Hi, darling. Where you?" His husky South African accent came down the line and her legs almost went to jelly.

"I'm walking to a meeting at the event planner's office for the event on Monday night."

"Good! Well, work hard today and I'll see you tomorrow. You know they've booked me into the Fairmont?

"Oh, no. You don't want to come to my apartment? It's amazing."

"Darling, I'll do whatever you want. Listen, I have to run – I'll call you in the morning when I land."

"Okay, cool."

Jemima ended the call and kept walking along the left side of the street out of the sun. At 9.45am, it was already very hot, and she noticed a digital thermometer outside a pharmacy saying it was now twenty-seven degrees. She wasn't surprised: the white cotton dress was sticking to her back after only five minutes. She also couldn't help noticing how immaculate everything was: there wasn't a coke can, a cigarette stub, or even a stray leaf on the streets. Suddenly, she remembered being told that street washers start scrubbing the tarmac around 4am.

Jemima looked in the windows of the little boutiques, most of which were filled with either very expensive clothes or fancy furniture. She passed a little antique jewellery boutique and stopped to look; there were such exquisite pieces in the window alone. A pair of aquamarine and amethyst chandelier earrings caught her eye; they were beautiful and intricately designed, despite being big and bold. There was also a sweet brooch of a Panther; she wondered if it would bring her luck if she bought it! With a smile, she guessed at how much the items were and whether she could justify putting them on the company credit card.

## Chapter 10

---

# Offices of Renata René Productions, Boulevard des Moulins

Jemima arrived at the event planner's office opposite the smart-looking tourist office on Boulevard des Moulins and pressed the intercom. Just as she was about to press it again, her phone rang. It was Mr Vogel.

"Jemima, good morning, how are you?"

"Yes, all is fine, thank you. I'm just at the event planner's office for the meeting," she said, wondering when he was going to let her know about any developments on the heist. She still felt unable to tell him hers. She had basically let the thieves get away with millions of euros' worth of high jewellery.

"Good, well, let me and Alexa know how it goes."

"Of course."

"Now, I know it's not in your new job description, but... I need you to pick up my wife's new Ferrari from the garage in Monaco and bring it out to us in Cap Ferrat. I take it you drive?"

Red Ferraris started flashing in front of her eyes. Suddenly, she didn't know if it was the heat, whether the sun had moved around and she was no longer in the shade, or whether or not this was even reality. Looking at her reflection in a dark window pane, she could see that her hair was frizzing like anything, and her French Sole ballerina shoes were stretched across her already swollen feet. If she turned up at a Ferrari garage looking like this – they'd call the police.

"Um, yes, of course? Today?" She was excited to take the car out of for a coastal drive but couldn't believe this was more important than the millions of dollars that were stolen yesterday afternoon.

"We're away for the weekend on the coast, so as long as it is there before Monday morning, that will be marvellous. Anna will send you our villa's address. The security guard will let you in when you arrive," he continued. "I have told them at the garage to expect you. It is the one on Avenue Princesse Grace."

"Right, urgh, okay…" She was about to let on that she had never driven anything snazzier than a Fiat Barchetta and joke that at least they were made by the same company, but thought better of it.

"It is her birthday tomorrow and the car is a surprise for when we get back on Monday," he said, sounding excited.

"Okay, Mr V," she said, but the phone had already gone dead and there was a voice coming through the intercom.

*"Oui, allo?"*

*"Allo bonjour – c'est Jemima Fox-Pearl pour Madame René."*

*"Ah oui, Jemima. Allez-y. C'est au cinquième étage,"* came a pleasant French voice from the intercom. The speaker buzzed open the big glass and brass doors for Jemima to go up to the fifth floor.

Jemima wondered if Petrina's mother would be at the meeting. After all, it was her movie that they had sponsored. She was quite fascinated about meeting the woman in person. Jemima walked through the marble-floored and richly-wallpapered hall to the large lift at the end. When it arrived, she stepped inside and pressed for the fifth floor. She couldn't help but notice her carefully applied makeup, particularly her mascara, had already slipped. Jemima felt incredibly nervous about looking like a poor English girl compared to the elegant French and American woman she was about to meet. She half wished that she hadn't swum that morning and had attempted to make her Carol Joy blow dry last longer, or even splurged on one that morning. Alexa had said they had a salon in the Fairmont Hotel, and she passed at least two hair salons on the way here.

"Salut!" The door to an office opened as she stepped out of the lift and walked across the small, dark landing to it. As she was about to step through, a very pretty, dark blonde girl with the bluest of eyes smiled at her and held out her hand.

"How are you? I am so pleased to meet you. I am sorry – I could hear the door buzzing but I was on the phone to Amex and couldn't get away. Come in. Oh, and I am Céline."

"Jemima." Jemima shook her hand, noticing that her English was perfect, and they walked into the most incredible office she had ever seen that was world's away from Mr Vogel's, though his wasn't really a real office. This whole place was in white; it was almost spacelike.

"Oui, I know." Céline acknowledged her surprise by smiling. "Renata René likes white! By the way, she is running late, as she is coming from Antibes where she has an event tomorrow. And Mrs Lindberg should be here any moment now. Would you like a cup of coffee?" she asked, walking towards what Jemima imagined was a kitchen.

She nodded and sat down as she heard the coffee machine start – Nespresso, no doubt. She'd be buzzing if she had another strong

French coffee. Jemima looked at her chair, noticed it was white snakeskin leather, and felt she recognised it. It was probably the one she saw in the window of one of the expensive furniture shops on the way here.

Jemima looked about her and absolutely everything was white, even the matt-like carpeted floor. The walls were alabaster with large white wooden frames containing black and white photographs. To her right, she saw two doors that must have been street side but were closed; to her left were two more closed doors and a little room which she presumed was Céline's, as it was open and the office looked a lot more lived in. The only glaringly non-white object was a huge palm tree planted in a white square pot with white pebbles about the base. There weren't any photographs of events that they had organised, which she thought was unusual.

"Here you go, take this and I'll show you around." Céline came back and handed her a small espresso-sized white cup and saucer.

"Thanks. Don't you get a little entranced by the colour? Well, the lack of it!"

"Yes, but I am used to it. To be honest, it is better than what it was. Follow me. This will make you smile."

Jemima followed her to one of the two closed doors she guessed would face on to the street.

"This is Renata's office, and this," she said, walking to the second door, "is the meeting room." Céline opened it and went in. Jemima looked out of the huge panoramic window that led out onto an extensive terrace.

Jemima took in the view. It was far more than streets and rooftops, like the one she had in London, although wintertime in the capital enabled her to see past the bare trees to Buckingham Palace. Her current view was amazing. Jemima could see all the way down to the Mediterranean; just a few glamorous buildings were in the way, including the Casino and the Hotel de Paris.

"Do you like it?" The French woman brought her mind back; she hadn't realised that she had quietly left the room and returned with a tray of coffees, juices, and pastries, which she placed on the large white glass table.

"Oh my gosh. Yes, it is possibly the best view I have ever seen from an office!"

"Mrs Lindberg has arrived. Would you like to sit down? I'll bring her in."

\* \* \*

Fortunata Lindberg was as glamorous as her name, and still as beautiful as Monsieur Renault had described her to be back in the seventies. Dressed a little like the author Jackie Collins, Fortunata was wearing a cream silk shirt under a black trouser suit, the jacket of which was lined with leopard print. She wore a pair of emerald and diamond earrings that Jemima recognised as David Morris and had a huge emerald ring next to a thin diamond set wedding band; the suite of jewels only intensified her deep green eyes. She was about the same height as Jemima but wearing towering heels underneath her trouser suit, and her dark brown hair was blow dried to perfectly fall down her back. In fact, she could easily have been Lucky Santiago, one of Jackie's protagonists. However, she had a worried air about her when she took a seat opposite Jemima at the large table and accepted the coffee – black, no sugar – that Céline gave her.

"I must leave you. Madame René is having problems getting back from Antibes and I am trying to sort out a helicopter or boat so that she doesn't miss the meeting. *Je suis tellement desolée.*" Céline apologised and closed the door behind her.

Jemima looked at Fortunata, who she knew had become friendly with Alexa Vogel two years ago when the movie was being made.

"Oh dear, what shall we do if she doesn't turn up?" asked Jemima.

"I believe that your Head of Security is coming to discuss the logistics with Madame René. I hope that he isn't too put out that she isn't here? I suppose we should have gone to meet her. It probably would have been more sensible." Fortunata kept looking down to tap at her phone, and Jemima reflected back to the minor security issues that had happened at Vogel since she started a year ago, and knew that Philip Goldsmith, the Head of Security at Vogel, would most definitely be put out.

"It's really hard getting around Monaco – maybe he is stuck in traffic? These Grand Prix structures have completely blocked off the usual routes around the town." Then, changing the subject, Jemima asked a question she already knew the answer to, since she was never one who could sit in awkward silence. "Do you know Monaco well? I imagine you've been to lots of Cannes Film Festivals?"

Fortunata hesitated a little before she looked up from her phone. She sighed, put it down, and seemed to relax.

"Well, I do come down to the Riviera quite a bit, but this is only the second time I have been in Monaco in about thirty years. I grew up here, you see, but I've only been back a couple of times since I met my husband and we left for the States."

"Didn't you want to see your family or did they come with you? To America, I assume?" Jemima added, wondering if she was being too friendly or, indeed, inquisitive. She didn't want to be unmasked too early in her diamond detective role.

Again, Fortunata paused, but this time she put her phone firmly in her handbag, which was a crocodile skin Hermes Kelly, and Jemima couldn't help but notice the appropriateness of it. After all, they were here to launch Fortunata's remake of Grace Kelly's most famous film before she became Princess of Monaco.

"It is rather a coincidence that I am making a movie about a cat burglar on the Riviera. My father was just that – for several decades. He is no longer alive." Fortunata smiled sadly and Jemima realised that she couldn't push it any further.

Jemima could just imagine Fortunata complaining to Alexa about her and being sent home immediately for ruining the investigation!

# Chapter 11

---

# Fortunata's Story

As Fortunata listened to the pretty English girl chat away in front of her, she started to think about the place where she had grown up and then escaped, and how it was so lovely to be back here amidst the very many happy memories she had of this magical princedom by the sea. The filming of the movie hadn't taken place in Monaco itself – well, only one scene had been shot there, but she hadn't been able to attend, because Patrick had needed her back in New York City. She poured herself another coffee from the pot and, for the first time in years, added a small brown sugar cube. She watched her hand slowly stir the spoon around the pretty china cup and let her imagination drift back a few decades.

Fortunata had been born in January 1957, almost exactly nine months after her parents met. She was named after her father's nickname and her mother's Italian heritage. Her parents had married quickly and quietly, so she was born legitimately, which was important in the strict Catholic society of Monaco in the fifties. Her early years were not for want of anything. For as long as Fortunata remembered, she was given anything and everything a little girl could possibly need, let alone want. She never really knew what work her father did, but when she was eight years old in 1965, he opened La Pantera. It started as a family run Italian bistro – Pierina asked her Italian mother to cook, and her three brothers to be waiters. Lucky was the maître d' and face of the place. He would spend the early mornings speeding along the coastal route to Ventimiglia and further afield to Genoa to buy the produce and wine that made La Pantera the best Italian restaurant outside of Italy.

Although her father said it was named after his wife's family, she much later discovered that it was actually named after the first piece of jewellery he stole: the Cartier Panthère ring from his mentor and benefactor, Duchess Tatiana. La Pantera was far enough away from the confines of The Rock and its palace to be able to have more freedom than most restaurants, and, by the end of the sixties, it was firmly established as one of the top places to see and be seen along the Riviera. Everyone who was anyone came, including Princess Grace's old Hollywood friends, who would sometimes spend the summers enjoying the regal treatment that they got off the back of Her Serene Highness. The tables would spill out over the empty Boulevard between the restaurant and the sea, and, during the summer, most evenings became an unofficial party, with the beau monde sailing their boats and mooring them out in the bay. It wasn't unusual to see one of Pierina's brothers acting as the tender's valet, picking people up from their boats and depositing them back after closing, which could be anything up until 2am.

When Fortunata was six, the family moved from a tiny one-bedroom apartment above a tabac near the railway station to a prominent house. Fortunata grew up with the rich kids of the principality. She was always fascinated by the world of Hollywood and loved to listen to the actors and actresses who frequented La Pantera and talk into the early hours about life in the movies. It was through the film producer, David Niven Jr, son of the old English actor David Niven, that she met her future husband, Patrick Lindberg, at a party in honour of his birthday. David Jr knew Fortunata through her parents's restaurant, where he was a regular. Patrick had spotted her at the old actor's infamous pink villa, La Fleur du Cap, but only plucked up the courage to ask her to dance after several nightcaps outside La Pantera, where her uncles, who were long past being mere waiters, couldn't see. He had been in his late thirties, blond, Swedish-American, and devastatingly good-looking; she was just twenty and longing to leave her small, closed community on the Rock. He quickly whizzed her off to live the American Dream, and they had their only child – a daughter, Petrina on Valentine's Day 1978.

Patrick had funded her first film – produced alongside his old friend David Niven Jr and starring a young Glenn Close in a tiny walk-on role – that she fitted in amidst her Broadway theatre work. Over the years since then, Glenn had become a friend and was now one of the three main roles in the remake of To Catch a Thief, her other baby. There had been more than five years of negotiations to get the green light to do this movie, the original version of which had brought Grace Kelly down to the French Riviera in the first place. Eventually, with the agreement of the estate of Alfred Hitchcock, the only way it was allowed to proceed was that a percentage of all global box office takings and the full cost of tickets to the premiere would go to The Princess Grace Foundation.

As she had explained to the girl from Vogel, who was now standing out on the balcony, Fortunata had been back to Monaco only twice since she had left over three decades earlier. Once for her mother's funeral, and then to meet with Prince Albert, seeking permission to hold the premiere in the open-air cinema next to the palace. She had also secured the two hottest Hollywood actors of the moment: Richard Wakefield, an Irish actor, who had recently won the Best Actor Oscar for his portrayal of Prince Andrei in the hugely nominated epic War & Peace, and who was being tipped to play James Bond, and Evie Talbot, a beautiful Irish-American actress who happened to bear a huge resemblance to Grace Kelly herself, with honey blonde hair and piercing blue eyes.

The story had been slightly reworked and was more like the original 1952 book by David Dodge. Very few people knew that there had been a book, but, like many Hitchcock movies, Hitchcock had based his famous film on quite an unknown story. David Dodge had been an American travel journalist and author who wrote his greatest book based on a true story that had happened to his family whilst living in the hills above Cannes. Fortunata had read the book as a girl when her teacher had given it to her, in order to improve her English, and she had fallen in love with the romance between Francie, a rich American girl on holiday in the South of France with her mother, and John Robie, an older, ex-cat burglar being trailed by the police for a new series of thefts. It seemed to coincide with the spate of burglaries happening around the coast from time to time. Little did she know, then, it was her father. But it had been, and his imprisonment and subsequent escape caused humiliation for her mother, and for the restaurant to go bankrupt for lack of business. Fortunata thought that, if she could remake the movie before one of her rivals did, and donate to the foundation in her mother's memory, then she would be able to set some wrongs right.

Fortunata had found out about her father's decades as the Snow Leopard only after he had disappeared. Her mother had called her in tears, begging her to come home, telling her all about Nico's moonlighting – quite literally – as a cat burglar. However, before she had a chance to return to Monaco, her mother was found dead, her body washed up in Fontvieille, having supposedly jumped off the Rock of Monaco.

Fortunata had never told anyone, not even Patrick, about what her mother had left buried at the spot she jumped from, but she knew her daughter was suspicious of the stunning sapphire that she had recently been photographed wearing. And, with a sense of panic rising in her veins, she couldn't help but wonder as to who had planted the seed of suspicion in the girl.

## Chapter 12

# Vogel Boutique, Casino de Monte Carlo

Jemima and Fortunata decided to leave when Renata René and Philip Goldsmith called to say they couldn't get into the centre of town.

Philip was in touch with the security at the palace and was remarkably relaxed. After all, "If they can keep the King safe, how on earth could the palace guards not be able to protect the jewellery?"

Jemima didn't want to remind him that Prince Albert wasn't a King, but she just hoped he knew what he was doing. He had been working for the company for as long as they had a store in Monaco, so she was sure he was pretty sussed up on the local security. Therefore, her job of looking after Evie Talbot and her jewellery during the premiere and gala should be a walk in the park.

As Jemima walked towards the main glass doors on the ground floor, leaving Fortunata in the cool of the building to make some calls, she saw a flotilla of Ferraris speed past. Dismissing, for the time, her mission to pick up and drive Mrs Vogel's new Ferrari out to Cap Ferrat, she thought she would nip down to the boutique and see if the director, the Comtesse de Ré, had picked anything out for her to borrow for the gala in two days' time. She also wanted to discover more details about the heist.

Jemima stepped through the doors on to the pavement and the heat hit her. It was only about an hour since she'd gone inside the cool interior, but outside the marbled pavement and structures of the building were so polished that the sun's reflection blinded her. With her eyes screwed, she dug around in her bag for her Tom Ford sunglasses. She took them out of their huge case, pushed them on to her face, and opened her eyes.

Leaving the office building, Jemima crossed over Boulevard des Moulins, one of Monaco's main thoroughfares. She walked past the tourist office, through the pretty palmed Jardins de la Petite Afrique, and crossed Avenue des Spélugues, which, in a couple of weeks, would have Formula 1 cars speeding down it to La Place du Casino. She passed the Café de Paris that was, as ever, full with tourists and continued towards the impressive Casino. It was impossible not to notice the police cars and officers. That wasn't a surprise. She just wondered how the thieves managed to burgle four stores within a hundred metre circle. Monaco was one of the safest places in the world, partly due to its high police presence at every street corner. Except if you were a gemstone, it seemed.

Jemima wasn't stopped this time as she walked up the steps of the Casino to the Vogel store. Smiling politely at the guy who had prevented her from having Petrina arrested the night before, she walked into the thankfully air-conditioned atrium of the Casino. Again, she thought briefly of Fortunata and her daughter. How could such a lovely woman have such a corrupt daughter who, from all intents and purposes, seemed potentially poised to ruin her mother's night by being involved in a raid on the gala? It seemed completely unconscionable. She just hoped that Philip was right and that the security was seamless.

An elegantly dressed doorman opened the large glass door to the Vogel boutique and Jemima stepped inside another of her company's diamond boutiques. The glossy interiors followed the brand's theme of green and gold. No one would have guessed that only twenty-four hours earlier there had been a heist with €20 million of jewels taken from this store alone, some of which she had seen on the boat last night. Other than two empty wall cabinets, which had been shattered, the five remaining glass cabinets, attached to the green silk-papered walls, were full of the most brilliant and bright diamond jewellery with the largest of gemstones. Necklaces, earrings, and rings set with diamonds in every cut possible sat proudly, waiting to be bought by the luckiest of women, or indeed their husbands or boyfriends. Emeralds, rubies, and sapphires as large as quails' eggs, and surrounded by diamonds, were set as rings or pendants suspended from strands of smaller stones. Jemima knew the collections well, but, in Monte Carlo, they had the biggest and best each summer to attract the kind of clientele who spent the sunny months on their boats and in their villas and gave the Riviera its rich reputation. Jemima was relieved to see that the aquamarine and diamond 'parure' that she hoped to borrow for the gala was still there, or rather a similar one to that which had been stolen.

This summer, the master jewellers in Vogel's workshops in Hatton's Gardens's Saffron Hill had worked even harder to produce extra pieces that could be lent to film stars and VIPs for the premiere of To Catch a Thief. It was these pieces that needed to be protected from the Pink Panthers and Petrina on Monday night.

Vogel's boutique director for thirty years, since the day they opened the doors of their first store outside London, was Diane la Comtesse de Ré. She was an extremely elegant French Monegasque aristocrat, in her early eighties, who had known Prince Rainier III, the current Prince of Monaco's father, since childhood. She therefore had a front door into the Princely family and didn't hesitate to use it, discreetly, for the good of Vogel, who had 'stolen' her from Cartier all those years ago.

*"Ah, Jemima. Bonjour. Comment allez-vous?"* She said, sitting at her own gold and marble Louis XVI desk by the back wall of the boutique. You'd never guess that she was a day older than seventy; she had no doubt been under the knife more than once.

"Bonjour, Comtesse." Feeling, as ever, like she should be curtsying, Jemima continued. "I hope that you are okay after the heist yesterday. How terrifying," she added, remembering the CCTV video on Mr V's phone.

"Yes, it was terrible." The aristocratic lady said. "Poor Julie—" she nodded to one of the store assistants "—has only been working with us for a few days. She still has a mark on her back. But Jean-Pierre has had to stay at home. He's too terrified to come in." Jemima's thoughts flickered back to the man they had seen being shouted at with a gun to his head.

"I was with a client at the hotel," she continued. "Alors! Thank you for coming to see me. Let's go through the pieces we are lending to the actresses for the gala. Julie?" She nodded to the pretty, dark haired girl who went into offices behind and came back a few minutes with some of Vogel's most important pieces – the haute couture of their jewels – on two large, blue, velvet trays. She placed them on the Comtesse's desk and Jemima sat down in one of the matching Louis XVI gilt chairs, remembering to place her bag on the other. It seemed rather unseemly to put in on the floor, even if it was marble. "Now, Mrs Vogel and Alexa haven't, as yet, chosen what they are going to be wearing – they might put on their own pieces – but these are for Madame Close and Mademoiselle Talbot," she said.

Jemima looked at Glenn Close's tray. On it was a ruby and diamond parure, which is a matching set of necklace, earrings, and a ring that sometimes includes a bracelet and brooch. The necklace had two strands of 3-carat marquise cut rubies, interspersed every third with a 3-carat marquise diamond; they came together with a large oval ruby of about 8-carats, surrounded by brilliant diamonds, from which was suspended an even larger oval ruby at about 15-carats, and again surrounded by more diamonds. The earrings and bracelet followed the same style using marquise and oval cut rubies and diamonds. The Comtesse opened the large oval ruby and diamond on the bracelet to reveal an exquisite watch hidden beneath. "Madame Close told me that she hates not knowing the time!" she said with a knowing smile, and Jemima imagined that the Comtesse was also punctual.

Evie Talbot's pieces, a sapphire and diamond demi-parure of necklace, bracelet, and ring, were less opulent, reflecting perhaps the age of the twenty-three-year-old actress; a necklace as large as Glenn's would have drowned her tiny frame. The Princess Grace huge pendant earrings were absolutely exquisite. Each piece had a pear-shaped sapphire, which were, in turn, surrounded by round, brilliant white diamonds. The sapphires were an unusually pale blue – almost cornflower blue. Suspended from below one of the white diamonds, there was a pavé set diamond bell, from which hung a large pear drop set with sapphires in a mystery setting that had been made famous by Van Cleef.

"Mr Vogel has replicated the earrings using the original Van

Cleef and Arpels drawings and gouaches perfectly. After all, he also made the original pair!" The Comtesse smiled as though it was a miracle. "These are the earrings to celebrate the gala and the opening of the Jewel Museum of Monaco; Mr Vogel is incredibly generous to be gifting them. We were going to be displaying them over there," she continued, pointing at the now empty and glassless cabinet, "but *grâce à dieu* we didn't. These only arrived yesterday with Mr Vogel and we didn't have enough time to mount them properly in the cabinet with the original gouache renderings."

Jemima watched as the Comtesse pulled out a grey vellum parchment paper with the original sapphire and diamond earrings made by Van Cleef, perfectly painted on in water colour. The new Vogel pendant earrings really did look exactly the same. Jemima knew that gouaches were rare and now only painted for pieces of high jewellery. "We are going to display them together in the Museum." said the Comtesse. "Do you know the story of the original earrings – the sapphires around which they were created?"

"Not really, no," Jemima said, although Alexa had told her – she could tell that the old lady would no doubt tell her more interesting information. She loved jewellery stories, particularly when they involved a mystery.

"*Alors*. Princess Grace's godmother, a wealthy Pennsylvanian woman called Pauline McCloskey, bought a pair of sapphire and diamond earrings from Barbara Hutton that had once belonged to Tsarina Maria Feodorovna. The two large pale sapphires surmounted above the pear shaped pendants of the earrings," she pointed to the relevant parts of the earrings on the gouache, "had originally been set in a brooch alongside a 197-carat pale blue sapphire. Cartier had bought that *énorme* sapphire after the Dowager Empress's death in 1928 and sold it a year later to a famous opera singer, Ganna Waleska, who commissioned them to make a piece of jewellery for her using it. They called the stone the Romanov Sapphire and set it in a sautoir, from which hung a 256.60-carat Mogul carved emerald drop. The opera singer wore the incredible piece of jewellery at the wedding of Woolworth heiress Barbara Hutton and Prince Mdivani a few years later. Miss Hutton so loved the unusual colour of the sapphires that she asked Cartier to find some similar ones. They had actually bought the identical pair of 98-carat sapphires at the same time as the large one, but Madame Waleska hadn't wanted them, so Cartier set them each with a diamond surround as a pair of earrings for Barbara Hutton, who was now a European princess. Move forward twenty years and one evening at a Manhattan party, Pauline McCloskey commented to Barbara Hutton, who was no longer a princess," the Comtesse added grandly "how much she loved the sapphires. She said that they were the most exquisite pale blue and would be the perfect wedding present for her goddaughter, Grace Kelly. Miss Hutton, now married to the tennis player, Gottfriend Von Cramm, practically gave them to Madame McCloskey. Barbara had so much jewellery and rather looked forward to dining off the story that the new Princess of Monaco had earrings that had once belonged to her." She took a sip of water from the crystal glass and poured one for Jemima. "Well, they were sent to Van Cleef in New York, of whom both the older couple and Grace Kelly were clients. Van Cleef used their special mystery-setting technique to create the pear drops which were then added to the bottom, but could be unclipped to return to their first incarnations as either a brooch or a simpler pair of earrings – the pear shaped sapphire and diamond cluster surmounts. The McCloskeys brought them over here on the boat in April 1956 for Grace's wedding present."

Jemima wondered if that was what the envelope from Flora's grandmother, Viscountess Fairfax, contained – notes about these Romanov sapphire earrings. After all, she had discovered at Christmas that Barbara Hutton was indeed an ancestor of her best friend.

"You know the rest of the story," the Comtesse said rhetorically, before continuing. "A few nights before the Royal Wedding, after which the McCloskey's would no doubt give their goddaughter the priceless present, the Hotel de Paris was burgled. Three suites belonging to the guests were ransacked and the Pennsylvanian pair had $50,000 worth stolen., including one turquoise and diamond necklace that she was going to wear at the ball after the wedding and the sapphire and diamond earrings for Princess Grace. Oh and a coral and diamond necklace. They were never seen again, nor was anyone caught, although we had our suspicions."

"The Snow Leopard, Nicolai Poparic." Jemima said.

"*Oui.* It was awful when we found out the Leopard's identity. We had all been friends with Nicolai and his beautiful wife, Pierina. They had the most popular restaurant, in what is now Sass Café. Over the years, jewels were stolen from unwitting guests but never the residents. Until one day in the early eighties, after the Princess died, he broke into the apartment of a Greek shipping heiress – Mrs Livanos. He was finally caught and imprisoned at the gaol on the Rock. Of course, when he was questioned about all the other thefts that had happened over the years, he always denied stealing the earrings from the Hotel de Paris that night in April 1956, and no one could prove him wrong."

The door of the boutique opened and in came a very wealthy-looking couple.

"Jemima, I must leave you," the Countess said, seeing the glamorous clients.

Jemima nodded and Julie swept away the two trays of priceless pieces of jewellery, while the Comtesse took the couple over to open a wall cabinet they were clearly interested in. She took her bag from the adjoining chair and slipped out of the boutique, not forgetting how the Vogels didn't like their non-sales staff being in the same room as clients.

Jemima was fascinated by the story she had just been told, and had an inkling there was more than just a simple connection to Fortunata's decision to hold the premiere of her movie where her mother had been so humiliated.

# Chapter 13

---

## American Bar, Hotel de Paris

Jemima walked down the steps of the Casino building, crossed the road, and was almost knocked down by a yellow Lamborghini. It was unlikely she'd be able to collect Mrs Vogel's Ferrari today; it was already 3pm and there was no way that she'd get to Cap Ferrat and back, shower, and dress for dinner with Mrs de Bourbon by 8pm. After all, she had until Monday morning to do so. She felt like she needed a cool drink and some time to think, so she walked up the steps of the Hotel de Paris.

The palatial hotel, housed in a beautiful Belle Epoque-era building, had opened in 1863. Since then, it had hosted innumerable famous faces, including the Kelly family and friends for Princess Grace's wedding. It also featured in two James Bond movies and is one of the backdrops to the Monaco Grand Prix. The American Bar was not only the hub of the hotel; it was also renowned for being a bit of a pick-up joint after 6pm.

The hotel atrium was as busy as ever and Jemima noticed Laurence Graff walk up the steps to his store. Like Harry Winston and Sidney Vogel, they had all come from having very little to being the kings of the diamond world. Jemima also spotted a few celebrities. It wasn't surprising; the film festival started along the coast in Cannes in a couple of days and maybe some of the stars had come to Monaco for the weekend beforehand and to attend the premiere of TCAT. She laughed at the acronym she'd heard Fortunata use earlier.

Jemima sat up at the bar and, refusing the barman's suggestion of a glass of champagne, asked for a citron pressé – a typical Riviera drink of lemon, ice cold water, and lots of sugar.

"Jemima!" she heard from behind. Wondering who on earth it was, she slowly and nervously turned around. "I just spotted you through the doors when I was coming back in after my lunch break!"

"Yves!" she said in relief, remembering that she had been a little unfriendly the night before.

Yves had said he was a friend of Renault, so Jemima decided it wouldn't hurt for her to spend some time with him. Besides, he knew practically everything there was to know about jewellery on the Riviera; he might be able to shed some light on what they were doing to catch the thieves, and how close they were to getting them. After all, if Petrina was proved to be the woman from the heist yesterday, then she wanted to make sure she found the Vogel Vanderpless diamond before Petrina was caught. Otherwise, they'd never get it back. However, she didn't want to talk about that here – it was too obvious. Everyone in Monaco knew Yves. And every wall in Monaco had a very well-tuned ear, so she organised to meet him in a little café she knew in Beausoleil early that evening before her dinner with Henrietta de Bourbon. But not before she asked how everything was at Graff.

"As you know, the Graff boutique wasn't burgled, but Renault is coming to talk to Mr Graff about security over the summer, and where they are with yesterday's heist. After all, it doesn't mean they won't hit Graff next time. I will find out what I can, Jemima, and tell you later."

"Thank you, Yves. Can you find out where Interpol thinks the Panthers will attack next?" If she knew their timetable, or at least Interpol's predicted one, she might be able to find the diamonds she was sent here to retrieve. Petrina and her gang could be locked up before wreaking jewellery havoc at the premiere.

"I can tell you that. It's the David Morris Jewellery luncheon tomorrow at the Hotel du Cap Eden Roc."

"How do you know?"

"Well, my boyfriend is one of the waiters," Yves said, and she remembered the hot guy he was sitting next to you yesterday.

"He looks more like a model!"

"He works for Renata René Productions when he isn't on a fashion shoot."

Jemima realised that he'd probably be working at the Vogel x To Catch a Thief gala on Monday night; it was the same events company and probably the reason why his boss, Renata René, couldn't make their meeting, as she was busy with her event at Eden Roc.

"Can he get me an invitation?"

"I don't think so, but I am sure he can get you into the event without one! Anyway, better get back to work!" Yves winked, kissed her on both cheeks, and strode out of the bar, no doubt to head back to the store on the first floor of the hotel.

Jemima paid her bill, slid off the stool, and left the bar. Before heading out of the main doors into the heat, she decided to take a look at the windows of Vogel's main rival in the fine jewellery world. Graff Diamonds had a boutique towards the back of the hotel's atrium. Sidney Vogel and Laurence Graff had known each other for years – years of outbidding each other when it came to buying the best diamonds. Maybe if she couldn't get her old job at Vogel back, she could go to Graff. Although the pink conch and diamond earrings at David Morris that she'd seen two days earlier were amazing, and she knew the wife of the owner from her days as PR at Gina Shoes, she would have to be careful not to rock the boat too much tomorrow at David Morris. She would also be sure to take her iPhone this time.

* * *

Beausoleil, 6pm

Almost exactly two hours later, Jemima Fox was sitting as far away as possible from either the Casino or Hotel de Paris, without leaving the country. Well, actually, she had left the principality: that is, by one street. Until halfway through France's Second Empire, Beausoleil had 'belonged' to Monaco, but, in exchange for four million francs, the village, along with the villages Menton, Roquebrune, and Cap Martin, was sold to France under the empireship of Napoleon III. When he died in England in 1872, his widow Empress Eugenie had built herself an incredible summer house, Villa Cyrnos, in Roquebrune-Cap Martin. You can just about see it from a boat just off the coast and Jemima was hoping to visit it one day. How, she didn't yet know!

"Jemima," Yves announced as he entered the little café and walked towards her.

It was certainly a strange place, somewhere people were coming to get a little beer and sit out in the sun, but it was also an Asian café with a display of slightly odd-looking pastries and Tupperware filled with rice and noodle salads, plus some greasy looking fried prawns.

"Yves, thank you for meeting up with me again," Jemima replied, already nervous about saying too much about why she wanted all this information. After all, she was undercover in her role to get back the Vogel diamonds, and it was only a few months ago that she was suspended from Vogel for telling someone something and being over heard by that horrid gossip columnist Steven Price from The Weekend Post.

"So, tell me, what is all this coat and knife business? Why do you want to know the Pink Panthers' schedule?"

"Ha ha, it's cloak and dagger, but I guess your version is more modern." Jemima said. "Go on, tell me – you first."

"*Alors…* last month, there was a big heist, *un vol au bélier* – you call it a 'smash and grab' – at our boutique in Dubai… you might have seen it on the news? I don't know if they showed it – they're not really newsworthy this time of year. Too many of them!" Yves laughed nervously.

Jemima had, of course, read about it: the '*vol au bélier*' for this heist concerned two Audis that smashed through the gated entrance of the luxury Wafi Mall. One of the Audis had then rammed into the front of Graff Diamonds; three masked men ran in and out of the store in a matter of minutes, then jumped into the two getaway cars and sped at a dangerously high speed out of the mall. The cars were later found burnt out and the Panthers had taken over $3.4 million of jewellery.

"Well, Renault told Mr Graff that a combination of the same DNA from the Audis was found in Van Cleef and Vogel after the heist yesterday. They therefore know who the thieves are. Or at least some of them."

"Oh my God!" she gasped. "Who was it?" she was surprised that she'd not been informed of this development at her own company.

"Well, one from Van Cleef was definitely a Milos Poznan."

Jemima immediately started Googling his name. He was the thirty-year-old son of a Serbian tycoon, who had been caught driving the getaway car from a heist at a boutique in Rome the year before, but got off. His defence team, which just happened to be Petrina's law firm, argued that their client had no idea who the two men threatening him with a gun were whilst he was innocently driving past the Damiani boutique on Via dei Condotti in his Maserati. As a matter of fact, the two men were discovered to be Pink Panthers and had gone down for a good few years.

"How come he's not in prison now if his DNA was recently found in Dubai?"

"They can't find him and no one knows what he really looks like. It was later discovered that he wore a latex mask to each court hearing. And his lawyer also said that she had no idea that it wasn't his real face!"

And neither did Jemima, but she knew what his boat looked like, and bet she knew who his liar of a lawyer was at Nortakers! She should tell Renault to get his DNA from the boat, if he believed her.

"But what's even more thrilling…" Yves started again, his eyes wide open with excitement.

"Yes?" Jemima prompted.

"The infamous Snow Leopard's DNA was also found. And… in Vogel. Renault is very excited; his father spent decades trying to prove it was him who stole the jewels from wedding guests in 1956 and a whole host of other jewellery thefts over the years. But there are two things that don't add up." He held up one finger. "Everyone thinks he is dead – that he drowned while escaping from prison in the eighties, because the rocks below are treacherous – and, if he was alive, he would be almost ninety-years-old by now, and–" he held up a second finger "–he always stole heirlooms and antique pieces from private persons, not stores. So, what was he doing in Vogel yesterday afternoon?"

Jemima knew the answers, but, as she unable to say so, she just opened her eyes equally wide and gasped at all the right moments.

Before she could ask anything else, her iPhone beeped with a text message:

Jemima! You're in Monaco!

It was Spyros, a Greek friend in London who was launching an eco-private jet company. He'd started his no-frills airline, AnyJet, a decade earlier, but, having discovered how to fly aeroplanes without emitting greenhouse gases, his time was now taken up persuading celebrities and VIPs to fly EcoJet. The Cannes Film Festival was his first big event. He was running a shuttle from London Heathrow and Charles de Gaulle in Paris; at the moment, his electric-propelled planes couldn't fly further than three hours without stopping to recharge. EcoJet was one of the main sponsors of the Festival. Talk about holding the whole film world in your hands. What if the battery ran out mid-flight?

Jemima apologised to Yves and replied in the affirmative to Spyros. Just as she was about to put her phone back in her bag, she received a reply asking her for dinner later.

"Damn!" she said out aloud, remembering that she was having dinner with Mrs de Bourbon at 8pm.

"Jemima, you're in Monaco and being asked out by a Greek. You won't be eating until at least 11pm!"

"Well, I guess it's good to line your stomach, so why not twice?"

She texted Spyros that she would be free after 11pm and asked where should she meet him. He replied immediately, saying that he would pick her up and to send her address.

"Yes, that is another thing that they do here; taxis are impossible, so, if the men have manners, they'll collect you and pay the cheque!"

Jemima knew she was going to love living in Monaco.

"Now, your turn. What is with the secrecy and meeting in this back of beyond," Yves asked, looking around the café snobbishly.

"Can I trust you?" Jemima asked, knowing she had been told to trust no one, and she hardly knew this guy. But it wouldn't be the first time she had opened her soul to a stranger, and she thought again about spending the summer with James.

Her phone beeped again; it was Alexa. Believing it to be a sign, Jemima changed her mind and made up an excuse.

"I'm on annual leave… I really wanted to come down here as my boyfriend is involved in the festival and invited me to a couple of events. I said that I was on a family holiday. Let's just say that he's not quite family yet!" she winked.

"How exciting! Your secret is safe with me. Oh, Jacques says he can get you into the party if you are at the kitchens for the Eden Roc Restaurant and Grill, around 1.45pm. Of course, make sure you're wearing the right outfit for a diamond luncheon by the sea. And, lastly, if he pops the question – you know where I am!"

Jemima thanked him, laughed, then picked up her bag and sunglasses from the table. She gave Yves a quick kiss, ran out of the café, down the cobbled path, and bought a bouquet of peonies from a small stall in the market on her way.

# Chapter 14

## La Radieuse, Boulevard d'Italie

Jemima walked into the apartment. Dumping her bag and the peonies on the floor, she quickly walked to the shutters in the sitting room to fling them and the windows wide open. The room was so hot, despite keeping the glare of the sun out, and she realised that there was no air conditioning, so she'd have to buy a fan or two. Her bedroom was the same: scorching.

Jemima found a vase in the kitchen, put the flowers in it, and opened the fridge to see if there was any cool water inside. There was a bottle of Domain Ott rosé wine, some butter, and milk, but not much else. However much she wanted a glass of the delicious pink liquid, she firmly closed the fridge, having poured herself a glass of milk. The milk would, at least, line her stomach before dinner: she was starving again. Feeling a little sick from all the running around in the heat, Jemima put the glass on the bedside table and went back to get her phone to read Alexa's message. She unlocked the phone, went to her message, and noticed that there was a photo attachment. Opening it, she saw it was a screen capture of one of the CCTV frames of the female figure from inside the store.

Jemima, we have had this scanned and the proportions taken. They all match Petrina's exactly. Several antique pieces of jewellery were taken from each of the four boutiques, according to Interpol. We had in fact €30 million taken, mostly from the Royal Riviera and the Caribbean Collections – fortunately, not the Princess Grace sapphires.

Another message pinged through.

Interpol are on high alert at Hotel du Cap for the David Morris luncheon tomorrow.

Jemima congratulated herself for already knowing and managing to wangle a way to get in, not that she would tell Alexa Vogel, of course: she wouldn't want her to be dining with rival jewellers, but, if she was going to catch Petrina, then she needed to follow her, and it was pretty obvious that she would be there.

After taking another sip of milk, she lay back on her bed, exhausted from the heat, and fell fast asleep.

\* \* \*

Jemima was awoken by a huge seagull that was railing, squawking, and squawking. Although she didn't really like these huge birds that swamped Monaco, thank God it had shaken her awake. She checked her phone to see if anything more had come through from Alexa – nothing – and saw that it was 7.30; she only had half an hour to get ready for the first of her two dinners.

Pulling off her sticky shoes and clothes, Jemima padded across to the bathroom and switched on the shower, before stepping in and letting the scorching water wash off the day's dusty Monaco dirt. Feeling refreshed, she decided to work out what to wear. The card had just said supper, and she wanted to make a good impression, but an old lady wouldn't expect a dress and heels. Jeans and a pretty top would suffice, alongside a pair of Greek sandals that she'd bought in Paros the previous summer.

*   *   *

Almost as soon as Jemima knocked, she heard a lilting "Come in!" through the crack in the door of the apartment at the top of La Radieuse.

Jemima pushed the door open to a small entrance hall wallpapered in typical English Colefax and Fowler. Two of the three white doors in each of the three walls were open a little bit and through them came a smell of tomatoes, garlic, and basil infused with Chanel No 5, as well as the sound of Françoise Hardy's immutable voice from a crackling record. Jemima's tummy started to rumble with the delicious smells from the kitchen.

"I'll be five minutes." The voice sounded huskier now, and echoed from one of the rooms. "There's champagne in the fridge – *sers toi*!"

Well, why not, Jemima thought as she walked towards the smell of cooking. Madame de Bourbon's kitchen was through the right hand door and, unlike her hall, was very modern, as though it had been installed only yesterday. Jemima's experience of French apartment kitchens was that they were tiny and old, as if they were only used to make tea and coffee. She picked up a crystal flute from the marble topped counter, opened the heavy fridge door, and found a bottle of Pol Roger inside, already open with a silver teaspoon in the top to stop it going flat. She poured herself a glass and took a delicious sip of the sharp, bubbling, amber liquid.

Not wanting to the stay in the kitchen and get her freshly washed hair smelling of food before she went out with Spyros later, she walked to the French windows at the end of the room and out on to the balcony. It stretched across the whole front of the building. The view was similar to hers but had the whole panorama of Monaco's share of the Mediterranean, as well as the seaside city itself. And what a view it was, Jemima thought, with a little jump in her tummy, as she gazed at the sparkling sea below and the beautiful old sailing boats moored a few hundred metres out.

"Isn't that yacht glorious? I have spent many a day aboard her," came the same husky voice from behind her, causing her to jump and spill a little splash of champagne over the side of the balcony railings. "Oh, I am sorry, I didn't mean to startle you, my dear."

Jemima turned around to see the most beautifully elegant lady. She looked very similar to the octogenarian model Carmen Dell' Orefice, with slightly Slavic facial features and a tall, thin frame clothed in a beautiful, flower-embroidered silk pyjama suit. Her white hair, with a few remaining silver flecks, was styled elegantly and tucked behind her ears to reveal exquisite amethyst and Paraiba tourmaline earrings which fell like flowers. She realised that it was the same woman she had seen that morning at the newspaper kiosk, and wondered where her two little terriers were. They were probably asleep on her bed like her own terrier was inclined to do.

"Hello, Madame de Bourbon," Jemima said, smiling, whilst realising that how one dressed in Monaco gave a whole new name to the meaning of a casual supper. Her Topshop jeans and Antik Batik peasant top didn't seem the right kind of casual. "It's amazing. So beautiful. Whose is it?"

"My ex-husband's," Henrietta de Bourbon answered without venturing further, and Jemima knew how annoying it could be to see it every day outside your window. "Call me Henrietta."

An ex-boyfriend of hers had lived just off the bus route she once took to work; she'd often see his ancient VW Golf parked on the side of the road and, despite hating the useless car when they were together, seeing it every morning began to upset her so much that she started to take a different bus.

"There's a bit of a chill, let's go inside," the old lady continued, despite the sweltering evening heat. "I'm afraid that I was going to have a young man to dinner tonight, too. However, he called earlier to cancel. He is very interesting – works for the FBI, or rather is training to do so. Colton Bond is his name, if you come across him. I thought it would be more interesting than just talking to me." Jemima recognised the name but couldn't think why.

They walked along the balcony and entered a drawing room through the next pair of French windows, and the room couldn't have been more English. It reminded her of her grandmother's in Dorset, with its eau de nil coloured walls and large comfortable sofas, filled with plump velvet and tapestry cushions. The floor was wooden, like hers, with a large pale green and cream rug in front of a large fireplace. Towards the back of the room, before you reached a pair of high doors, there was a baby grand piano topped with lots of photographs. Jemima walked over and saw one of Princess Grace and what must have been Henrietta when she was much younger.

"Were you friends with Princess Grace? She was so beautiful." Jemima leant forward to peer closer at the photograph, conscious that perhaps she was being a little bit rude.

"Do sit down, I'll tell you all about it. Would you like some more?" Henrietta asked, holding up the bottle of Pol Roger she had somehow managed to retrieve from the fridge, unless it was another one that had been sitting in an ice bucket.

"Thank you, yes. I'd love another glass."

Henrietta filled up their glasses, replaced the bottle in the cooler, and sat down on the elegant armchair next to the unlit fire.

"So, tell me... is the apartment to your liking?"

"Yes, it is wonderful, and this view–" she pointed out of the French windows "–is spectacular. I might never leave!" she said, laughing.

"I have lived here on and off since I first came in 1956 to cover Grace Kelly's wedding for *The Tatler* Magazine. So, gosh, that is almost sixty years! This was my mother's and stepfather's pied à terre that I was lent for a fortnight that spring and summer."

"Wow, you were here for the wedding? What was it like? Was that when the photo was taken?"

"Yes, it was taken a couple of days before the wedding, at one of the many parties we went to that week. If I am honest, it was quite chaotic. I am sure Prince William's one last weekend was too, more so from what I have heard. But let's go and get ourselves some supper, and then I'll tell you what I can remember."

They walked through to the kitchen and Henrietta told her that her maid had made some fresh pasta and a ratatouille type sauce. "She has been with me since she was quite young, as her mother worked for my mother. However, she is starting to lose her eyesight, so her cooking is not as good as it was!" Jemima, already feeling a little tipsy from the two large glasses of champagne, was relieved. Hopefully, the pasta would soak it all up.

"Help yourself." The old lady, who looked as though pasta had never passed her lips, pointed at the pans on the stove, as she put down a couple of very expensive-looking Spode china plates on the side. "Knives and forks are in the drawer to the left of the stove." Then, looking at her watch, she suggested that they go back outside to eat at the table on the other balcony.

As they took their plates into the warm Riviera evening, Jemima noticed that the boat had gone – disappeared like a ghost.

That must have been the 'chill' she spoke of earlier. In its place was a mega-yacht, with several decks and a helicopter on the front. She'd never seen anything like it.

"Oh dear, the Russian is back," Henrietta sighed, staring at the superyacht.

Jemima wondered what she would prefer; this Russian with his vodka palace of a boat, or Henrietta's ex-husband's sailing yacht. She glanced at the Cartier watch on Henrietta's bony wrist and noticed the time was 9.10pm. She had ages until she needed to shimmy downstairs and change into her next outfit.

"Who is the Russian? Roman Abramovich?"

"No, another oligarch. Peter Petrovich."

Jemima almost spat out her champagne; Petrovich was the surname of the guy who had bought the Vogel Vanderpless in the auction, part of which had been stolen by Petrina. This was his boat – she wondered if it was the same man, and if he was also on the Riviera to get back his missing diamonds.

"Do you know him?" Henrietta asked.

"No, not at all, but there is a client of Vogel called something Petrovich." Jemima replied.

"That is more unusual than it sounds. His grandmother, Grand Duchess Tatiana, was part of the Romanov dynasty – one of the few survivors. She knew my mother and stepfather well. In fact, they probably entertained her here. He was Russian, my stepfather. She was a collector of Russian Romanov jewellery. She tried to buy a lot of it back from those who bought it after the Revolution, when it was sold by the Communists or indeed by its owners who'd managed to smuggle them out of Russia and needed to buy houses and food."

"I don't know anything about the Russian Revolution –

although my father is a huge Russophile, and I am hoping to take him to St Petersburg one day."

"They had the most incredible jewellery collections that ever existed. Would you like some more pasta?"

"No, thank you, although it was delicious. Please, tell me about the wedding."

Henrietta put down her fork and picked up the full glass of champagne that she had poured herself after refilling Jemima's, then leant back in her chair.

"It was quite an extraordinary few days." Henrietta took a sip and put her glass down, before pushing her white hair back from her face and giving a little shake of head, as though to remove any remaining strands. "But it was my great friend, Margo Peters, who had the most fun experience. I was busy being very English about the whole thing. Trying very hard to embarrass neither my mother, not that she could ever have been embarrassed, nor *The Tatler* – which was terribly 'posh and PC' in those days, not at all like it is now."

Henrietta went on to explain that Margo Peters was the daughter of a friend of her mother's and the young FBI man who was supposed to be joining them was, in fact, Margo's grandson. The mothers had been childhood friends in Ireland. Margo's mother had gone to America with her parents before the war and never returned. Henrietta had never met Margo before she had arrived in Monaco on the same boat as the Kelly wedding party, but they very quickly became firm and, consequently, lifelong friends.

"This photograph–" Henrietta had gone to collect it from the piano and pass it to Jemima "–was taken at a party held in what had been Empress Eugenie's villa in Roquebrune, Villa Cyrnos.

Apparently, Grace had wanted to play her in a movie that was being mulled about in Hollywood but, of course, she became a Princess instead and gave up her film star career."

"That brooch is incredible!" Jemima said, looking closely at a large floral affair pinned to one of the girls in the photograph.

"Quite so. The girl wearing it was Maree Frisby, an old friend of Grace's. She became very good friends with Margo on the boat on the way back to the United States. Anyway, Maree's aunt had given her that brooch, or left it to her in her will. She wore it most nights and was nervous about leaving it in the hotel: it was very special. It was by the world's oldest jewellers, Mellerio of Paris, and had once belonged to Napoleon's niece, Princesse Mathilde." Jemima did wonder how Henrietta knew so much about jewellery. "However, it just so happened that it was stolen a few nights before the civil ceremony, along with jewellery from several other wedding guests, including some sapphires that were to be a wedding present from Grace's godmother, Mrs McCloskey."

"Who was it?" Jemima asked, not wanting to let on that she already knew all about the sapphires.

"Well, it was a bit of a mystery. No one was ever caught at the time, nor the jewels found. It was said that it was the chauffeur of Prince Rainier's mother – it turned out he had been a convict. An ex-jewel thief, who she'd taken pity on when he was released from jail. They could never pin it on him. They searched his dwellings and found nothing. Princess Grace, however, believed that it was The Snow Leopard."

"Why?" she asked.

"I remember my friend Margo, who worked at MGM, telling me that she had heard that Grace Kelly – before she became Princess, and after filming To Catch a Thief – thought that it was too much of a coincidence that that there had been several burglaries in the early fifties in Montenegro. She had wanted Hitchcock to make a sequel based on this mysterious burglar, nicknamed The Snow Leopard!" Henrietta laughed and took another sip of champagne. "She was particularly excited about a piece of jewellery that had supposedly belonged to Catherine the Great and was stolen from a Russian Duchess while she was holidaying in Budva. In fact, I believe that it was Petrovich's great-grandmother – the Grand Duchess Tatiana."

"How did she know your stepfather?"

Henrietta smiled and raised her shoulders. "I have no idea. Europe was full of White Russians who'd fled their country around the time of the Revolution, taking their jewellery with them as a means of survival."

Jemima's phone pinged from her bag that had been left on a sofa, and she suddenly realised it must be late. The sky was completely dark and there were faint sounds of music coming from down below. The revving of expensive engines driving up and down the streets signalled it was time to meet Spyros. The two hours had sped by, and she was a bit sad to end it.

"I must go, but thank you so much for dinner. It was delicious, and I loved hearing about the wedding. What an experience! Despite the sad jewellery thefts."

"Oh, everything in Monaco is an experience, my dear." Henrietta got up and Jemima followed suit, picking up her plate and glass, before following the old lady into the kitchen and placing them in the sink. She asked if she could wash them for her.

"My maid will do the dishes in the morning when she arrives to make my breakfast."

Jemima smiled. "Henrietta. It was so nice to meet you and,

again, thank you. And I do so love the apartment I am in. You must meet my boyfriend when he arrives."

Henrietta led Jemima back through the sitting room, where she picked up her bag and noticed a black and white photograph of a beautiful lady in furs, a long silk dress, and a large diamond tiara. She looked very like Henrietta, or indeed Katherine Hepburn.

"My mother," Jemima was told.

She nodded, thinking that it was such a shame that it was no longer the era of wearing tiaras, they were so elegant and glamorous, and was led through the hallway to the main door of the apartment.

"Goodnight, my dear," said Henrietta.

"Goodnight, Henrietta."

# Chapter 15

---

# Spyros's Lamborghini Miura

As she walked down the stairs to her own apartment, Jemima opened her clutch bag and took out her iPhone; it was almost 11pm and Spyros had texted to say he'd pick her up promptly at 11pm from outside La Radieuse.

"Dammit," she said aloud to herself.

Jemima ran the rest of the way down, careful not to slip on the old stone steps. She opened the door, kicked off her flat shoes, went into her bedroom, pulled off her jeans and top, and, without caring what it was, pulled a dress out of her wardrobe. Slipping it over her head and running into the bathroom to touch up her makeup, she noticed that it was another Harvey Nichols number: a gorgeous pale pink sequin dress from Pinko which she had been unable to resist. She grabbed a pair of black heels from the wardrobe to match her clutch, threw on some lipstick and a pair of Panetta chandelier earrings, and ran out of the door, slamming it a little too hard.

Waiting outside in a 1972 yellow Lamborghini Miura was Spyros the Greek. Jemima smiled as she crossed the small pavement, noticing that he had jumped out his side of the car to dash around and open her door. He was of average height, had dark black hair with a few strands of white around the ears, and his open-necked pink shirt, tucked into blue jeans, revealed quite a grey-haired chest. He was wearing a pair of Superga trainers. He didn't dress like a billionaire on a night out in Monaco at all.

"Welcome to Monte Carlo, Miss Fox," he said, giving her a kiss on the cheek and a hug.

"Thank you, Spyros," she said. "Where are we going?"

"Well, first I will give you a little tour," he said, once they were settled in their seats. "And then we go to Sass Café before a little dance, perhaps at Jimmy'z!"

"Ahh, Spyros – the perfect welcome party." Excited for having cocktails and dancing, all thoughts of missing diamonds were gone as quickly as the Lamborghini took the sharp Monaco corners.

Jemima had been to Monaco a few times before, but she had not been to the eastern part of the principality, where both the Monte Carlo Beach Club and Country Club had their grounds. Spyros wound his way confidently through the streets, passed the red clay tennis courts of the country club, and out towards Roquebrune, the little village next door.

"Are you kidnapping me, Spyros?" she joked, wondering where on earth they were going.

"No, my dear! Ha, you English girls are always the funniest. We are going to pick up a friend who is joining us. He lives in the most beautiful house in Cap Martin."

Although it was dark, they were speeding along the coastal road, and Jemima could just about make out the shadows of large houses against the orange haze from Monaco. She wound down her window and inhaled the cool air, the sounds of cicadas barely audible above the noise of the classic car. It was so much better than sitting in stationary traffic in London. Maybe she wouldn't want her job back in London, after all. Before long, they were pulling up outside a pair of formidable-looking gates. Spyros stopped and dialled his friend from his very 1980s car phone, speaking something incomprehensible in Greek. Within a moment, the large gates opened and out walked what could be Spyros's twin brother.

"I'll jump in the back," Jemima said, before turning around to see there was no back seat. "Or on his knee." She inelegantly clambered out of the car to let the Greek sit in the passenger seat, before she got back in and balanced on his knee.

"Well, this is a nice surprise," the new man said.

For a second, Jemima cringed, then realised that she had better get used to these kinds of comments whilst in Monaco.

"Marco, this is my friend, Jemima Fox. Jemima, Ilias Dimitriades."

"Hi," she said, not wanting to swivel around on his knee, for fear of causing any undue excitement.

Before he lapsed into anything untoward, Jemima decided to do what most men like and ask him questions about himself. "These houses are amazing. Have you been here long?"

"Villa Cherbourg is my French grandmother's house. My family rarely come as they are always in Greece, but I prefer France at the moment; too many problems in Greece."

"Do you know many of these houses?" Jemima asked, looking through the window at the huge gates lining the streets that no doubt hid huge houses.

"We are just coming up to what was once Empress Eugenie's house – Villa Cyrnos. It is on the left, just up here. Very beautiful but only visible from the sea. It's uninhabited." Jemima made a mental note to Google the Empress; she had heard her name quite a bit recently.

"Yes, I have heard about it. Why has no one bought it?"

"I don't know," he said, and she could feel him shrug his shoulders. "Apparently, there is a horde of treasure buried somewhere in the garden! Haunted, too, I guess." Jemima was shaken up and down on his knees as he laughed, and she could feel her tiny dress ride further up her legs. She felt a sense of rising panic as remembered she was wearing the smallest pair of panties.

"My great-grandmother," Ilias continued, "the Princesse of Cherbourg, used to have the Empress over for tea. They would take it in turns to host at each other's villas on either side of the Cap – to compare views, I think. Of course, the Empress's was much more impressive, with a little tower to view the sea and impeccable gardens. She recreated a mini 'court' there. At least, that is the story I was told as a child. I'll see if I can find someone to take us inside. Your Queen Victoria used to stay there, too." Jemima was excited about this new bit of local info… she thought that Henrietta de Bourbon might have a few bits to add to the story as well, and could probably organise for her to visit.

"Right, you two – enough flirting," Spyros interrupted; he wasn't keen on not being the centre of attention. "We're almost here."

Jemima flushed. She had a boyfriend, and Ilias Dimitriades couldn't be further from whom she'd flirt with even if she didn't. She remembered her friend Delfine warning her that, in Monaco, some people thought you were flirting even if you were talking to a man. Thank goodness James was arriving the following day, so she could put rest to any ideas that she was on the hunt for a rich man.

Eventually, they pulled up outside a restaurant and exited the vehicle before a valet took it. Spyros led the trio along the pavement to the red canopy-covered tables – and what was Monaco's most popular summer spot – Sass Café. Tables were squashed together, with barely a gap to squeeze through, not that most girls needed one: with the highest of heel and thinnest of legs, they seemed to glide through the minute cracks in the white table clothes. Bowls of pasta were discarded and uneaten, ice buckets filled with bottles of rosé and champagne were almost outnumbering glasses on the tables, whilst cigar and cigarette smoke fought above expensively coiffed hairstyles. Jemima was relieved that she had not only changed into her teeny dress and high heels, but had also managed not to eat too much since returning from South Africa, so she didn't look too out of place amongst the Russian models and hangers-on treating the Monaco pavement as though it were the runway.

Spyros led them through the throng to a long table at the back of the outside space, against the canopy that was already half-filled with seven or so people. He walked over, opening his arms out to his friends, who, upon seeing him, jumped up to greet him. Marco following and Jemima just behind.

*"Ciao, Spyros! Che mervilloso,"* one of them exclaimed in delight to see the dashing Greek.

Jemima looked at those gathered round the table and suddenly took a sharp intake of breath and clung to the back of an empty chair. She felt sick as blood drained from her face. In the middle of the table, with her back against the canopy wall, was Petrina, sitting snuggled up to what looked like James, his face hidden underneath her hair and hand as they passionately kissed each other, seemingly unaware of their fellow diners. She recognised the tattoo of a leopard that she had first seen in Cape Town, and another one of the infinity sign, like an elongated figure '8'. Hearing her host had arrived Petrina flicked her hair back to reveal one single chandelier earring hanging like an icicle from her left ear. Jemima didn't want to stare, but the very large pear-shaped diamond hanging from an equally huge turquoise cabochon looked remarkably similar to one of those missing from the Vogel Vanderpless necklace – the one she knew Petrina had, and that she was supposed to be getting back for the Vogels and Mr Petrovich.

Petrina looked up. "Ah, Jemima Fox, I wondered if I would see you on the Riviera this summer," she teased.

All Jemima could do was smile and breathe a huge sigh of relief. It wasn't James, although she couldn't imagine there was anyone else in the world who could possibly look more alike.

The guy pushed the table away from him and stood up, leant over, and stuck out his hand. "Milos… nice to meet you. Jemima, was it?"

Jemima was careful not to let her emotions show but she recognised his Balkan accent from the previous night. This must have been the Milos Poznan that Yves had told her about. And the Milos od Montenegro, was obviously his boat.

"Yes, hi." She smiled at him and then, with a huge effort, smiled at Petrina.

A surge of confidence seeped through her body when she remembered what Alexa had said, 'Think like her, be like her'. She also advised Jemima to make friends with the American girl,

"Well, I didn't have to wonder if you would be here, Petrina," she continued with a smile. "I'm so pleased. And your boyfriend looks remarkably like mine! How funny. In fact, if I didn't know James was arriving tomorrow – I'd have called him out for cheating on me!" She laughed, knowing that she had won the first round, and walked over to where Spyros was sitting at the far end of the long table, put her arm on his shoulder, and asked where he would like her to sit.

"Right next to me. This is your welcoming party!"

So, what on earth is she doing here, at my welcome party, Jemima thought, whilst smiling enthusiastically. "Thank you, Spyros, ever the gentleman!"

# Chapter 16

---

# Sass Café, Avenue Princesse Grace

Sitting ensconced between the two Greeks, Jemima couldn't help but be flabbergasted at Petrina's gall to not only wear some of the diamonds that she had stolen from the Vogel Vanderpless but to wear them to Jemima's welcome party. She just had to be careful not to drink too much Domaine Ott rosé, otherwise her tongue would get the better of her.

Jemima was keeping a careful eye on James's doppelganger when a guy she thought she recognised came towards the table. He was good-looking, in a very preppy American way, and looked like he'd grown up between the Upper East Side in Manhattan, and either the Hamptons, Nantucket, or Newport. His looks would normally go hand in hand with easy confidence and being the life and soul of the party, but this American seemed quite nervous as he made his way through the crowded terrace of tables.

Jemima noticed Petrina catch the newcomer's eye and, with a quick jolt of her head, beckoned him to come over.

But Jemima got there first and, jumping up so that Ilias's hand fell from where it was working its way up her thigh, she stuck out her hand to the new guy. "Hi! I recognise you – I can't think from where though."

"Hey, yes, we met at Cecconi's a couple days ago. Colt Bond." He stuck out his hand to meet her.

Of course! But what a coincidence that he was here and clearly knew Petrina. She looked back at Petrina and the man sitting next to her; he really was the spitting image of James, except there was something strange about his eyes. Or was it just the lighting?

Didn't Henrietta de Bourbon mention this guy's name only a few hours earlier? He was the grandson of her great friend and worked for the FBI. He couldn't be a very good secret agent if he was friends with a Pink Panther without knowing it!

"I can see you know, Petrina." Jemima stated. "It is a small world. Meet our host, Spyros, and I'll get you a glass of wine – as you can see, we've run out!" She'd overcome the shock of seeing what she assumed was part of the Vogel Vanderpless necklace, and was now more surprised that whoever had 'ordered' it wasn't more impatient to have their prize. Petrina had kept the diamonds for over a month now; talk about sitting on hot ice! Jemima needed to find out who the big boss was, as well as get all four diamonds back, but she couldn't just pull it off Petrina's elegant ear and run to Renault at the police station.

It was way past midnight. Monaco was still ablaze with bright young things – and the not-so-young – but Jemima could see that Petrina was on edge. She spotted a spare chair opposite Petrina and moved around the table to it. Then she noticed Petrina's date look over her shoulder, as though he'd seen a ghost. Suddenly, she felt someone put their hands on her shoulders and, before she could jump, a kiss was placed by her ears – her most erotic area – and she swung around to see James standing over her. Her heart skipped a beat, as it always did when she saw James, and she leapt up to hug him. After several glasses of pink champagne, on top of the wine she'd had with Henrietta, Jemima felt more than a little bit tipsy, but she wasn't about to let anyone think she was drunk. That'd only be playing into Petrina's hand. No wonder Milos had thought he'd seen a ghost; James and him could be identical twins, she thought. It was just the eyes that were a bit different. It was uncanny.

"James," came Petrina's unmistakable purr behind Jemima. "How are you?"

"It's Petrina, isn't it?" he replied, as Jemima smiled into his shoulder, feeling his strong South African torso with her hand and not caring about her obvious PDA, which in London she would have shied from. He was hers and none of these Monte Carlo gold diggers were going to get a chance. And definitely not Petrina Lindberg, if she could help it.

"Yes, and this is my boyfriend – Milos Poznan," she replied as the two men shook hands over the table, now littered with empty and half-empty wine glasses, the uneaten plates of food having been taken away.

"Milos, how nice to meet you."

"And have you met Spyros? He's our host – in fact, it is your girlfriend's welcome party we are attending." She laughed.

"How kind. I must thank him for making my darling girlfriend so welcome here. But first, I need a drink." He sat down, pulling Jemima onto his knee. "Another glass of champagne, sweetheart?" he asked.

"That'd be lovely – although, I really should have some water as well. We're meant to be going to Jimmy'z and I think I've drunk too much," she whispered to him.

James ordered pink champagne, knowing that it was her favourite, and water. Within seconds, a waiter arrived with a magnum of Cristal Rosé Champagne and a bottle of San Pellegrino.

"Oh my God, James, that is going to be so expensive!" she whispered to him as the waiter opened the champagne, half laughing, half shocked.

"Sshhh," he whispered back, aware that Petrina was watching him, and then, leaning into Jemima further, so she couldn't lip read him, he said, "you might quite like my room at The Fairmont. It is directly below Petrina's parents. And I heard something earlier that will interest you."

"So, James," Petrina called over the table, leaning as far forward as possible to give him a direct view of her cleavage. "How did you know where to find Jemima? She told me you were arriving tomorrow."

"I have my spies," James replied, much to her visible annoyance and Jemima's intrigue. How did her boyfriend know she was here, and why was he already here? "Glass of champagne, Petrina?"

Petrina nodded so slightly that her earring barely moved, and Jemima realised that she was staring at it; she needed to sober up and not let 'the cat' catch her out.

# Chapter 17

---

## The Fairmont Hotel, Avenue des Spélugues
## Sunday 8th May

Jemima awoke to her iPhone buzzing under her pillow and, for a moment, couldn't be sure it was the telephone making her head vibrate and not her hangover. She decided to wait until whoever was calling was announced and turned over in the crisp sheets, wincing at her headache.

"Number Withheld," shrilled a muffled electronic voice.

"Well, this is a déjà vu, don't answer it," James groaned.

Jemima thought that she must change the phone's ring tone setting as she reached out to answer, silently cursing the caller who, she realised as she turned the screen over, had chosen 8.30am for their impromptu wakeup call. They'd managed a bare five hours sleep.

As she raised the phone to her ear, however, James grabbed it, cancelled the call, and threw it to the floor.

"James! That could have been important!"

James put an arm around her and pulled her back next to him. "Well, in that case, you won't want to hear what important info I found out last night about a sapphire brooch or were they earrings?" he mumbled into her hair.

Jemima remembered a vague conversation they'd had in the restaurant about Petrina's parents. "The sapphires! Of course, you were going to tell me," she propped herself up on her elbow, one hand on his chest.

"Can't we have sex first?" He made to move her hand further down his body.

"Sex soon, talk first," she replied defiantly, stealing the line from a Harold Robbins novel she'd recently finished.

James pulled himself up and propped his back against one of the huge white pillows that the super king-sized bed was liberally scattered with.

"So," he said, yawning and reaching for the room service menu. "I was having a scotch on the balcony before leaving to come out to meet you. I'd seen you get out of that car at the restaurant, on the way here from my client's apartment, so I thought I'd come here and change first. You seemed to be in good hands, after all." He raised an eyebrow and Jemima smiled mischievously back at him. "Of course, my girlfriend wouldn't be tucked up in bed on her first night on the Riviera!" he continued.

"Second!" she laughed. "But, yes, you know me too well, my darling. Were you a little jealous when you saw Spyros and Marco get out of the car with me?"

"No, not at all – they're not your type," said James, eyeing the coffee section of the menu a little too studiedly.

He was jealous, thought Jemima. She giggled and kissed him. "Go on."

Before answering, James picked up the room's telephone. "If you could please bring us some breakfast: two omelettes, and coffees and croissants." Hanging up, he turned back to Jemima, and explained how he'd been standing on the balcony, sucking up the atmosphere after being stuck in an airplane, when he heard Petrina's name mentioned above him. "It was a woman's voice with a French-American accent," he said. "She was worried that Petrina was involved with her father. I wouldn't have taken much notice but she said, "...who everyone called Snow Leopard, who it seems is not dead after all," which I thought pertinent to your investigations here."

"Go on," Jemima said again, intrigued and now impatient.

"So, then an older man's voice asked her about what she was going to do, how she had always promised to avenge her mother, should it turn out he wasn't six feet under, after all, and she said that she didn't know. And then she said, "Unlike the beautiful sapphire and diamond brooch and earrings which Petrina seems intent on finding out about..." which is what really interested me. You told me that part of your task was to prevent Petrina from getting her hands on a pair of special sapphire and diamond earrings. There were some mutterings that I didn't understand, and she said that she was going to give them back, and if Petrina was in contact with her father, then maybe she could unknowingly help lure him to the authorities once and for all. She then mentioned these earrings again, and how Petrina had been asking after them – and that's what led her to believe her father wasn't dead and he wanted them back. That was before she said something about she had "...always thought it was part of my father's stolen loot but didn't really know for sure. My mother left them for me to find under a particular palm tree.""

"The woman was definitely Fortunata," gasped Jemima, wide-eyed. "She has the Romanov sapphire earrings that were originally for Princess Grace and which she is intending to return to the Monaco Royal Family. They were also created so that the sapphire and surmounts could be removed from the pear drops below, clipped together and worn as a brooch." Remembering what the Comtesse de Ré had told her about the day before at the boutique.

"Woah!" said James. "And I thought I was solving your mystery so you can retire and be a kept woman for the rest of your life." Jemima, now looking for her phone, didn't look up.

"It's just too impossible," she wailed. "How am I going to catch them out? Fortunata is so lovely – I don't want her going down for harbouring stolen goods! But why does she have them? She said that her mother left them for her, so did her mother steal them from her husband, the Snow Leopard?" she said, defeated. "Renault's father tried to catch the old Leopard thief, back in the Sixties and Seventies, to no avail. And Alexa has told me that I need to catch Petrina red-handed with the Vanderpless diamonds. It was so obvious that Petrina was wearing one last night. She was winding me up – making it look like something from the jeweller de Grisogono – and how the hell am I going to get it from her? I couldn't exactly rip it from her ear!" She retrieved her phone and flopped back onto the bed exhausted from her venting, then looked up slowly. "What do you mean be a kept woman for the rest of my life?" she asked, her heart beginning to beat faster. James turned to look at her, struggling not to smile, and didn't say anything.

"I said, what did you mean?" Jemima urged, crawling across the bed as the sheet slipped to the floor.

Her body was suddenly covered in goose pimples and her nipples were hard and pointed, which had nothing to do with the breeze whispering in through the wide-open windows. James was still smiling, and she realised he was looking down at his own body. Pulling herself up to his bare torso and leaning against the pillow, she pulled away his side of the immense silky white sheet to reveal a Vogel ring box balanced on his pubic bone amidst the blond tufts of hair. She stared at it, her face only centimetres away, and then raised her eyes to look at him.

James raised an eyebrow. "Still want to talk first?"

"Touché!" said Jemima, glancing down. "Is this for me?"

"Well, I don't see anyone else here, do you?"

Jemima leant back, her buttocks on her ankles, and picked up the beautiful green box with the Vogel logo embossed in gold on the top. She hesitated in opening it: she had been waiting for this moment for as long as she could remember, but wanted to savour the exciting but scary anticipation. Momentarily, Jemima remembered looking in the elevator mirror back at Vogel HQ, after her tipsy lunch with the jewellery editor of *Tatler*, just before the whole Vogel Vanderpless saga started. She had looked at her ring finger and told herself that one day she'd have a Vogel rock on it…

"Come on! Open it!" James was unusually impatient.

Jemima held it in her left hand, while her other prized open the stiff lid of the jewellery box. She took in a sharp breath. Inside was the most exquisite ring she'd ever seen. A huge beautiful bluish-purple oval tanzanite, which must have been at least 8-carats, surrounded by two oval halos of the whitest and brightest of diamonds, which followed through on to the shoulders of the thin band. She looked up at her new fiancé, her eyes full of tears, and smiled, unable to speak.

"I hope that is a yes?" James asked gently, before reaching out and taking the ring from the box. "Let me try it on for size." He slid the ring on to her finger, like a perfectly fitted glove.

"Yes! Yes! Yes!" Jemima squealed, her eyes darting between the ring, which glinted in the sun streaming through the window, and his face.

Jemima knelt with her knees either side of James's thighs and put her hands around his head, bringing it towards her. She leaned forward to meet his lips and kissed the man who had changed her life in so many ways. It seemed strange she had met him only five months ago. She'd had no idea that this was coming until he gave her the Vogel box: Jemima Fox-Pearl engaged! And to this man. This incredible, kind, beautiful man.

James shifted down the bed beneath her and, in turn, she stretched out her legs, so that their naked bodies lay together. She felt him harden beneath and slid further down, her newly bejewelled hand tracing his rippled torso and resting on his tummy button, whilst the other clasped his penis so her lips could encircle it. She moved up and down, feeling it harden even more, and then shifted her hips back up his body, letting him enter her. He fitted her as perfectly as the ring on her finger. For the first time in her life, Jemima felt completely happy, as though all her worries had flown away with the wind breezing in and out of the window. And then all thoughts completely disappeared as she came so sensuously, while simultaneously feeling him fill her with his own ecstatic juices. Satisfied, they lay next to each other, until James held up her left hand and examined the beautiful ring, and Jemima realised that there was something about it that didn't ring true.

"I don't recognise this ring from any of Vogel's collections?" she said to James. "I know they rarely use tanzanite; it's deemed semi-precious, but it's the most exquisite gemstone. This deep blueish-purple is so rare in these stones!" she gushed, holding her hand up to the light, breathless from the excitement and the sex. "And these diamonds – they're so clear, they must be D-Flawless! My darling, this ring must have cost you an arm and a leg!" She looked over to her fiancé with a guilty look on her face.

James smiled. "You don't recognise it because I commissioned it."

"What? How?" Jemima knew full well that only billionaires bought bespoke Vogel jewellery.

"The tanzanite came from my mother's engagement ring. My parents met in Tanzania. Mum was working in New York for Tiffany at the time. Tiffany were the first to use tanzanite in their fine jewellery, and Mum took the first journalist press trip to Tanzania to cover it. That's where she met my father, in the hotel they were all staying at near Mount Kilimanjaro, where tanzanite comes from. My father was working for De Beers in Johannesburg. In fact, he was doing a bit of an undercover operation for them at the time!"

"So, basically, he chatted your mother up to find out what Tiffany was up to?" Jemima's teasing covered the fact she was hugely touched. After all, she knew that James's parents had been killed in a road shootout in South Africa a few years ago and thought of how much it must mean to him that he had used his mother's ring for her own engagement ring.

"Kind of." Although he was smiling, his aquamarine eyes held traces of tears.

"Tell me more," Jemima asked, touching one of his cheeks. "I'd love to have chatted jewellery with your mother. Your grandmother never mentioned that she had worked for Tiffany. I knew she'd been at Dior."

"She went to Tiffany after two years at Dior. She didn't work for them long – just enough to meet my father. In fact, I think they sent her to Tanzania because she was South African. They probably thought it was the same country! My grandmother hated her being in New York. Too far away."

Jemima didn't say anything. She remembered how lovingly James's grandmother, Rosemary, had spoken of his mother. She sounded like such a special woman, and Jemima wished they'd been able to meet.

"So, your father bought her a tanzanite ring, not a De Beers diamond one, to ask her to marry him. How heavenly! You still haven't explained how you got the most expensive jeweller in the world to add all these exquisite diamonds to mine?"

"Well, and this is the bit you'll really love…" said James.

"How can I love anything more than wearing your mother's gemstone?" she interrupted,

James smiled like a naughty schoolboy. "Well, the diamonds are what was left over after they set the Vogel Vanderpless."

"What!" Jemima's shriek could have been heard way out to sea.

"Yes, well, I do know a little bit about diamonds and diamond cutting," James smiled. "Dad worked for De Beers, after all! I just so happened to ask Danny at the charity auction what happened to the remainder of the diamonds after they had cut the rough. I had a feeling those stones might be a worthwhile investment." He smiled.

You don't know how worthwhile, if they're from the Cullinan! thought Jemima. She was hugely impressed with James's knowledge, and remembered back to when Danny Vogel taught her all about the *rough diamond to sparkling jewel* process. When diamonds are mined, the good are sorted from the 'duds', ready to be cut and polished into sparkling stones, just like the ones in Jemima's engagement ring. Rough diamonds, as the original uncut and unpolished stones are called, are much larger than the gems they end up as. Diamonds have stringent criteria and grading systems to determine their value, and Jemima knew that a diamond cutter will want to ensure that each diamond he or she has cut is of the highest quality possible. To achieve this, some of the diamond will be discarded during the cutting process due to 'inclusions' in the stone caused by imperfections – anything from dirt to gases. The least number of inclusions a diamond has, the higher its clarity, and therefore the higher the value. The Vogel Vanderpless was a D grade flawless diamond, meaning that the stone contained no inclusions, and its colour was of the most perfect white that a diamond can be. When Sidney Vogel bought the huge rough diamond at the auction house Bothebie's in early December, the carat weight was 723. To achieve its impeccable final grading, he told Jemima that the diamond went through rigorous planning and plotting to see what could be kept and what had to go. More than half was disposed of, most of which would have been diamond dust, which is used in polishing machines to polish other diamonds, or turned into boart, which are industrial diamonds. Occasionally, however, and depending on the shape, size, and quality of the left-over 'satellite' pieces, they can be polished and used in smaller pieces of jewellery. The tiniest pieces are called melée diamonds and are often used in pavé settings. The rest is discarded as dust.

"And – what, did he say?" Jemima continued.

"He said there were very few left that could be used in jewellery by Vogel, as the quality was between VVS2 and VS2, but no doubt they would be used in something. They're still almost perfect white."

"So, you're saying that these diamonds are some of the satellites from the Vogel Vanderpless?" Jemima asked, starting to shake.

If what James was saying was true, it meant that she, potentially, had parts of the world's largest and most famous diamond on her finger. Now she wanted to know even more if her predilection was correct; that the Vogel Vanderpless diamond was the infamous other half of the Cullinan.

"Yes, that's what I am saying!" he said, laughing and stroking his fiancée's hair. "I spoke with him just after you left with Mr Vogel to go back to London and told him that I'd buy what was needed to create this, and, hey presto, you've got it forever."

The doorbell rang to announce that their breakfast had arrived. As James wrapped a robe around himself and went to answer the door, Jemima collapsed back down onto the bed and stared at her beautiful piece of jewellery.

Now – more than ever – she wanted to find the missing diamonds and catch the cat, Petrina Lindberg.

# Chapter 18

## Hotel du Cap, Cap d'Antibes, France

"What time is this luncheon at the Hotel du Cap?" James asked a little later, as Jemima held up the dress she'd been wearing the night before and wondered how on earth she'd be able to get across Monaco in it without looking like a tramp – huge engagement ring or no huge engagement ring!

James caught her worried look. "There are some clothes boutiques in the hotel," he said, kissing her forehead. "Grab something that's not too expensive, I've got a honeymoon to pay for," he said with a smile. "And put it on my room account." He walked into the bathroom and passed her one of the hotel's creamy towelling robes and a pair of their matching, embossed slippers. Jemima quickly wrapped the robe around her and pushed her sore feet into the slippers.

"The luncheon's at 2pm," Jemima said. "We should leave around 12 noon at the latest. I have to pick up a Ferrari beforehand." She laughed and rushed out of the room before there were any more questions.

James watched his fiancée leave with an expression of bemused adoration.

Jemima hurried down the hall. There was a lot to do and she wanted to have a quick swim in the hotel's rooftop pool to get rid of her hangover before heading back to the apartment, where she would change into something suitably sexy for a diamond pool party, before collecting Mrs Vogel's Ferrari and driving along the coast to the most beautiful hotel she'd ever heard of – so she could drop it off on their way back to Monaco. She hoped that one of Mr Vogel's villa staff members would give them a lift the rest of the way. She knew that, with Monaco's Grand Prix barriers, she'd have to be quick in the pool. It was only a week to the race, and the roads were becoming more impossible to navigate with each passing day.

Twenty minutes later, with a new bikini under her robe and a little Missoni kaftan from the reduced rail in a bag, Jemima took the elevator up to the pool. Just as she emerged onto the rooftop, she spotted Petrina's father walking up the steps. Watching him, she grabbed a towel and followed him to where he joined Fortunata, whose face was concealed under a large white straw hat. Their loungers, which had a tray of coffees and croissants placed between them, looked out over the ocean. Quite by chance, Jemima's bed – where she had left her belongings earlier – was directly behind theirs, but facing towards the pool. Jemima knew that she didn't have much time. Whipping out her phone, she texted James to join her for a quick swim and then dived into the pool. Jemima power swam twenty lengths of the long pool, and, by the time she got out, James was lying in the sun with a copy of the weekend's *Financial Times* shading the sun from his face, his ears firmly on Petrina's parents.

"Nice bikini!" James smiled as she approached.

"Oh, yes, I thought I might as well get one so I could leave it here for the future. Although I hope you'll be moving into my apartment before too long? After all, we are engaged now!" she said, feeling yet another surge of excitement as her eyes drifted to her ring.

"Of course. I need to work, though – this isn't a holiday." One of James's major clients in his financial institution lived in Monaco, and had put him up at The Fairmont.

"Nor me!" she protested as she wrung her wet hair out on his torso and jumped on to her lounger before he could pay her back.

She lay down and asked, in a whisper, if he had heard anything else interesting.

"They were just talking about the David Morris event. It seems they're going as well," James answered, pretending to read a long and boring article about tax evasion.

"Oh, good. I'll know someone other than you; I'm not meant to be going to a rival jewellery house's party," she whispered.

"I think you have a very good reason, Mademoiselle Clueso!" James muttered back, stopping quickly as the waitress arrived. "Here are our juices. Then we'd better go and get changed."

While James got dressed into something appropriate for a film-star filled diamond luncheon at the Hotel du Cap, Jemima took a cab back to her apartment to change into a beautiful, cornflower blue Chloe maxi dress that had a sequin embossed bodice. Quite Grecian, she'd thought, when she'd plucked it from a rail at Harvey Nichols. She carefully applied her makeup, put up her hair in a messy bun, slipped into a pair of white Superga trainers, and, carrying her Gina heels, dashed out of the apartment.

Running as carefully as possible to avoid ripping the hem of her chiffon dress, Jemima went down the narrow path to the Avenue Princesse Grace and along the road until she reached the

Ferrari garage where, after flashing her ID, she was shown to Mrs Vogel's new Ferrari. Or rather her new classic Ferrari. It was the most beautiful car that Jemima had ever seen – a scarlet red 1962 250 California Spyder. Jumping into the driver's seat, Jemima picked up James at the foot of the hill below his hotel and the famous Fairmont Grand Prix hairpin bend, and they were soon out of Monaco, picking up speed as they burned along the coastline. With some time to spare, they drove the scenic route along the coastal road through the pretty villages dotted from Monaco to Cannes, and Jemima thought what a glorious day it was to get engaged.

Leaving Eze to go West, Jemima spotted the sign to Cap Ferrat, where they'd be dropping the car off on the way back. A sudden worry flashed through her mind as a lorry passed a little close in the other direction; the garage had told her that she was at the wheel of an €8 million car. Her attention, however, turned to Petrina and whether she'd be at the party with her mother and father. She wondered if a raid was planned, and what had happened to the jewellery that the Panthers had stolen two days previously.

The roof was down on the car and Jemima and James sat in amiable silence, one of his tanned hands resting on her slender thigh. Once she had parked her thoughts on Petrina, Jemima couldn't help catching glimpses of her ring. The central tanzanite seemed to become bluer under the azure sky, and, once again, she felt a delicious little shiver: the diamonds were part of the same stone as Vogel Vanderpless. Therefore, as Mr V had said on Friday, they were 99% certain to be part of the British Crown Jewels! She wondered briefly if Grace Kelly had ever felt this happy when she married Prince Rainier and became 'Queen' of the Riviera? And then, of course, her mind drifted back to the original Van Cleef earrings, the ones with the Romanov Ceylon sapphires that Fortunata had worn recently as a brooch and brought to Monaco to give back to Princess Grace's family. God, this was complicated. She should just focus on tailing Petrina to get the Vogel Vanderpless stones and find out if there was a heist planned for Monday night.

They drove through Nice and Antibes, before turning off the main road to head down to the 'Cap' where the Hotel du Cap was located. Like Cap Ferrat, Cap d'Antibes juts out into the sea and the coastline is full of the most beautiful villas and mansions. They cruised through a large white stone entrance and along a perfectly manicured drive up to the house, where a valet came forward to take the car.

"Oh gosh, do you think he will look after it?" Jemima whispered to James, having grown very fond of the car on their drive.

They pulled to a stop in front of the white chateau that was the hotel, and stepped out. Jemima gazed up at the pristine façade. Built in 1869 as a private house by the owner of the French newspaper, Le Figaro, Cap Ferrat had always provided an inspiring place for writers to relax and write.

"Yes, my darling." James gallantly held his arm out so she could balance as she changed her shoes. "I imagine they probably look after cars like this all day long."

They handed the keys to the valet before heading up the steps into the exquisite atrium of this famous and fabulous hotel.

"Do you want a drink before we go down to the event?" James asked, looking at his watch and seeing that they were over half an hour early, something that was very unfashionable for a fashion party.

"Yes, why not?" said Jemima. "But I'll just have a citron pressé."

James walked to the bar and placed their order. Afterwards, they made their way across a sumptuous drawing room, past two tall French windows draped with blue and white curtains, and through to a terrace beyond with wicker tables.

"He's bringing them," James said as they sat down and took in the surroundings.

Jemima looked about her. Everyone who was anyone stayed here during the Cannes Film Festival, and she almost jumped with delight when she saw Jane Fonda chatting to friends on a nearby table. Looking over the terrace balcony to the gardens below, she saw several stunning people make their way down to where the luncheon was being held at the Eden-Roc Restaurant by the sea.

"You think we should go?" James asked, sensing her nervousness.

"Well, I didn't tell you, but…" Jemima took a deep breath. "We're not actually invited. We have to go to the kitchen door and wait for Yves's boyfriend who is working here. I said I'd be there at 1.45pm."

"Right." James, as ever, took it all in his stride. "Well, it's 1.42pm now, so we'd better go quickly if we're going to catch him." They moved quickly through the increasingly busy terrace bar to the steps that led through the plush gardens to the restaurant at the bottom.

"Jemima?"

Jemima turned around as she was being practically pulled through the pretty gardens full of rhododendrons and hydrangeas by her determined fiancé.

"Rosie!" She let go of James's hand and turned to greet her

friend. "How gorgeous to see you!"

"Darling, we're going to miss getting in," James said with a touch of impatience, while his fiancée was hugged by a blonde woman. She was dressed glamorously in a maxi dress and heels with a huge pair of dark glasses covering most of her face.

"So, who's this?" Rosie asked after a mutual admiration of each other's outfits.

"Oh, sorry, Rosie, this is my boyfr… fiancé, James Courtney."

"James, this is Rosie Vantomani, a friend of mine. She's another hugely successful PR–" Jemima winked "–whose clients' dresses are normally on most of the actresses during the festival."

"How nice to meet you, James!" Rosie flashed a winning smile. "And Jemima, what's this about a fiancé?"

"Happened this morning," she said, waving her huge ring whilst beaming at James.

"That is fantastic! Congratulations – champagne will be flowing, so what a way to celebrate! But James, what do you mean you won't be getting in?"

"We're not actually invited, but I need to be in there.' Jemima answered. "Long story, darling – will tell you another time."

"Come in with me! I am staying here and organising the fashion show! A couple of actors on my table have dropped out – you can have their seats."

Jemima could have kissed her. "You're a star!" The girls walked down in a more relaxed fashion to the party at the seaside restaurant, while James rushed on to alert the waiting waiter.

The Cannes Film Festival is, without doubt, one of the most glamorous events of the movie world, perhaps even more so than the Oscars. Although there are hundreds of industry insiders hustling for financing, spending ten days on the French Riviera is no hardship, particularly if you are staying at the Hotel du Cap Eden Roc and attending glittering fine jewellery luncheons, with the sparkling sea as the backdrop.

As the group approached the sleek white building, with its terracotta slated tiled roof through the small copse of tall Corsican pines, they heard the lyrical sound of a harp coming from the entrance hall of the villa-style restaurant. There were already lots of beautiful-looking men and women walking up the steps towards the sound of the music and chatter coming from inside. Chauffeurs were dropping guests off, and some had come down from the main hotel via white golf buggies with Hotel du Cap emblazoned on the canopies.

Inside, they were greeted by the sight of a glass cabinet with the most exquisite array of diamond and pink conch pearl jewellery that had been created by the party's host: the British jeweller, David Morris. As they went further in, they saw a crowd around another cabinet – a taller, full-length one. Eager to see what they were looking at, Jemima carefully edged her way through the throng. Inside the huge cabinet was the South African swimwear supermodel and wife of Hollywood star Greg Sylvester, Josette Von Arnette, posing in an exquisite silver dress that clung to her curves. She was adorned in a large, black opal, Paraiba tourmaline and white diamond necklace and matching chandelier earrings. Set with large oval opals interspersed with diamonds and the translucent turquoise Paraiba tourmalines that came from Brazil, the necklace hung down Josette's décolletage, ending with a large medallion formed of a large black opal surrounded by smaller opals, diamonds, and tourmalines. The earrings, in the same stones, had three large pendants hanging from a central clip. The whole ensemble was hugely dramatic, and Josette looked incredible.

Jemima squirmed out of the ever-growing crowd and found James. He was already holding a Bellini and chatting to a man by the railings above the sea, which was crashing against the rocks below. The view from the restaurant terrace was wonderful: you could see across the sparkling water to the Lérin Islands. Jemima grabbed a glass of Pol Roger and joined them. She had seen her friend Delfine in the crowd and wanted to introduce her fiancé to her at some point. Delfine had been in banking but now invested people's money in movies, so it wasn't surprising that she was here – it was one of the major movie social events of the festival calendar.

"Hi, babe, this is Jim Fleming," James introduced her, as she got up to the two men. The man with a large smile and tanned, unshaven face, who was in his mid-fifties, leaned forward to kiss Jemima on both cheeks. He was dressed in a white linen suit, with a blue shirt open at the neck and a slightly squashed Panama on his head.

*"Enchanté,"* he said. "I gather that you are staying in Monaco for the summer?"

"Well, yes, although it might be only a couple of weeks. It depends," she said unguardedly, then immediately regretted it, knowing what was coming next.

"On what?" he enquired.

"Diamonds!" She tried to laugh it off, but continued, having noticing that she had piqued his interest. "My company is the official jeweller of the remake of To Catch a Thief, which is premiering tomorrow night at the cinema on the Rock of Monaco."

"Ah, yes, Vogel!" The man smiled and clapped his hands. "I know the family well. I will be attending the party."

"Jim is one of Prince Albert's oldest friends, and my newest," Delfine explained as she came up to them and gave Jemima a huge hug. "They were at school together in Switzerland. Jim is everyone who is anyone's 'man in Monaco'."

"Wow, so you are a sort of fixer?" Jemima asked, and then wondered if that sounded rude.

"Well, yes, I suppose you could say that." He handed her his card with a wink before saying goodbye to them and drifting off to speak to more people.

"Oh dear. I do hope that I didn't offend him?"

"No! Don't worry at all!" said Delfine with a laugh. "He is a fixer and loves it! He would never have given you his card if he was offended. You don't want to lose it, by the way; he rarely gives his details out to anyone. I'd put them straight into your phone," she advised, before Jemima introduced her to James.

A large gong sounded and everyone was asked to find their seats.

"Oh dear, I'd hoped there wouldn't be a placement." Jemima started to worry as Rosie came up to the group.

"Don't worry, I've already spoken to the maître d'. They've put you in the seats that are suddenly vacant on the same table as me," the PR reassured her. "I'm glad to see you've met Jim – he will definitely come in use during your stay down here! He got us this venue. And de Grisogono are doing their annual party here in a few days."

As they wandered over to the tables, Jemima saw Petrina arrive with her parents. She decided she would make an effort to follow Alexa's advice and be friendly, so she went over and greeted the family cheerfully. She was immediately addressed fondly by Fortunata and introduced to her husband, Patrick. But she couldn't help but notice Petrina looking around elsewhere until she caught sight of James, and smiled confidently; Jemima realised that Milos wasn't with her. Suddenly, Jemima had an idea, and she secretly slipped off the engagement ring and put it in her little clutch bag before Petrina spotted it.

"It is so nice to see you again, Jemima," Fortunata continued, obviously not having spotted her by the pool earlier that day. "I am hoping that we can pin down Madame René, although she called Alexa and I on a conference call last evening and seems to be completely au fait with what needs to be done. Of course, she has organised premieres and events in Monaco for years!" She pointed out a very elegant lady, well into her sixties or even seventies, who was air-kissing everyone and introducing them to Jeremy Morris, the owner of David Morris.

"She looks like she could have been doing this for centuries!" Patrick Lindberg teased.

His wife admonished him with a smile. "She's probably no older than you, darling!"

"How are you after last night, Jemima?" Petrina asked, sipping a glass of Pol Roger pink champagne while handing one to her mother.

Jemima went on the charm offensive. "Not 100%, I'm afraid. It's easy to have a little too much fun on the Riviera, isn't it?" She smiled conspiratorially and was relieved to see Petrina smiling back. "I hope that we're on the same table as we barely got to speak last night. Is your lovely man Milos not here?"

"Oh, he's got some business today," Petrina said airily as her parents talked to someone else who'd come up to them. "But I see his doppelganger is here!" She indicated James a few metres away from their group with a tilt of her glass and smiled mischievously.

As they chatted and Petrina relaxed a little, Jemima wondered what business the jewel thief was up to, and how her plan would pan out this time.

"He's a bit pissed off with me," Jemima said, nodding at James. She held tightly on to her bag, knowing the ring and her future were safely inside, and took a breath – an idea was brewing in her brain. "We had a fight last night. He said I was too drunk at the party – said I should be more like you... more sophisticated." She knew she was playing into Petrina's hands. "I think he wants to split up," she added, getting carried away with herself.

"Really?" Petrina replied, looking as smug as ever.

Before Jemima could reply, they realised Petrina's parents had gone to their table, and Petrina went to join them.

Fortunata was already sitting down next to Mr Morris. She was, after all, an important client, who was wearing a beautiful pair of turquoise and diamond earrings that Jemima knew were from the brand's spring collection.

Jemima walked casually over to James, who was now talking to Josette, finally free from her glass cabinet but still wearing the exquisite opals.

"And you must be Jemima? I hear congratulations are in order?" the supermodel said, and Jemima was relieved that her Gina shoes meant that she was almost as tall as the two South Africans. "Josette Von Arnette," she said as she kissed Jemima, who was trying to mouth to her fiancé that she needed to talk to him urgently, on both cheeks. "I know your husband-to-be from South Africa. What a catch!"

"I'm so pleased to meet you! And yes, I know – I am so lucky," said Jemima, relieved that there was no way Petrina would have heard her. "I'm so sorry, I have to grab James quickly!"

Jemima pulled James away as Josette said she'd catch up with them later.

"What's going on, and where's your ring?" asked James quietly.

"I've got a plan," Jemima said. "Alexa wants me to befriend Petrina, so I can somehow get into her room at The Fairmont. She wants me to see what the safe's code is, so that they can go in and retrieve the diamonds, which, I forgot to mention, Petrina was wearing last night. They were dressed up as a De Grisogono earring. They're definitely still in her possession. So—" Jemima felt so giddy with what she was about to ask that she took a sip of water from a glass that had been left precariously on the stone wall of the terrace "–I want you to befriend Petrina. Flirt with her. She's really into you. Don't tell her or anyone else that we're engaged. Moan about me instead. I've hidden the ring in my bag for the moment; it's safe, don't worry. She's much more likely to let you into her room, than me. We need to pretend we've had a huge fight and are not talking to each other."

James looked at her incredulously.

"You don't have to sleep with her!" She laughed. "Well, I'd rather you didn't anyway, but needs must," she winked, "and I want to get these earrings back and her behind bars before she can ruin tomorrow night. And then you and I can sail off into the sunset and get married!" She smiled as she walked away from her suddenly-secret fiancé.

## Chapter 19

---

# Eden Roc Restaurant, Hotel du Cap

J emima and James walked to the tables separately. Jemima hated what she was asking him to do but she just couldn't figure out any other way of getting the Vogel Vanderpless diamonds back and somehow prevent a heist during the premiere the following evening. Of course, she thought as she sat down, the heist was probably already in motion. It would have taken months of planning, with Milos doing just that now.

Jemima whispered to Rosie that James was going to sit with Petrina, who raised her eyebrows and said that Petrina had already swapped the placement, so Jemima was now sitting next to Jim Fleming on her left and an up-and-coming American movie star on her right. Jemima didn't mind at all; Jim was clearly going to prove a useful person to know, and the actor looked just like Christian Slater, one of Jemima's secret crushes since she'd seen Robin Hood: Prince of Thieves back in the early 1990s. The tables were exquisitely decorated in a pink and white theme – the jewellery designer's colours – with posies of coordinated coloured peonies and pink Swarovski crystals sprinkled all over the white linen table cloths. The pink Pol Roger was still flowing, and, as Jemima made small talk with Jim, she realised that he was great friends with her first boss, the author and producer, Simon Astaire. She had a feeling that she was going to be able to trust this guy and that he was going to be of use in the coming days.

"This food is absolutely scrumptious! Although I seem to be one of the few women eating," Jemima said as their starters of caviar and truffled oysters were replaced by salmon fillet, huge, shelled pink prawns, and mint infused new potatoes with a cucumber, avocado, and rocket garnish. Jim, she noticed, had a rather larger plate than anyone else and had smiled gratefully at the waitress when she'd placed it in front of him.

"I love food." He smiled.

What a relief it must be for the chef, Jemima thought.

"I've got to eat lots and try to stop drinking the Pol Roger," Jemima smiled back. "I've got to drive my boss's car back to Cap Ferrat."

"And who's your boss?" he enquired, taking a bite of salmon. "I see that you have suddenly removed your engagement ring?" he whispered. "Trouble in paradise?"

"Can I trust you?"

"You should never ask someone that. They'll immediately know they're about to get something to use against you or indeed tell elsewhere," he said, without any sort of condescension. "But yes, you can. A protégé of Astaire's is a 'proctectee' of mine."

Jemima went on to explain in hushed tones why she was in Monaco, and why she had persuaded her fiancé to flirt with Petrina, who she then explained was the granddaughter of the notorious Snow Leopard.

"You are very brave," said Jim when she had finished. "If she is anything like her grandfather, I wouldn't want to get between her and jewels. He was as dangerous as his namesake: he's killed, and more than once probably." He took another sip of champagne. "I should know. I dated his daughter."

"Fortunata? She is over there on the top table with her husband."

"Yes, I was supposed to sit over there, next to her daughter, who I see is now next to your... fiancé." He smiled and she was sure she could see a feint flush under his bearded face. "She was one of the sweetest girls I knew. Her mother, Pierina, was also lovely, but had a sadness in her eyes."

"She died fairly young, didn't she? People keep saying it was tragic."

"Oh yes, terribly sad. She threw herself off the Rock, you know. She was found washed up in the foundations of Fontvieille in the early eighties, I think it was. Just after her husband had escaped from prison."

"Who did he kill?"

"He drowned an old fisherman who wouldn't transport him from the rocks below the prison to safety."

"Oh my God. I had no idea!" she said, shocked.

Jim was now washing down his poached salmon with Domain Ott rosé wine, and she remembered that she had to stick to the San Pellegrino water for a while. "I had better warn James."

"I would. I didn't know anything about Petrina, or indeed this Milos character, until recently, but I think I know who he is." As Jim proceeded to fill her in on Petrina's partner in crime, some of which she already knew, she texted James to meet her in the bathrooms as soon as the plates were cleared. She couldn't see him or Petrina, and was starting to worry.

"So, Milos's stepfather, Pyotr Petrovich, owns Force Russia and most of those islands over there," Jim was saying as he gestured towards the coast. "Ile Sainte Marguerite."

"Pyotr Petrovich!" she almost shouted, pronouncing the first name as Jim had – in the correct Russian way: *Piotur* – the same name as whoever Petrina and Milos had been going to meet after the heist on Friday? Was this the Peter Petrovich who Henrietta had told her owned the huge yacht, was a client of Vogel, and had bought the Vogel Vanderpless at auction? The same necklace whose four main diamonds had been stolen by Petrina. The very ones she was in the South of France to get back? What was going on?

"Yes, you know him?"

"Well, a Peter Petrovich is a Vogel client."

"Yes, that's him. Obviously, Peter is the English pronunciation of Pyotr." Jim advised.

"Obviously." Jemima answered, feeling very naïve.

"His grandmother was a White Russian who spent the last two decades of her life holed up between that island and her apartment in Monaco, trying to get back all of the Romanov jewels that had been sold off after the Revolution."

Jemima had heard as much from Henrietta the night before – everyone was seemingly connected. A waiter came to take their plates.

"Right, I haven't spoken to anyone else all lunch," Jim said. "Neither have you, for that matter. I am sorry for monopolising you."

"Not at all, Jim, you've been incredibly interesting!"

The plates were cleared and Rosie and her team were about to start a fashion show when Jemima saw Petrina walk away from the tables towards the swimming pool with James.

"Hi, my darling," James sat down next to her in the seat that

Jim had recently vacated and Jemima looked back over towards where Petrina had just gone. How had he got back so quickly?

"Don't worry - our seceret is safe. That Milos guy turned up, so Petrina told me that I'd better make myself scarce or he'd be jealous! It's very unnerving looking at someone who looks like my mirror image." Goodness Jemima couldn't believe that had mistaken them. She must have had too much champagne and grabbed a glass of water from the table.

"You're far sexier than him," she placated, relieved that she wasn't going crazy, was just a bit tipsy. "So, she thinks we've broken up?"

"Yes, but she is a smart girl; she got top marks at Harvard Law School. She actually defended Milos in a Pink Panther trial in New York last year."

"Yes, I Googled him yesterday. Jim just told me about him, too. Sounds super suspicious. Particularly as his stepfather owns one of those islands." She pointed out at the Lerin Islands. "He's also the same guy for whom I am trying to get back the diamonds from Petrina! Why can't he get them himself?"

"What? This is all way too much to take in," James said, shaking his head. "Thank God for my own job! It's a piece of piss compared to this. Anyway, have you been chatted up by the Panama-wearing Englishman?"

"Yes, I have actually, and it proved very interesting. Anyway, we shouldn't be seen talking!"

"Petrina is fascinated about you and your job. I also saw her receive and send a few messages to that guy from last night, Colt Bond. Several of which contained your name."

"Really, why?" She suddenly shuddered, despite the mid-afternoon heat when she remembered Jim's fatal warning.

"Duchess!" They were interrupted by another previous boss of Jemima's who was passing by on her way to the pool where the diamond fashion show was taking place. "What are you doing here?"

Jemima got up while explaining to James that Lina Kirke called her 'Duchess' because of her posh English accent. The women hugged each other, and Jemima made the introductions.

"Lina, this is my fiancé, James Courtney," she said, hoping, once again, that Petrina was far enough away not to hear her. "James, this is Lina Kirke of Gina Shoes. She dresses, or should I say, 'shoes' all the stars during the Film Festival, including me!" She laughed and put her beautiful blue high heeled shoe up on her chair for a second.

"We've also supplied the shoes for the show. We're working with Rosie. Anyway - it's about to start. Come and sit with me," said Lina.

"I'm going to the bathroom," James said, knowing they couldn't be seen together, plus he'd seen a polo friend of his heading to the bar and was more interested in talking to him than watching swimwear models pose around a pool.

Jemima and Lina found the only two seats that didn't appear to be taken, just as Shirley Bassey began to sing Diamonds are Forever from the side of the pool. Ten models, dressed in bikinis and swimsuits that matched the many colours of the jewels and shoes that they were wearing, followed Josette as they slinked down the steps past guests and down to the pool terrace. The infinity pool was dug into the side of the rocky cliff, on top of which Jemima sat in the front row and was trying not to fall over the side into the pool. The ten junior models walked precariously around the opposite edge, teetering on their tall heels. As the girls left, Josette dived into the turquoise pool, still wearing the opal and Paraiba tourmaline suite of necklace and earrings and the turquoise shoes, much to Lina's seemingly shocked face. Jemima winced; the gorgeously expensive shoes wouldn't be good for anything after their dunking. Josette was still underwater and, for a split second, Jemima, along with the rest of the crowd, started to panic, but then she surfaced to the relief of the onlookers. It didn't last long, however. As she came up from below, there was a sharp intake of breath from the hundred people watching. The jewels she had been wearing had disappeared.

Jemima glanced around the audience, looking for Petrina and Milos, and realised that she couldn't see them. The last chords of the song died away and it was then that Jemima noticed she could hear a boat speeding off. She carefully craned her neck to look over and recognised the sleek shape of Milos's black super boat heading towards the Lerin Islands. She was just about to yell out that they had taken the jewels when Josette disappeared under the water again, only to reappear with the most exquisite suite of emeralds and diamonds around her neck and on her ears. She swam to the side of the pool and carefully got out – now with a pair of emerald shoes on – and followed the ten younger girls back along the edge of the pool.

Everyone looked into the pool to see what had happened. Were the original jewels lying on the bottom of the pool? They were the same colour, so it was quite impossible to see without falling in. It was then that Jemima saw the magician David Copperfield go up to Josette and stand between her and Shirley Bassey before they, and the rest of the models, all bowed. David Copperfield had clearly magicked away the jewels and somehow swapped them under the water. The crowd applauded – a clever magic trick!

Jemima heard her phone vibrate from inside her bag and dug it. She had two texts on her phone, one from James, and one from a number she didn't recognise. She unlocked the screen, and read:

Ha ha! Got you!

It must be Petrina. How on earth had she got her number? Jemima realised that she had been played, and Petrina knew what game she was playing. Dammit! She felt a hot flush appear on her cheeks and walked slowly over to the bar where James had texted to say he was waiting for her to take the car to Villa Vogel in Cap Ferrat.

# Chapter 20

## Vogel Boutique, Casino de Monte Carlo
## Monday 9th May

Jemima awoke in her apartment the morning alone; she hadn't wanted to text James to see which room in The Fairmont he'd woken up in: his or Petrina's. Despite the pool fiasco the night before, they'd decided it was best if he continued to pursue Petrina, to see if he could get any further. In need of some good quality time, though, they had arranged to spend the day together after his meeting and before the gala.

After the diamond fashion show, they left before the David Morris evening party began, dropping the Ferrari off at Mr V's sprawling seaside villa before being driven back – rather sedately – by his chauffeur. Jemima was too embarrassed to tell James about the text and the trick. She was even more determined for him to find out where the Vogel Vanderpless jewels were, and get Petrina locked up for a long time. Perhaps Pyotr Petrovich wasn't the same Pyotr that they'd met on Friday night and had no idea that she had his missing diamonds. She had no proof of the Friday night theft either, but maybe James would find some of the gems in her room safe at The Fairmont. They had decided not to stay together that night. Hopefully, there was only twenty-four hours left of the pretence. Jemima was dropped off first, before the chauffeur headed back to Cap Ferrat, dropping James off on the way.

Jemima got up, showered, put on a chic dress that was appropriate for a meeting at the boutique, and placed her precious ring in the bedside table drawer. She proceeded to leave her apartment with a strong sense of butterflies playing havoc in her stomach, and felt a wave of fear that she was jeopardising her future with James by putting her job first. It suddenly seemed silly and dangerous to be putting them both at such risk when a peaceful and happy marriage awaited them, and she mulled it over as she made her way to the Vogel boutique. There was finally going to be a security meeting that morning with Philip Goldsmith, Alexa, and Renata René. She wondered if the event planner knew anything about the potential for a Panther heist, and the thought struck her that it would have made more sense to target David Morris yesterday – as Yves had said was Interpol's projection. It was far easier to speed off into the sunset in a boat full of jewels, than from the Princely Palace. And, if not Petrina and Milos, then what about the other Panthers? After all, there were the other four who had targeted the Casino Square stores on Friday.

The heat was yet again hitting the streets, and Monaco was steaming at only 9am; it seemed hotter than the past few days, if that was possible. Jemima was relieved to enter the cool of the Casino building. She hadn't ever ventured into any of the ornate gaming rooms, but she knew that they were beautifully and elaborately decorated in the original Belle Époque style of the Casino's inauguration in 1863. She couldn't imagine James was much of a gambler either, but perhaps, when her job on the Riviera was done, they could go for a little flutter. Jemima giggled to herself at the thought of her and James as an old Riviera couple, glued to the gambling tables in their late years, with Jemima bedecked in diamonds and dark spectacles, a glass of champagne permanently pressed into one hand.

"Ah, Jemima, I missed you yesterday when you dropped my mother's birthday present off. I suppose you had fun driving it, though?" Alexa was sitting with la Comtesse, drinking coffee from an elegant green and gold Spode china which matched the rest of the boutique.

"Yes, thank you. It was great fun!" She hoped that there were no scratches or, indeed, that it had been reported as being at the Hotel du Cap.

"Good. I'm glad to see you brought it back safely," Alexa said imperiously.

Philip Goldsmith arrived at that moment with DI Paige and, for once, Jemima was relieved to see Paige, still in his Inspector Clueso coat.

"Apologies for missing the meeting on Saturday," DI Paige said. "The traffic was impossible from Nice. It wasn't much better this morning, but I got a lift in with Madame René, who I met at the Nice helipad. She's outside talking to the Casino director."

DI Paige looked flustered and Jemima thought that the poor man would have spent a month's income to make sure he didn't miss the meeting. This was, after all, an important day of security for all of them.

"We must be paying Renata too much if she comes to meetings by helicopter!" Alexa sniffed, despite personally demanding the highest of standards and being worth billions.

"It is actually the same price as a taxi during this time of year, and far faster," La Comtesse said, defending her old friend, just as the elegantly coiffured lady in question walked in.

Alexa motioned for everyone to sit down and fresh coffee was served by a smiling Julie. Every single detail of the event and security for the night was covered with a fine-tooth comb. Philip seemed remarkably relaxed compared to the Somerset House gala back in April, and Jemima wondered if the heat had got to him. Like DI Paige, he wasn't really dressed for the Riviera; the rainy English version maybe, but by no means the sunny French one.

"Now, Jemima, Evie Talbot, and Glenn Close are both staying at The Fairmont. Fortunata has put them up there, rather than across the road in Hotel de Paris. Apparently, she feels funny about the Hotel de Paris. I have no idea why," said la Comtesse.

Jemima knew why: it was where her father had stolen all the jewels before the Royal Wedding in 1956.

"Philip will accompany me to the hotel with two security guards," la Comtesse continued while Alexa tapped away on her iPhone. "I would like you to meet us there at 5.30pm and come up to their suites. Obviously, Fortunata's team know the actresses well and will be escorting them up to the rocher, with our guards following subtly behind."

"Jemima, I am presuming you will be suitably dressed?" Alexa enquired condescendingly, and Jemima was relieved that Rosie had lent her the most exquisite haute couture gown of the palest blue silk lace that she had seen on a rail backstage when she had gone to the bathroom after the fashion show yesterday.

The French women, however, looked shocked at Alexa's impertinence. La Comtesse announced that Jemima was to choose some jewellery before she left, which she would bring with her to The Fairmont that evening.

"Merci, Madame la Comtesse. I will be wearing a pale blue Ralph Lauren Couture," Jemima said, so Alexa could hear. "Which

I have been lent," she added quickly, so her boss didn't think it had gone on the company credit card.

*"Parfait. J'ai une idée d'une suite d'un collier, boucles d'oreille et bracelet en aigue-marines et diamants. C'est une partie de la nouvelle Collection Méditerranée."* The boutique directrice suggested a parure of aquamarines and diamonds. She was clearly infuriated with Alexa's rudeness, and didn't approve of her inability to learn French, despite her father having had a villa in Cap Ferrat for most her life.

Alexa was now calling the Carol Joy Salon at The Fairmont to make an appointment for later that day. Jemima listened carefully to make sure she didn't arrange one at the same time; she didn't feel like sitting next to the woman any longer than she had to.

Finally, Madame René went through the evening's agenda. Afterwards, they all left, except Philip, who was back to his normal self and insisted on triple-checking all the details.

# Chapter 21

## The Fairmont Hotel, Avenue des Spélugues

Jemima had spent the rest of the morning and afternoon wondering where James was, as her texts and calls had gone unanswered. Strangely he hadn't turned up at her apartment after his morning polo game at the Monte Carlo Polo Club with the friend he had seen the day before at Hotel du Cap. Jemima had booked her hair appointment at Carol Joy for 3pm, and now, as she went up in the hotel elevator to his room with her hair neatly coiffured, she was starting to worry. Had Petrina done anything to him, as Jim had predicted?

On the way back to Monaco the previous day, James had updated Jemima on all he had learnt. Petrina had told him that she would be with her mother all afternoon at the palace, preparing for the gala. They had been lent a suite of rooms to use to freshen up and change in before the guests arrived at 6pm, so she wouldn't be returning to the hotel that afternoon. James had, however, told Jemima that Petrina had mentioned she had hoped to see him at the party, which was good news – James was still the best way into Petrina's safe. As he was no longer going with Jemima, she'd left his name with the event security, and instructed him to bring his ID. Vogel had become incredibly worried about all the jewels that were going to be on show and had insisted on photo ID for all guests.

When Jemima arrived in James's room just after 4pm to see what was going on, she found his mobile on the huge bed, the screen showing several missed calls and a voicemail from the same number ending '666'. She knew that number and pulled her own phone from her bag. For the umpteenth time that day, she reread the text Petrina had sent her the day before <<Haha! Got you!>>, which had also enabled her to memorise much of the phone number, ending in the unforgettable '666'. Jemima remembered her History of Art studies at school; her favourite poet and artist, William Blake, had a Biblical painting entitled 'The Number of the Beast is 666'. It seemed too appropriate for Petrina not to realise the significance. Or maybe it was a fluke.

Before plucking up the courage to listen to the messages, Jemima hung up her beautiful blue gown and put the same shoes and bag that she'd worn yesterday by the side of the closet, looking at them with excitement. She then pulled off the smart work dress and put on a cool silk La Perla robe she had found behind the bathroom door.

Once Jemima was ready, she plugged her earphones into James's phone and went out to the balcony. Despite the several missed calls, Petrina had only left one message. It confirmed her hopes that he hadn't awoken with her in bed that morning, but it did tell him how much she loved spending time with him, and how she would get rid of Milos, so they could spend time together that night, before congratulating him on "Dumping the stupid English girl".

Jemima ended the call using her headphones, but continued staring out to sea, trying not to shake. Horrible thoughts seeped into her mind, and she wondered if James had, in fact, dumped her, and that was why he'd left her at the apartment alone last night. She tried to focus on the view instead.

To the left, she noticed Henrietta's ex-husband's beautiful sailing boat moored back in front of La Radieuse, off Larvotto Bay. To the right, Pyotr Petrovich's mega yacht was motoring in from the direction of Cannes. She supposed he was coming to the gala; it was one of the opening events of the 2011 festival. Her thoughts flicked to Fortunata, and she wondered why on earth the film producer was holding such a sensationally high-profile movie at the same spot where her mother committed suicide all those years before.

Vanderpless diamonds, sapphire earrings, muttered Jemima to herself; the pieces of jewellery that kept cropping up where they were least expected. Petrovich. And that damned Petrina.

Wrapped in the silk robe and leaning on the railings, Jemima looked both below her and to either side, just to make sure no-one could hear her muttering, although it was unlikely with the sound of the sea swirling against the rocks below. She felt like screaming in anger, hurt, and embarrassment, and wished she could just let it all out. Damn Petrina and damn Alexa for getting her mixed up in all this Monte Carlo business, and damn herself for getting James involved in Petrina's dangerous life. Jim Fleming's words were coming back to haunt her. And damn James. Where the hell was he, she thought, as she stormed back into the room. She decided then and there that there was no way Petrina would steal her fiancé as well as all these diamonds. James was far more important than lumps of glossy rock. She would do her PR job and cover the event this evening, then hand in her resignation tomorrow. She would write novels and travel around the world with her future husband.

Maybe she'd even become a jewellery editor of a magazine; she had always wanted to, and knew enough about jewellery now to write for any of the glossies.

Jemima turned from the turquoise Mediterranean Sea, slid open the French windows, and stepped through, having heard a door close.

"Babe, I am so sorry," James said as he threw down a huge bag emblazoned with the Cape Town Polo Club logo that contained his sticks and other polo paraphernalia. "I am sorry," he said again, walking over with his arms open. "I have no excuse other than we just couldn't get back into the city. The bloody Grand Prix traffic. Even by boat, you know. There is some serious security over your do tonight. Colt told me that apparently the ports are on high alert! I hope your guests are already on their way." He smiled at her proudly.

Jemima's hurt and fury faded fast. She believed him; everyone she'd been due to meet in the past few days had had problems getting into Monaco.

"Colt?"

"Yes! The American guy from the other night at Sass. After a couple of beers, he let slip that he's not known Petrina long; his brother married your assistant earlier this year, and the girls are friends. Sounds like they've both got it in for you – the girls, that is. She's asked him to keep an eye on you. Which, of course, I wasn't happy with…" James saw her face and changed the subject. "But I am so happy you're here. I have been thinking about doing this to you ever since I left you at your apartment last night." He undid the tie on her silk robe, letting it slip to the ground, and then gently pushed her down on to the bed.

Jemima was trying to ask him about what Colt had said but

couldn't concentrate; James had crouched between her legs and started to lick the inside of her thigh, before moving slowly up. She felt his tongue inside her and immediately orgasmed, her body shaking with the delight of him and what he was doing to her.

"So," she said, some minutes later, pulling him up towards her.

When James was next to her, Jemima undid his white polo jeans, before standing up off the bed and leaning over to pull them and his boxers off, whilst letting her silk robe slip to the floor. James pulled up the polo shirt covering his insanely athletic body, and she proceeded to crawl up between his legs that were splayed open in his relaxed state. She licked and nibbled the top of his large penis and, as he began to stiffen, she continued, "So, it seems, my darling, that you've signed up for this for the rest of your life." She moved up his body and sunk down with him inside her.

They spent the next hour making love on the bed, before Jemima realised that she only had thirty minutes before she had to meet the Vogel team downstairs in the foyer. She suggested James join her in the shower and walked across the room to the bathroom, where she noticed how bedraggled her hair looked in the huge mirror. She laughed; it was no longer the elegant up do that she'd had done before he arrived.

Jemima pulled open the glass door of the shower and turned on the hot water which came gushing out of the square shower head. When she could see steam appearing, she pulled all the pins from her hair, put them on the side by the basin, and then stepped back inside. She let the piping hot water scald her as much as she could bear, before turning the temperature down. She loved that most men couldn't stand extreme temperatures as much as women. She heard the shower door open behind her; James pushed her gently against the marble wall, so he was under the torrent of water. She felt him gather her long wet hair, twist it up on her head, and leaned in to kiss her behind her ear and on the right side of her neck. Suddenly, with one hand, he pulled her hips out and up to him, and then he was inside her. He grabbed her hands and pushed them up above her head, sliding himself inside her as the water poured down upon them. They came together so soon, with such intensity, that she felt like she was drowning in the lack of the control she had over him. He withdrew and pulled her lips up to his.

"I guess I should have booked my hair appointment for later?" She smiled, stepped out of the shower, and wrapped herself in a towel.

James laughed and apologised as he turned off the water and followed her, taking the big towel she passed him.

"So, you still want me to pretend to Petrina that I'm no longer in love with you?" James asked.

Jemima's happiness evaporated as she winced with worry, thinking back to what he had said about why Colt Bond was on the Riviera.

# Chapter 22

---

# The Premiere of To Catch a Thief, Le Rocher de Monaco

Jemima left the hotel in the same car as Evie Talbot, while the Comtesse de Ré went with Glenn Close in a separate blacked-out Mercedes S-Class, each with their own Vogel security guard.

Dressed in diamonds and couture gowns, they were settled on the back seat, making their way through the traffic. Jemima had, surprisingly successfully, managed to slick back her hair behind her ears with some of James's pomade, so her aquamarine and diamond earrings glittered spectacularly from her ears. She thought that she'd put on a bit too much smoky eyeshadow, but then, she had put the whole look together in ten minutes.

"I must get the name of your hairstylist," said Evie, as the car slipped past a parade of similar black cars, all with blacked-out windows.

"It was Carol Joy downstairs in the hotel."

Jemima looked at the huge Princess Grace sapphire and diamond earrings that Evie was wearing. They were incredibly beautiful, and she suddenly felt so sad that Princess Grace never got to wear the originals. She thought how generous it was of Mr

V to gift these exquisite and exact replicas to the new Jewel Museum of Monaco. She knew that they were worth well into the six figures.

Due to the security around the jewellery and the stars, it had been arranged for them to have a window of half an hour where the road was closed to other traffic. The route they took from the Fairmont Hotel to the Rock of Monaco was part of the Grand Prix circuit and their chauffeur seemed intent on using the opportunity to behave like a Formula One driver. After going down the famous Fairmont Hairpin, they sped through the tunnel under the hotel adjacent to the sea, before hurtling around Port Hercules to the Rascasse corner that was below the Rock. As they reached the corner, the car turned up the hill to the outdoor cinema where the premiere was being shown. It was Europe's largest outdoor cinema, situated only a popcorn's throw away from the Palace of Monaco, in which the gala was being held after the film.

Their car pulled up to park outside the entrance to the cinema, next to that of the Comtesse and Glenn Close, and Jemima could see the enormous red carpet was already ablaze with the flashing of the paparazzi. As they waited to be told to get out, she asked Evie if she ever got nervous walking the red carpet.

"Yes! But then I haven't done many – this is perhaps the most glamorous. I mean, Monaco is literally one of the most glamorous places that I have ever been to!"

"Isn't it? Sometimes I never want to leave."

"Do you have to?"

"Well, maybe my fiancé could get a permanent job here and I could write books by the sea!" she joked dreamily.

"Well, let me know – maybe I'll star in one of the film adaptions of them, if I don't mess this one up. Right, our doors are about to be opened! I guess I'll see you in there… you don't have to walk the red carpet, lucky you. It's the most nerve-wracking part of the whole night!"

Although Jemima thought it would be quite fun to parade up the red runway with a plethora of the world's most famous people, she was quite relieved to be going through the 'civilian' entrance with la Comtesse. She watched Evie meet with her onscreen amour, Richard Wakefield. Glenn Close followed in the most gorgeous gold gown with a matching cape over her shoulders. Uma Thurman, Jane Fonda, Robert de Niro, and Kirsten Dunst were just a handful of the celebrities she saw arrive to see this off-circuit screening. Monaco, being much more dignified than London's Leicester Square, meant that there were no hordes of people screaming, but there was still a bit of a crowd standing outside the entrance, with their backs to the blue Mediterranean. It really was the most exquisite setting to watch a movie.

Jemima found la Comtesse and together they went through a side gate and found themselves being shown to seats that were quite a way from the actresses they were supposed to be accompanying, but, fortunately, they could see them, along with the guards who were guarding the jewels. However, every single star had the equivalent amount of jewellery on – so, as Charles Renault had promised, security was of the highest level. Philip Goldsmith would be relieved and very impressed, she didn't doubt. Even he couldn't possibly find fault. She just hoped that Petrina, who she hadn't yet seen, wouldn't find one either. It was just all too perfect to be ruined by Petrina and the Pink Panthers.

Suddenly, it was 8.30pm and waiters in coattails and bowties were walking around handing out bags of sparkly popcorn – Jemima guessed they was supposed to look a bag of diamonds –

and filling everyone's glasses with champagne. Since she'd made the decision to stick with water, she reluctantly refused her favourite drink and sat up as high in her chair as possible, looking for James, just as her iPhone vibrated in her clutch bag. She pulled it out and saw a message from him.

You look completely beautiful, future wifey... I can't wait to see you on our wedding day. Maybe I'll have to get you those jewels to wear more often... with nothing else!

Jemima looked around for him, but it was hard as there were so many people and still a bit glary from the sun setting over the sea.

I am standing up on the other side of the audience, near the back under the trees.

Oh yes, my darling, there you are. But where is Petrina?

James looked insanely dashing in his black tie, with the setting sun behind him.

She is talking to a bodyguard called Ivan. I can't work out who is he guarding but he came with a Russian friend of hers. I recognise him from somewhere.

Jemima wondered how long it was before the Pink Panthers would descend on the event. Surely, it would be after the movie; they couldn't hold up an open-air auditorium of five hundred people. Her heart starting to pound with nervous excitement, and she remembered that she had to concentrate on Evie, not the Pink Panthers. That was what Interpol were for. And James was going to get back the Vogel Vanderpless diamonds; that is, if Petrina hadn't already handed them over to Petrovich.... Jemima hadn't seen Fortunata yet, but was pretty sure that she wouldn't be wearing the original Romanov earrings – she would surely give them back to the Royal family privately? After all, the Vogel would be donating the replica Romanov earrings to the new Jewel

Museum that was being unveiled at the same time. Jemima couldn't help wondering if that was on the Pink Panthers' program of events in the future – although she had heard that the Head of Security for the Tower of London had been instrumental in advising the director of the new museum.

Enjoy the movie and see you in your room bright and early – with the diamonds, I hope!

Lekker! he texted back, which made Jemima laugh. It was South African for 'great', and she'd not heard James say it since his grandmother admonished him for it.

The crowd started to go quiet, just as the Comtesse touched her arm. Jemima looked up from her phone to see Fortunata onstage, wearing a parure of emeralds, not dissimilar to the Vogel ruby parure that Glenn Close was wearing.

"Apologies for the late hour, but even Hitchcock couldn't control the sun!" There was a small chuckle from the audience. Fortunata continued to give a small speech about how much the original movie meant to her and how she could never replicate it, so she decided to focus on the original novel by David Dodge. She thanked the cast for promising not to watch the original Hitchcock ones, if that hadn't already seen them. "So," she continued. "All that is left to say is that I hope you enjoy our movie, thank you for coming, and I look forward to talking with some of you at the gala afterwards. Oh, and if there's anything you think I've got wrong, because you did watch the Hitchcock–" She paused for effect "– It's too late to change, so do read the book and then come back to me."

"It's for sale at the FNAC in the Metropole centre," someone in the audience called out.

Everyone laughed when Fortunata said, "Merci, Adrien!" And they realised that it was Adrien Bonpoint, the well-known

President of the French retail chain FNAC.

Fortunata smiled as the crowd laughed and clapped, and then left the stage so the film could begin.

* * *

At the end of the film, Jemima realised that she hadn't seen the original Hitchcock version, as she had confused it with his Rear Window, but thought Fortunata's was brilliant. Glenn Close and Evie Talbot were so good as mother and daughter, and Richard Wakefield was a very dashing retired cat burglar. La Comtesse and Jemima got up and went to meet the two leading female stars, already being whispered about as getting Oscar nominations for their performances. It was now almost 11pm, but Monaco wasn't about to go to bed, and many of the guests were still on US time. They found their movie stars, with the jewels still in place, and followed the crowd that was walking towards the gala room in the Prince's Palace.

Jemima looked about her at the ornate room; it was simply exquisite and, at the far end, she could see the large white and gold doors that led to what was to be The Jewel Museum of Monaco. It had a large red and white ribbon tied in front of it and was due to be opened by the Prince at midnight, with Evie Talbot handing Mr Vogel the earrings, who would in turn give them to the Prince to display in a glass cabinet in memory of the earrings stolen before Princess Grace's wedding.

Jemima saw James chatting with Petrina in the middle of the room. She looked absolutely beautiful in what she recognised as emerald and diamond David Morris earrings that her mother had no doubt bought her after the lunch at Hotel du Cap. They perfectly matched her one-shouldered, toga style, silk dress and made her eyes even greener. She was overwhelmed with jealousy. Suddenly, a man appeared with a glass of champagne and said it was a present from an admirer, nodding to James who then looked over at her smiled when Petrina wasn't looking. She decided to forgo her ban on alcohol and drink this one; she needed it after seeing them looking so good together, far better than she ever would with him. She drank the golden liquid quickly and went to look for Evie who had disappeared for the bathroom a while ago; she could see the bodyguard that had accompanied them, and who was assigned to the actress for the event, walking about on his own. It was now almost midnight and she could see the Vogels standing near the doors to the about to be unveiled museum. Where was Evie with the jewels that they were presenting to the prince for the museum?

Jemima searched the bathrooms but saw that Evie wasn't there, so she quickly went to the loo. As she went to wash her hands, she noticed that her reflection in the big ornate mirrors was looking very blurry and she was swaying slightly. Surprised that the champagne had gone to her head so quickly, she made towards the door to get some water from a waiter, but the door that she came through was locked. She tried another one and it opened to a rose garden outside.

Suddenly, she felt a heavy thump on the back of her head, and everything went black.

# Chapter 23

## Princess Grace Hospital, Monaco
## Tuesday 10th May

Jemima awoke with the most awful headache, so much so that she quickly closed her eyes again after only a brief flicker of them being open. She felt sick and sore throughout her whole body, but the pain in the back of her head was unbearable. The only time she'd ever felt even half as bad was back in April when she had been poisoned by Paul Pratt at the Somerset House gala. This wasn't a hangover, she thought, as she tried to make sense of her surroundings. Someone had spiked her drink. It hurt to lie on the back of her head, so she turned over and opened her eyes to look at James. But James wasn't there, and Jemima suddenly realised she wasn't in his bed. White sheets, sweaty mattress, the smell of bleach. She was clearly in a hospital, or was it a prison? She could barely move; the bed's siderails were firmly up from head to toe. She'd never awoken in such a confined space and could imagine a coffin wasn't much different. Jemima sat up and immediately thought that she was going to be sick. Luckily, someone had placed a grey cardboard bowl next to her, but nothing came up; she hadn't eaten anything last night. In fact, she hadn't eaten anything much since lunch at Hotel du Cap two days previously.

Vague memories started coming back to her. The evening had gone so well, despite having to see Petrina and James together. But she couldn't remember a heist. Was there one? Was it all a bluff to distract Interpol from something else? She spent much of the evening with Evie, or at least keeping an eye on her and her jewellery. Were they still safe? She then recalled searching for the film star in the bathrooms, after noticing Evie go in there while being tailed by a different security guard to the one they had arrived with. Yes! It was the odd-looking guy who had been outside Vogel in London when she went to meet with Alexa. How strange – what was he doing 'guarding' Evie Talbot or, indeed, the jewels? He definitely did not work for Vogel. And what had happened to the original guard, Ismael, who had travelled with them from The Fairmont?

Jemima looked around the room and saw her beautiful Ralph Lauren gown lying over a hospital chair in the corner, with her clutch bag poking out under the now muddy and ripped silk lace skirt. What the hell? She also realised that she was wearing a hospital gown. Jemima tried to get out of the bed but couldn't work out how to lower the rails. Just as she was about to call for help, the door opened, and a doctor and a nurse came in.

*"Bonjour, Madame,"* the doctor said in a non-descript tone. "We need to take another blood sample before we can let you go." He motioned for the nurse to come forward.

She pushed a trolley towards the bed and Jemima automatically pulled up her left sleeve for the nice-looking, elderly lady, who smiled sympathetically and made Jemima want to cry. What the hell was she doing here? And where was James?

"Why am I here?"

"Well, it appears you were found unconscious in a rose bed in the palace gardens. You were brought here to the Princess Grace Hospital at around 1am, and we tested you. You sustained a nasty bump to the head and are suffering from concussion. You also had very high levels of Rohypnol in your blood."

"What? How?"

"It is often slipped into alcoholic drinks," he said, while the nurse gently put the syringe in her arm.

"I only had one glass of champagne," she said, feeling confused.

"I am afraid that is all it takes."

Jemima thought back to the glass of champagne that James had sent over. What was it the waiter had said when he brought over the champagne? From an admirer nodding at James... or was he nodding at Petrina? Had she spiked her drink? Jemima wouldn't put it past her, and she put her hand to the back of her head. It was still throbbing, and she felt a huge lump that was agony to touch.

"Is my fiancé here?" She looked at her hand; of course, the ring wasn't there because she hadn't put in on. She felt her ears and neck. The jewellery wasn't there. She took in a sharp intake of breath. "My jewellery! Where is it?"

"Don't worry, it is in the hospital safe. I will get it for you when you leave," the nurse said in near perfect English as she put the phial of blood into a clear plastic bag. *"Monsieur le docteur, je vais verifier cette sangue,"* she continued, addressing the doctor. She proceeded to leave the room, pushing the trolley to have Jemima's blood tested. After telling Jemima that she couldn't leave until her blood was clear of any trace of the drug, and that the police might want to question her, the doctor followed.

When the door closed, Jemima started to cry; she felt so unwell, her head was pounding and she had no idea what had happened, or where James was. She wondered if Evie was okay. She was supposed to have been looking after her and the last thing she remembered was looking for her in the bathrooms. She pulled herself up with the rails, so she was on all fours, and climbed over the top of the bed, before landing with a thud on the cold floor.

Jemima could now see her beautiful blue Gina shoes, with much of the silk on the heels ripped and the white plastic showing through. She grabbed her bag and, feeling sick again, sat down on the dress and opened the clutch. Her phone wasn't there. She had definitely not forgotten it at the apartment: after leaving it behind when she saw the jewels on Milos's boat, she'd vowed she wouldn't make that mistake again. It must have been taken. She flicked through the contents of her clutch rapidly, trying to find any scrap of evidence that might tell her what had happened. It was then when she saw Jim Fleming's card. She'd have to call him and ask him to help; after all, she didn't know James's number off by heart and the only other number she knew, other than her own, was her parents' landline number in Dorset. She was definitely not calling them! She hadn't even told them that she was engaged, for goodness' sake.

The nurse came back in, on her own this time, carrying a tray of breakfast. She saw Jemima crying on the chair, put the tray on the table by the bed, and came over to her and gave her a hug.

"Calm yourself, my dear." The old lady soothed her kindly, then said that there was payphone in the reception that she could use to call someone to collect her.

Jemima explained that she had no euros on her, and the pretty, blue-eyed, wrinkled face looked at her before whispering that her phone was in her locker and Jemima could borrow it, but she mustn't tell anyone. She also told her that she should have something to eat while she went and retrieved it. Pulling the wheeled table over to the chair, she grimaced at the tray.

"I apologise, the doctor instructed the simplest of breakfasts," the nurse said.

This explained the plain crackers, lump of cheese, and cup of tea that was in front of her. Not quite what she imagined a private hospital to provide. Despite still feeling sick, she was starving, and had eaten the crackers and cheese by the time the nurse had returned with her very old-looking Nokia phone.

"Thank you," she said to the nurse, who politely left the room.

As Jemima dialled Jim's number, she noticed that it was only 7.30am and he'd probably still be in bed after his night at the gala. Luckily, he answered on the fourth ring.

"Oui, Allo?"

"Jim! It's Jemima Fox."

"Ah, Jemima! Good morning, my dear. What a good party you gave last night," he laughed. "I barely saw you though. Was hoping for an introduction to the splendid Evie Talbot but then you both disappeared. Why are you calling me so early?"

"Oh, Jim!" Despite herself, Jemima almost giggled: she supposed it was the shock. "I'm in the Princess Grace hospital. I was drugged and they found me in a flower bed." It did sound ridiculous, she acknowledged to herself.

"What? How?"

"I have no idea, and yours is the only number I have to call, thanks to your business card. I don't know where James is or who brought me here. I've got no money to get back to my apartment, and someone's stolen my phone. This one belongs to the nurse."

She started to weep uncontrollably; this was a disaster.

"Okay, darling, stop crying and get yourself together. I'll be there in twenty minutes, I don't live far away. We will sort it all out."

Jim hung up and the nurse reappeared, holding a piece of paper and a towel.

"Take a shower, my dear. You'll feel better." She handed Jemima the towel and bashfully put the paper on the bed, before leaving the room again with the tray.

Jemima picked up the paper and noticed that it was an invoice for €987. She was astounded and was about to cry again before she realised that it wasn't going to help. Work can damn well pay for it, she thought, and again cursed Alexa for bringing her out here. She showered quickly and was just about to put her bedraggled dress back on when the nurse came back with a pile of clothes, explaining that an Englishman was waiting for her and had brought them.

The clothes were a teenager's pink t-shirt with Nikki Beach St Tropez emblazoned across the front, a pair of denim cut offs, and a pair of pink and white striped espadrilles. She just managed to squeeze into them and wore the shoes with the backs down. Putting her dress, shoes, and bag into the white plastic bag that she found in the room, she left, holding the invoice in her hand and hoping they'd at least let her leave with the promise of paying it at a later date.

Jim was standing outside the main door of the hospital on his phone. The sun was blazing, and he was wearing a Hawaiian shirt and khaki coloured shorts. He looked through the glass doors as she walked to the reception desk and smiled, before finishing his call and coming to join her.

"You poor thing," he said. "These are my daughter's, I'm

afraid. It's all I had in my apartment. She's with her mother in Paris this weekend, or I might have asked if she had something a bit more sophisticated!"

"Don't worry at all – it's just so kind of you to have even thought of this, let alone pick me up." She smiled at him as he leant over to kiss her cheek. "Now, somehow I have to persuade them to let me go without paying this very expensive bill for an uncomfortable bed and horrible breakfast! Or, indeed, without having to wait for the police to interview me – someone spiked my drink."

"I'll speak to them about the police and sort this out, and you can settle up with me later." He took the invoice from her and turned to the reception desk with a Platinum Amex card in his hand as the nurse casually handed Jemima back a bag containing her aquamarine and diamond jewels. They were probably used to seeing thousands of euros worth of belongings at this Monaco hospital, she thought.

"Now," said Jim, as he ushered her out to the waiting car. "You need to make a statement at the police station at some point today, However, on the way here, I made some calls and I know what has happened. I'll tell you in the car. It's not good news, I am afraid."

# Chapter 24

---

# La Radieuse

alf an hour later, they pulled up outside La Radieuse in his Toyota Prius. On the drive over, Jim had broken the news to Jemima that Evie Talbot had disappeared, presumed kidnapped. She missed her press call at 8am at The Fairmont and her room had been searched.

"She was last seen leaving the palace with a man at around 12.30am," said Jim grimly. "Who, naturally, is now the prime suspect. They are trying to find out – from the palace's security cameras – who the man was. But there are reports that it was a South African man. Could it be your James?"

"James wouldn't hurt a fly, let alone kidnap someone," Jemima practically screamed in shock, and implored him to go faster.

"Of course, I believe you and I will help you. But Renault and his force are looking for him. They no longer care about the jewels, I imagine. They are nothing compared to the world's most sought after actress being kidnapped in Monaco." Jim pulled up outside her apartment and got out to open the door for her.

"Get warm, get dressed, and eat something. It may take a while to get over the shock and the poison. I have to go now, I'm afraid; I have a breakfast meeting in Cannes regarding the Film Festival.

My friend Spyros is one of the sponsors, with his new battery-powered aeroplanes." He helped her up the steps and asked how to get in touch with her. They had tried her phone and it was still on but there was no answer; she thought it was probably up at the palace in a flowerbed. "Now you have my number," he continued. "Call me if you can, should you need to, and I'll see what more I can find out."

"Your email is on your card – I can contact you from my iPad," Jemima said. "Please keep me posted; there is no way James took this poor girl."

Jemima felt like crying again as she opened the door. She had been supposed to look after the actress, only a few years younger than herself and such a lovely girl. As she went up in the lift, her hands sweating from clutching the plastic hospital bag, she wondered if the earrings that Evie had been wearing were with her, or had James taken them off and given them to Petrina before kidnapping Evie? She stopped herself – James hadn't kidnapped anyone, nor stolen any earrings. He was supposed to be with Petrina getting back the jewellery she had stolen. He probably didn't even know anything about this kidnapping.

Jemima opened the door of her apartment and, despite the disaster surrounding her, felt a surge of relief to be 'home'. Although she wished she was back in Dorset at her parents's house, having never got mixed up in this mess.

Jemima went to her bedside table, turned on her iPad, and then slipped on her exquisite engagement ring, thinking what a fool she was to have got James involved. She knew it had been a horrific mistake. The iPad started beeping immediately with messages and emails, so, lying on her bed, she scrolled through everything. Nothing from James. They were all from Alexa and Mr Vogel, asking where she was, and sent around midnight last night, which was way before she was found and taken to the hospital, and seemingly before James was seen leaving with Evie. She dimly remembered feeling sad that he was with Petrina, and then, at one point, watching James and Petrina leave the gala dinner to go outside. He had glanced back as if to look for her, she thought, but he had his arm around Petrina's waist as he guided her through the large doors. Had she finally lured him in?

Jemima heard a phone ring from somewhere inside the apartment, jumped off her bed, and walked towards where the ring was coming. For the first time, she noticed an old pale-blue wall phone in the hall behind the kitchen door which she'd always left open since she arrived there a few days earlier. She picked it up, hoping that it might just be James – although how would he get this number? – and heard shouting down the line. It was Alexa.

"Jemima, what the hell happened to you? I should never have trusted you with this job! All you had to do was look after the actress and the earrings, and now both have vanished."

Jemima took a deep breath, wondered how she got the number, and plucked up the courage to be equally angry. "Alexa, I woke up in the Princess Grace hospital having been drugged and–"

"I seem to remember you saying that before."

"–knocked out." Jemima continued, ignoring her. "My phone was stolen and…"

"Those jewels Diane lent you?"

There was no concern for her welfare whatsoever. Bitch, Jemima thought.

"I have them with me," she looked at them in the plastic bag on her bed, along with her dress and the other bits.

"Good. Get them back to the boutique ASAP," Alexa said as a word rather than an acronym. "Now, your boyfriend was seen leaving the gala with Evie not long after midnight." It was James, she sighed. Alexa was supremely detached as she described the kidnapping of the world's most famous face, and Jemima wondered what Alexa was more worried about.

"I need you to find him," Alexa continued. "Interpol needs you to find him. In fact, you need to find him before Interpol does. Did you know that he was a kidnapper and a jewel thief? I gather he tried to get some of the satellite Vogel Vanderpless diamonds from Danny, for some reason. He was also seen with Petrina for most of the night – the girl you were supposed to be tailing to find the missing d…" She then stopped, suddenly before her voice rose to a shriek, "Are you all in this together?"

Jemima, seeing red, couldn't even find the words to reply. Instead, she slammed the old phone back down on its wall piece. She was so incensed and upset that she sat for a long time on the bed, head in her hands. *Of course* they weren't in this together with Petrina. James was supposed to have gone back with Petrina and found out the code to her room. He was not supposed to have left with Evie, let alone kidnapped her. He couldn't have done it, thought Jemima, stunned to find herself even considering it. She again wished she knew his number by heart so she could try to call him from her burner phone. If she ever got out of this mess, she'd memorise it.

# Chapter 25

---

## An hour later

After washing her hair, which was caked with dirt from the flowerbed, under a long, hot shower, Jemima heard a loud knock on her door. Again, thinking it could be James, she walked out of the shower, wrapped a towel around herself, and ran to open it.

"Jemima." It was Colt Bond. "Can I come in?"

"Umm, well I am in a bit of a hurry: my boyfriend is in trouble." She didn't mention anything about him potentially kidnapping one of the world's most famous actresses.

"That's why I'm here. Let me in. I want to help." Jemima opened the door.

Colt walked in and went straight over to the sofa in the sitting room. She followed him, water dripping all over the wooden floor.

"Petrina 'employed' me," he said, holding his hands up to show the inverted commas, "to follow you and tell her what you were up to. I didn't know why, to be honest, and now I feel like a real fool. I didn't want to but was persuaded by my brother's new wife." When he saw Jemima's baffled face, he added, "Zoe Weinberg."

"Zoe! My old assistant at Vogel. Oh, of course – her boyfriend was a Ned Bond. Now her husband! But why follow me?"

"Yes, her husband is my brother and apparently Petrina befriended Zoe when she got the job with you at Vogel. She must have something on Zoe, I have no idea what – which isn't great, as she is now part of my family. But I do know that Zoe kept her informed of the jewellery shoots that she went on, and then Petrina would tell her grandfather…"

"The Snow Leopard, but I thought he was only interested in heirlooms – Russian ones?"

"He was… but he was also the instigator of the Pink Panthers."

"How do you know all this?"

"Henrietta told me. She is my grandmother's oldest friend and we had dinner last night. They were here when The Leopard did his first thefts in Monaco."

"At the Royal Wedding," Jemima said, realising that his grandmother must be Margo Bond, née Peters.

"Exactly. Petrina mentioned something about the Pink Panthers that I'd read an article about these jewel thieves in The New Yorker a few months ago, and I just put two and two together. So, I just called a friend in the FBI. Apparently, the Panthers are thought to be going to repeat the move at the Prince of Monaco's wedding in July, with so many of Europe's royals attending."

Jemima slumped down on the sofa next to Colt, forgetting she was semi-naked and soaking wet. "Wow, they did most of the boutiques last week. I guess there are a number of hotels they'll hit during the Film Festival… but the wedding as well? These guys will stop at nothing."

There was a silence.

"Colt, you were with my boyfriend yesterday… did he say anything about Petrina?" she asked nervously, remembering that James had told her yesterday the same story – about Colt following her, on Petrina's instructions.

"No, nothing, except that he didn't like or trust the girl and that he wished she'd leave you alone. Oh, and he told me that you were engaged and that he was madly in love with you!" He smiled at her obvious relief.

"I have to go and find my boyfriend. Where's Petrina now?"

"Right," he said, not quite getting it. "She mentioned something about having lunch at somewhere called 55?"

"Oh my God, Club Cinquante Cinq," Jemima said, using its French name. "It's in St Tropez. How the hell am I going to get there? Has Henrietta got a car? Even so, it's about two hours away with no traffic!"

"No, she doesn't drive. Never needed to." He rolled his eyes.

"Shit. Umm, okay. Jim and Spyros are entertaining clients in Cannes, so they're no use. Delfine's old Mercedes convertible is too slow. Right, I'll just have to go back to the Ferrari garage." She got up and ran to get changed. "You're coming with me," she added, shouting from the bedroom.

Ten minutes later, dressed in white culottes from Stella McCartney, navy blue Chanel espadrilles and a white backless halter neck top, Jemima and Colt, the latter dressed in blue jeans and a pale blue shirt, raced up to Place des Moulins. They took the lift down to Avenue Princesse Grace and ran along the street, much to the surprise of the sedate septuagenarians walking their dogs. When they reached the garage, Jemima saw it was the same guy as before.

"*Salut!* My friend here absolutely loved the car that Mr Vogel bought for his wife but is actually looking for something a little bit newer and faster!" Jemima feigned laughter. "Is there any chance he could take that one out for a test drive?" She pointed to a brand new black coloured Ferrari 458, giving Colt a quick look.

"You 'ave lots of boyfriends, Mademoiselle Fox-Puurl," he said in a French accent with a snigger. "I am afraid that car is waiting to be picked up. But we are getting a similar model tomorrow afternoon. Can you come back then?"

"The thing is, we kind of want to test drive it today. You see, it's his birthday and we are going for lunch just out of Monaco? Not to worry, we'll go to McLaren down the road. If he likes it, he'll buy it, won't you, sweetheart?" Jemima looked at Colt and touched his cheek endearingly.

"Well, I suppose you can take it if you are back by the end of the day? Mr Poznan is coming tomorrow morning. But we will need to clean it. Don't go too far – we can't increase the kilometres too much. After all, it's new."

"You said Mr Poznan, Milos?"

"Yes."

"Oh, I know him well."

"You must not tell him, but I also don't want you to tell Mr Vogel to buy a McLaren next time."

"I promise not to. Thank you. Oh, and Milos Poznan is never up before 10am!" Jemima wondered where he was. He hadn't been at the movie premiere or gala. Maybe James really had usurped him. A fleeting moment of panic passed over her.

"Very well. Enjoy yourself, and please be careful, Mademoiselle. This is a rare model." He handed them the keys, not without a nervous look around to see if any of his colleagues were looking. "I would advise going by the coastal road to St Tropez.

The A8 is partly closed between Nice and Cannes because of an accident. There will be a lot of traffic."

# Chapter 26

## The French Riviera Coastal Road

J emima took the keys and, having mastered the coastal path to Antibes two days earlier, jumped in the driving seat and left Monaco by the same way as she had on Sunday, through Fontvieille and Cap d'Ail. She put her foot down and, out the corner of her eye, could see Colt holding on to his seat. He wasn't much of an FBI agent if he couldn't cope with her driving! They drove through Eze and passed the seaside restaurant Anjuna – music was already pumping out of the wooden hut at 11am. As they went up the hill towards the precarious corner at Cap Roux, Jemima looked out to sea in front of her and saw Petrovich's mega-yacht, now unmistakeable from the first time she saw it from Henrietta's balcony.

"Look!" she pointed ahead. "Petrina will be on that boat."

"Jemima, keep your eye on the road!"

She almost veered over the side of the cliff when the road turned a sharp right.

"Sorry!" She straightened the Ferrari and entered the tunnel. "Do you think you should call her and subtly find out if she has James? Maybe they have kidnapped Evie and she is on the boat with them?" she said with her eyes wide, looking at Colt again.

"The FBI will promote you immediately!" she said with a small smile; she was so worried about what she was going to find out in St Tropez.

"Road!" Colt warned as a tanker lorry came hurtling through the tunnel towards them. "Do you want me to call her?"

"Well, she did hire you to follow me, so she'll be expecting some sort of update. They poisoned me, knocked me out, and I ended up in hospital! Were you not waiting to see if I actually woke up?" she asked while nervously laughing.

"No. Yesterday, I decided enough was enough. Henrietta only consolidated my decision."

"Good. If you do call, please can you ask her about James before you hand in your resignation? And then you can check the roads ahead. If that is their boat, we'll likely to be there ahead of them, but not if the roads are blocked."

Colt looked at Google Maps. Jemima couldn't help but look over and notice the thick red lines along the roads between Théoule sur Mer and Sainte Maxime, which were then even worse along the last stretch through Ports Grimaud and Cogolin.

"It says it could take us three hours from here," Colt said through his teeth. "I guess all the traffic has been diverted from the highway."

"I guess," Jemima said. "Will you get the card out from my bag that says Jim Fleming? He might know someone with a boat." And she flung her small bag from her knee to his.

Colt dug in the bag to pull out the card, then dialled the number from his phone with the loudspeaker on.

"Hello? Jim Fleming." Jim answered after only a few rings and, as she drove what felt like about 100 mph along the tiny windy coastal road, Jemima shouted at the phone, "Jim, hi! I am on my way to find Petrina in St Tropez but the traffic is blocked almost the whole way there. We've just left Cagnes sur Mer. Can you suggest another route?"

"No, it'll be blocked everywhere. You'll need a boat or a helicopter! Don't worry. Spyros is collecting me from Tetou restaurant in Golfe Juan. Just your side of Cannes. Between Antibes and Cannes. Get there and we'll take you on. We're lunching at 55."

"That's amazing, Jim – that's where we're headed. But how long are you going to be there? I need to get to Cinquante-Cinq as soon as possible. Petrina is having lunch there with the Russian, and we just saw his boat go past."

"Jemima, dear, no one has lunch at 55 before 2pm."

"Okay, well, I need to find James. I think he might be with her, or at least she'll know where he is. Maybe Evie is also on the yacht? Anyway, see you at Tetou."

"Can you believe it? Spyros's boat is at Golfe Juan, and they're going to 55, too."

"Yes! I heard," Colt laughed and she laughed out of relief as well. "How do you know so many people down here?" he asked, impressed.

"I know them from London, really. That is the only good thing about never having long-term boyfriends; you make much more useful friends who are boys!" She laughed but felt distraught that her dream future with James could all be a lie.

Petrina's boyfriend couldn't be James's doppelganger by chance, could he? She was increasingly realising, after Colt told her that he had been tailing her since she spotted him in Cecconi's, that nothing Petrina did was by chance. She was a Pink Panther; everything was meticulously planned.

# Chapter 27

## Tetou, Golfe Juan, France

As they arrived in Golfe Juan, Jemima suddenly realised that she didn't know what Tetou was. Colt Googled it and told her that it was one of the most famous beach restaurants on the Riviera and had blue and white awning.

"What are we going to do with the car if we go by boat?"

"I didn't even think about that?" With her desperation to get to St Tropez and quiz Petrina as to where James was, she had completely forgotten about getting the car back to the garage.

"Are there any car parks around? I am sure we can get a lift back here somehow and I'll drive it back later. It's not like it'll be the only Ferrari around!"

"I can't see any on Google, but I guess there will be one at the station."

Jemima followed his directions and parked the car. There weren't any other Ferraris but Colt gave the station guard €50 to keep an eye on it. They just hoped it would be okay; they'd seen CCTV cameras outside the station building. They left the station and took a left down Avenue de Belgique, left again, and found themselves on the railway track that had dusty weeds spouting out from under the rails all over it.

"Are you sure we're going the right way?" Jemima said, letting out another nervous laugh as this was getting ridiculous.

"Apparently," Colt laughed back.

They crossed the tracks, entered a road, and, thankfully, walked in the shadow of palm trees between the pavement and a small beach called Plage du Soleil. The first white building was Restaurant Vallauris Plage, and just further along, with blue and white matching parasols and sun loungers on the narrow strip of sand, Jemima spotted another white painted building with an entrance on the road. 'TETOU' was written in large gold letters on a canopy over a brown wooden double door. Fletch opened the door for them and they entered the coolness of the interior.

Jemima spotted Jim sitting with Chuck Chaffinch, who'd been at the gala the night before, at a table just inside the wall near some French windows that were pushed only half-open, in order to stop the heat from coming in too much. As they walked towards them, Jemima glanced through the glass at the sea and thought how quaint and romantic the restaurant was. She could quite imagine the Danzigers from Scott Fitzgerald's Tender is the Night lunching and dining here. Colt and Jemima got to the table and Jim immediately stood up to greet them. She hoped that they could get going soon; she wanted to be there when Petrina arrived.

"Jemima, hello again. Hope you're feeling better." He gave her a hug before shaking Colt's hand to introduce himself. "Do you know Chuck?"

"No, I don't, hello, but I do know that you organised the Vogel placement and sponsorship with Panther Productions for the remake of To Catch a Thief," Jemima said, remembering the meeting with Alexa back in London. She leant forward to shake his hand. "Hi, Chuck. Jemima Fox-Pearl, Head of PR at Vogel."

"Ah, so you work for Sidney and Alexa? She's a great girl!"

"Yes," Jemima said, not quite agreeing with him, and he turned back to Jim who was sitting down in front of a large bowl of lobster bouillabaisse.

"I told him not to have the lobster. It's the amateur's choice!" Chuck said.

"I love lobster and bouillabaisse – makes sense to have them together!" Jim chuckled. "Sit down, you two. Do you want lunch?"

"I thought you were having lunch at Cinquante Cinq?" Jemima asked nervously.

She desperately needed to get there and find out where James was. Petrina would be having lunch in an hour and perhaps he'd be with her – she was sure that James had been trying to get hold of her all day, but her phone was still sitting under a rose bush at the palace. She probably should have gone to look for it, but time was of the essence and the palace gardens would now be closed to the gala guests. She'd have to get another one tomorrow and somehow get Vodafone to hook it up with her account. Once again, she felt relieved that she had the company credit card sitting in her bag slung over the back of her chair. "Where's Spyros?" she asked.

"Spyros is on his way. He's picking us up from here at 1.30pm. Chuck's not coming and he was hungry," Jim replied, as Chuck tucked into his non-lobster 'professional' version of the traditional French fish soup. "So, I joined him for a starter." He smiled. "Go on, order something. Food is notoriously late at 55."

Jemima felt another rush of panic sweep over her, but she was also starving, so she quickly ordered tomatoes topped with breadcrumbs, and begun eating a hunk of bread and some olives that were on the table, while Colt went for the same as Chuck, and was brought a bowl to help himself from the large terracotta tureen sitting on the table.

"This is one of the oldest and most famous restaurants on the Riviera," Jim explained. "Been here almost as long as the Hotel du Cap. The bouillabaisse is its signature dish, even Barbara Bush wrote about it in her memoirs." He nodded in approval as he pulled the last piece of white flesh from the lobster shell. "Everyone comes during the festival. Last night, Brad and Angelina were here on one table, and Jessica Chastain was on another. Robert de Niro and Jane Fonda also popped in on their way back from your premiere." Jemima had forgotten that she hadn't seen them at the gala dinner after the premiere… but then, it appears she'd spent most of the night in a flowerbed or a hospital bed. "Tonight, Chanel is holding a party with Vanity Fair France. It's a coup; they never close the restaurant for anyone… except Chanel and Chuck."

Chuck smiled. "That is kind, Jim. Cannes and Chanel are two of France's most iconic ideologies…"

"And Tetou!" Jim interrupted.

"Exactly, so where else to hold their Festival party?"

Jim turned to Jemima. "I secured it for them. You should tell Sidney and his wife to come along – Alexa, is it?"

So, she wasn't being invited and clearly Jim hadn't told Chuck about Evie Talbot, not that she imagined anything was put on hold at Cannes. Evie might be the hottest new actress in town this year, but there were many more to take her spot should she be kidnapped. A wave of panic swept over her for the second time since sitting down, as she again wondered what James had to do with all of this, if anything.

Their food arrived and Colt and Jemima ate quickly. Just as

they were finishing and glugging down glasses of water, Spyros walked up from the beach and slid open one of the French windows. He opened his arms wide in a welcoming exclamation, and Jemima noticed Delfine slip inside behind him.

"Eeets Jemima Foz! And Petrina's friend… Frank?"

"Colt," he corrected. "Colt Bond. Hi, Spyros." He got up to shake hands.

Jemima went over to her Dutch friend and gave her a kiss while the men greeted each other.

"What are you doing here?" she asked Delfine, very happy to have a girl there for company.

"Spyros was introducing me to one of his movie contacts. And now I am coming with you all for lunch! Although I wouldn't have minded staying here," she said, looking enviously at Jim's bouillabaisse.

"I'm on a bit of a mission."

"I've heard." Delfine said sympathetically, touching Jemima's arm.

"Okey dokey, pame, lez goh! I need to get my boat out of its berth soon or I get a fine. My friend, the marina chief, said that the owners are on their way back." Said Spyros hurrying his friends.

Jemima knew from Delfine's husband telling her last year, that a marina berth on the Riviera in the summer can cost thousands. In Monaco, you can only hire them for 51 weeks of the year – the Grand Prix week is sold separately and can be almost as much as the rest of the year put together.

"That boat?" Jemima said as they stood up. She looked out at the sea, desperate to get going.

"Yes, that is Pyotr Petrovich's mega-yacht," said Jim as the vast, liner-looking yacht headed in the direction of St Tropez.

"I know, I think Petrina is on it. Maybe my boyfriend, too. Is your boat fast, Spyros?"

"My dear, you have seen nothing faster!" Jim laughed.

"I'll get this." Chuck said, pulling out a wad of cash. "No credit cards here." He added to no one in particular, not that this would be new information to anyone but Jemima and Colt – the others were clearly regulars at Tetou.

# Chapter 28

---

# Club 55, St Tropez, France

S pyros's boat was just what a Greek tycoon should have. In fact, Jim was quite right. A Mystic C-5000 was just what you'd get if you were super wealthy, had everything else, and liked going fast. Jemima did wonder if Spyros's new eJet venture was to cancel out the carbon foot print his boat made every time it left its mooring. The pearl-coloured speedboat was so low on the water that you could barely see it behind the slightly more sober-looking sport cruisers moored along a concrete jetty of Vieux Port Golfe Juan. The sleek, pearly white vessel had a cornflower blue stripe running along the side and the blue and white Greek flag on either side. When they got closer, Spyros pressed the remote control in his hand and the flags opened up into the air like sports car doors to reveal the 'cabin'.

Spyros jumped in and held his hand out as Jemima stepped off the jetty and into the boat. The inside was as slick as the outside. It looked more like something out of a space movie than real life, with a shining aluminium and leather steering wheel, a bunch of dials around a computer screen, and four 'gear sticks' sitting upright behind a pad of buttons. When they were all in and sitting in the low racing car like blue and white leather seats, with their racing car belts strapped over their shoulders, Spyros, with Jemima sitting up front with him, pressed a button and the flag covered gull-winged doors came down to close them in.

"Those doors are awesome," Colt shouted from the back, as the sound of the engines were getting louder while they revved up.

"They're based on a 1952 Mercedes race car," Spyros yelled back.

"In French, they're called *portes-papillons*," Jim said, sitting next to Colt in the back, ever the fountain of knowledge, while Delfine secured large headphones over her ears.

Despite the shortness of the trip and the speed at which they about to go, Jemima wandered when they'd start to boil under the glass roof, through which the sun was already beating, and was relieved when the air conditioning suddenly started to kick in. As they made their way out of the harbour, the Greek expertly steering the 50-foot superboat through the narrow gaps between the row of boats in front, Jemima again wondered what she was going to discover when they found Petrina. She turned around to smile at Colt and just hoped that he hadn't texted to warn his Petrina what was going on – she wanted to catch her unawares. She also didn't think her trip to the hospital was a coincidence; she was pretty certain that the Balkan bodyguard she had first met outside Vogel on Bond Street had not only spiked her drink but hit her over the head with something, all on the orders of Petrina.

She just wondered where James and Evie Talbot were. And, of course, the earrings. What on earth had happened to them? Should she call Alexa back? She had probably lost her job by cutting her off. There was no point calling her now: the roar of the engines were too much. She'd call her when they got to Club 55.

It was now 2pm. They were right out in the open water, having wound their way out of the warren of other boats and gone far out so Spyros could go at top speed.

"It is now 28 nautical miles to St Tropez," Spyros shouted over the noise of the engines. "We should be there just after 2.30pm. Perfect time for lunch on the Riviera," he added with a smile, before instructing them all to put on headphones.

\* \* \*

They were earlier than predicted and had made it in twenty-five minutes, in what had been one of the most exciting rides of Jemima's life. Jemima didn't have time to feel sea sick and, when Spyros cut the engine down to calm cruising, she still felt as though her head was flying over the surface of the water at the equivalent of 150mph. Spyros powered the boat up towards the small wooden jetty that led to the sandy Pampelonne Beach, stopped it about one hundred yards away, and opened the doors while making a call. Within minutes, a small tender came out to collect them. Jumping into the small motor boat, Jemima briefly smiled when she saw the hot guy wearing a white T-shirt with Club 55 written across the front in bright blue. As they got to the wooden jetty and he helped her out, she saw Jack Nicholson with a young woman getting out of a tender on the other side, and was that Leonardo di Caprio following him?

They followed the famous actors down the jetty, Jemima being careful not to fall in the water from the mixture of nerves and excitement of being only an arm's reach from one of her and Flora's biggest crushes. She just wished she was here to have a long, relaxing, rosé-fuelled lunch, not as part of the manhunt for her fiancé. Jemima looked back as she walked on to the sand to see what she could only imagine was Pyotr Petrovich's mega yacht sitting prominently against the horizon a few hundred feet further out than the Mystic.

Being May and not July, the place wasn't as busy as the time she'd been with Delfine. But, of course, it was the Cannes Film Festival and there were enough celebrities and their entourage to have the restaurant buzzing. Club 55 was founded in 1955, when the famous French film director Roger Vadim and his then-wife Brigitte Bardot were filming And God Created Women nearby along Pampelonne Beach. At the time, the long stretch of white sand was only occupied by the occasional sunbather and fishermen, who went to a small hut to have a fish filleted and cooked before taking the rest of their catch home or to market. On the short journey there, Jim had told them through the headphones that after a long day filming, not long after the crew had all arrived in what seemed like no man's land, someone had asked the couple cooking fish over an open fire if they wouldn't mind preparing some food for the hungry men and women. Jean de Colmont and his wife were happy to help and Club 55 was born. Today, apparently, it is run by their son Patrice who is there throughout the summer and always happy to help serve those in need of delicious home cooked food, as he was that day.

*"Spyros, bienvenue!"* the tall grey-haired Frenchman said to the Greek when they walked in from the beach through the canopy-covered restaurant to what could be vaguely described as the front desk. Jemima kept her eyes peeled for Petrina the whole time.

*"Patrice. Comment allez-vous?"* It was the first time Jemima had ever heard her friend speak French. Clearly, the owner of Club 55 commanded respect.

"Your usual table will be free in five minutes. Or, would you like another?" the owner then asked in broken English.

Jemima wondered where this would be: there were none free that would accommodate six people, except out at the front under the trees.

"No, no, my usual. Thank you Patrice. We'll go to the bar." As they followed Spryos over to the little bar back on the way in from the beach, Jemima looked over at the tables under the trees, thinking how nice it would be to sit there.

She stopped mid-step. Colt and Delfine walked straight into the back of her.

"What's up?" Delfine asked.

"Petrina is over there." She jerked her head towards the tables under the trees, and Colt followed her gaze.

"Who's Petrina?" Delfine enquired as Colt asked simultaneously, "Do you want me to go over there?"

"No, she'll wonder why you're with me. I don't think we should be seen together." And, just at that point, Jemima spotted some girlfriends sitting in the middle of the restaurant. "I'm going to go and sit with some friends and then go up and ask where James is." As she started to walk over to them, she turned back to him, "will you explain to Delfine and the others?"

"Yes, sure. I'll keep an eye out in case you need me. Wave or something."

"Okay, thanks." Jemima smiled and walked over to the table.

Her four girlfriends were already pretty pissed from an empty bottle of Chateau de Pampelonne Rosé that was sitting on the table next to the untouched basket of whole vegetables that was the traditional starter at the restaurant.

"Jem! What are you doing here?" Alice Von Haeg asked, standing up and leaning over Emie Coote to hug her. "You're a bit early for the wedding?" She laughed as Jemima hung her bag over the back of a chair and sat down, taking a large gulp of the wine from the glass of whoever's place she'd stolen.

"I'm in Monaco for a few weeks for work," was all she said, the wine hitting her pretty empty stomach and giving her a bit of much needed Dutch courage. "Can't wait for Saturday!" she said, happy that her Belgian friend, whose parents lived in the most beautiful farmhouse a few kilometres away, was not on a pre-wedding detox like so many brides.

"Is James coming?" Emie asked.

Of course, none of them knew that she was officially engaged, nor had many of her friends met James. Jemima couldn't help but wonder if they ever would. Her heart stopped when her friend, Hope Carlton, the only one of them who'd met James, came back from the loo and told her, "You must be with him. I just saw him go through to the men's loos," as she refilled the glass that Jemima had just emptied.

"Really?"

"Didn't you know he was here? I noticed him earlier. He was sitting over there under the trees."

Without saying anything, Jemima walked over to Petrina. She was perfectly dressed in a white cotton sundress that was clearly far more expensive than the simple fabric belied.

"Jemima, I thought it was you. What are you doing here with my friend Colt?" Petrina asked, smoking a cigarette and hiding her face behind an oversized pair of blue mirrored Raybans.

"Oh, I bumped into him. He was chatting to my friend Delfine." She just hoped Petrina hadn't seen her arrive with Colt, but she couldn't tell if Petrina knew she was lying, as her green eyes were hidden.

"Why is James here?" she said, cutting to the chase.

"Where?" Petrina asked, looking around.

"Sit down. Have a drink." Petrina's table companion ordered and Jemima looked at the guy who she had not only seen in Vogel the week before, but was the new owner of the Vogel Vanderpless: Pyotr Petrovich. She wanted to ask if Petrina had returned his missing diamonds, but finding out about James was far more important. If it wasn't for the damned diamonds, James wouldn't be missing in the first place.

"I don't want a drink. I want to know why my boyfriend is with you today?" As she said it, she knew she sounded like a crazy jealous woman.

"You'll have to ask him, Jemima. I've not seen him since last night at the gala," she said. "Have some rosé – you'll feel better."

"I'm feeling fine, Petrina. Why wouldn't I?" Jemima knew Petrina was responsible for organising her unplanned night in the hospital, but she also remembered Alexa's advice on being friends with her. "But thank you." She eventually sat down. "I'll just wait for James."

"You'll be waiting a long time. I have no idea where he is. The last time I saw him was when he was talking to you. You were pretty drunk and talking loudly about how angry you were that he'd dumped you or something. And how you couldn't believe that he'd come to the event, although I'd invited him."

Jemima could feel herself getting redder and redder, and it wasn't the sun. She hated to admit it but that did sound just like her, particularly if she'd had too much white wine to drink. But she hadn't: she had only drunk fizzy water. Not even the Pol Roger that was flowing like a fountain had passed her lips. Jemima was about to ask what had happened to Evie when Petrina answered the question for her.

"It was lucky that Ivan had accompanied Evie to meet the Prince and his fiancée with my mother and Glenn," Said Petrina. "But it was James who later left with her as you'd disappeared. She wanted to go to the Casino, and then he was going to take her back to The Fairmont, where everyone is staying." Petrina took a sip of rosé and Jemima quickly stopped herself from doing the same from the glass the Russian had filled in front of her. "And now, I gather, she is missing?"

"Yes, apparently, she is, but I doubt that it's his fault. Maybe she decided to go for a walk before the press call and got delayed? I bet that she is back now and all is fine. You should ask your mother – surely, they'd be at the press call together? Who is Ivan anyway? I saw him outside Vogel the other day."

"He's part of my security team," the Russian answered, which kind of made sense. After all, he was in the store the day Jemima had her meeting with Alexa, but why was he opening the boutique's doors?

Jemima thought it best to find that out later and was about to go back to the subject of why James was with her when Milos appeared at the table.

"Aaah, my darling." He leant over her shoulder to kiss Petrina.

Jemima realised that Hope hadn't seen James at all; she'd seen Milos. His bloody doppelganger.

"So, you've not seen James since we had that argument at the palace?" she asked Petrina, annoyed that she had been confused and Petrina had played along.

"I've not seen him since he left with Evie Talbot," she reminded her. "Poor Jemima doesn't know where her boyfriend is," Petrina explained to Milos, who was now puffing on a Cuban cigar, their plates having been cleared and coffee brought out. "Sorry, ex-boyfriend," she added, looking at Jemima briefly.

Petrina and Milos turned away from Jemima and started talking in Montenegrin, while the Russian got up and went in the direction of the bathrooms.

Jemima was about to leave to go back to her friends when she heard her embarrassing personalised ring tone. The Run DMC tune was muffled and coming from Petrina's Chanel beach bag that was sitting on the sand, right next to Jemima's feet.

# Chapter 29

---

# Club 55 Restaurant

The bag was easily out of Petrina's eyesight but she really didn't want to be seen, even though their attention was on each other. She deliberately knocked her knife to the floor with her elbow as she picked up her wine glass, and, leaning down as far as possible – so her sunglasses also fell off – dug her hand deep into the bag and felt her iPhone vibrating. Then, very carefully, Jemima slid her phone out of the bag and put in on her lap under the table, so Petrina couldn't see. She also took out a Fairmont key card that was sitting in a side pocket of the bag, slipping it into the back of the iPhone case.

Turning the phone over, she saw she had loads of missed calls from James from the night before listed on the locked screen, as well as several from other numbers which must have been her trying to locate it. There were also a few texts from Mr V, including a recent one that must have caused the vibrating.

Jemima quickly hid the phone in a pocket of her culottes, got up, and, without bothering to say goodbye, went back to her girlfriends and sat down. She wanted to listen to her voicemail but realised that, without the pin number that she'd never set before leaving the UK, she couldn't. She wanted to scream.

"Wasn't that James?" Alice asked. "My God, he's good looking!"

"No," she said to them sadly.

With a shaky hand, she helped herself to a glass of wine and a piece of cucumber from the crudités basket, Jemima then unlocked her phone and tried to call James back. She'd call Alexa and Mr Vogel later, when she'd found her boyfriend. She didn't really care about the jewellery now; after all, Petrina had probably handed them back to her Russian friend.

James's phone was turned off, so she left a message and realised, strangely, that there were no texts from him. Surely he'd have texted? Maybe Petrina had managed to unlock the phone and deleted them, but then his calls wouldn't show up...

The phone rang, showing a withheld number, so Jemima answered it quickly.

"Jemima, Evie Talbot has been found in your boyfriend's room," said Alexa. "Her throat has been slit. And... all her jewellery, including the earrings, have gone. Where are you?"

"WHAT? OH MY GOD!" She shouted down the phone, and her friends stopped what they were doing to find out what was going on.

"The police want to talk with you and are going to your apartment. They think he might be there with you. Is he?"

"No! I have no idea where he is!" she said, shocked about Evie's death, as her friends turned to look at her with worried faces. "I am not in my apartment, and I am also looking for him. There is no way in the world that James killed Evie Talbot or stole your earrings." She was almost shouting now, and a few other tables turned around to stare at her.

"Well, you'd better get back soon. He was last seen entering his room at 5am with her. Another hotel guest saw, as well as the hotel's CCTV." As Jemima listened, she looked over and saw Petrina, Milos, and the Russian walk through the trees to the little wooden jetty, no doubt to go back to Pyotr's boat. She couldn't believe that she hadn't guessed that Peter and Pyotr was the same person, despite the completely different pronunciation of his name. She then realised that it was Milos who had left the gala and gone to James's room with Evie at 5am. It wasn't James who had killed her and stolen the earrings: it was Milos. And, thinking back to the previous night, Milos was wearing almost identical clothes to James; it was, after all, black tie. On camera they'd look almost identical, she thought, remembering Milos's odd eye and hoping that it would show up. She needed to get Renault to check the CCTV from the palace and the hotel. Jemima left the girls, saying she hoped to see them with James at Alice's wedding on Saturday, and went over to Spyros and Jim's table. A number of others had joined them and Colt was deep in conversation with an American actress who Jemima recognised but couldn't put a name too.

"Have you found your boyfriend?" Jim asked as she sat down on a spare chair between Delfine and him.

"No, but I need to get back to Monaco. Desperately. The police want to talk to me." She looked down the table at Spyros who didn't look ready to jump back into his jet-powered boat, and, just as she was about to ask if Jim could help, she heard one of the girls at the table gasp loudly. She looked down the long table and saw a blonde model scrolling down her phone's screen.

"Evie Talbot has been found murdered in Monaco. And there is a search out for some South African guy? It's all on TMZ and The Daily Mail."

Panicking, Jemima pulled her recently retrieved iPhone from

her bag and opened up The Daily Mail website. There was a picture of Evie at the premiere last night and a CCTV shot of her leaving with what could well be James but was actually Milos. And then a close up of the real James, her James, from his company's website.

Jim took the phone from her and scrolled, then looked at Jemima with disbelief and pity in his eyes.

"Hold on." He got up, walked over to another table, leant down, and whispered in the ear of a large-looking man that Jemima vaguely recognised from Annabel's – the nightclub in London. Jim then stood and beckoned Jemima to come over.

Jemima stood up, grabbed her bag, waved goodbye to an oblivious Spyros who was talking over several girls to a newly-arrived Ilias. She told Colt what was going on and gave him her number, and then walked past Elton John, who was sitting at a table with Naomi Campbell and Kate Moss, across the restaurant to where Jim was standing.

As Jemima reached them, she realised the man he was talking to was the brother of an older Persian guy she used to see out in clubs in her early twenties. He was a multi-millionaire playboy; even though he was married to a beautiful cosmetic surgeon called Fern Feather, a rather pneumatic brunette was sitting on his knee sucking his ear, while he chomped at a cigar. Despite his pink tinted shades, which gave him a rather sinister look, he smiled at Jemima and nodded his head at Jim. He almost tipped the girl from his knee and waved her off before picking up a huge iPhone from the table and making a call. She realised she was being given the once over and, although she didn't come close to any of the girls on this table in the sexy stakes, he clearly approved.

"Go out to the car park behind the restaurant and a guy wearing a head piece and a dark suit will meet you. Go with him and he'll take you back to Monaco."

"Wow, Jim, thanks. How did you manage that?"

"Bob owes me a favour." He kissed Jemima goodbye and wished her good luck.

# Chapter 30

---

# The Skies over the Riviera

As Jemima went up the steps from the restaurant, and passed a long queue of people waiting to be seated at the popular Riviera restaurant, she heard Elton John join in with the band that had been playing classic pop songs during the meal. Damn, she thought, she'd always wanted to hear her favourite song man sing live. This was typical of lunches at Club 55, which often had the added extra of celebrities actually joining in with "civilians".

Jemima walked along the pathway to the car park that was filled with Bentleys, Ferraris, and Maseratis and noticed that there were several men in dark suits with headpieces. Of course, it was the international uniform of a bodyguard. She wondered what Ivan was doing today; clearly he'd been outside Vogel waiting for his boss. But it seemed odd to think that he also was part of the Pink Panther gang. Petrovich obviously hadn't done his checks very well, unless Petrina had recruited him after he started working in the billionaire's bodyguard company.

"Are you Jemima?" a tall, dark-haired man said in an accent that she couldn't quite place.

"Yes."

"Follow me," he said, a bit ominously for her liking.

She did as she was told and climbed into the passenger seat of a Tesla Roadster. As the man drove soundlessly out of the car park, he explained to her surprised face that it was an electric car. What was it with these rich men and their sudden environmental consciences? She just hoped that it wouldn't run out of juice before they got back to Monaco. However, they were soon driving up a steep road into the hills above the coast towards Gassin. They wound their way through the beautiful hilltop village, past the church that her friend Alice was getting married in that Saturday, and out towards what seemed like the middle of nowhere. Her 'driver' spoke into his headpiece and she suddenly heard the momentous noise of a helicopter starting up.

The car stopped a few hundred yards from the silver helicopter, and a pilot in a white and blue shirt and a pair of jeans ran over to them. He opened Jemima's door while waving and giving a thumbs up to the driver, before shouting for her to come with him. Closing the Tesla's door behind her, and now understanding even more why Jim's friend had an electric car, she ran after him across the dry rubble field, keeping her head low. As the pilot helped her up into the cabin, he pointed for her to sit in any of the four large creamy white leather seats, put a black seatbelt on, and plug in her headphones. He proceeded to shut the door of the helicopter and ran around to the pilot's door, jumped in, and put on his own headphones. Jemima heard him through the inflight radio asking if she was okay. As he pressed a number of buttons, she could see through the glass divide. The headphones then went silent; she guessed that he was talking to someone else, probably air traffic control.

Within seconds, the immaculate machine rose quickly from the field and started flying towards the coast. They flew over Alice's parents's house – she could see a couple of marquees already up for Saturday's wedding – before heading out over the sea and the ubiquitous boats of all sizes that now looked toy-like as they floated in the blue-green water. The pilot introduced himself as Richard and said that they would be at Monaco Heliport in about twenty-five minutes. He then informed her proudly that the helicopter was one of only three special edition Airbus EC145s with Mercedes-Benz style twin-engine turbines; it was made in Italy for Mercedes and had bespoke interiors. Jemima looked about her, and it really was luxurious; the leather seats, which faced each other in pairs, were as soft as silk and looked like they'd rarely been sat on, and the floor was wooden veneer with a white leather strip down the middle. In the middle of the two rows of seats was a large matching bolster that she rested her arm on. The pilot told her that there were drinks inside.

Jemima was very thirsty after having only rosé since her quick lunch at Tetou, so she pressed a black button near her elbow and the bolster top slowly opened. Inside was a tiny fridge with two mini bottles, one of Pol Roger and the other Evian, as well as a Toblerone. Tempted to unscrew the plastic champagne cork, she sensibly took the bottle of water, closed the fridge lid, and then noticed that the lid of the bolster had a screen on it. She half-smiled to herself as she glugged down the cupful of water; she had definitely travelled in some pretty luxurious vehicles since she had left Monaco only a few hours earlier.

As they flew over Cannes, Jemima could see white marquees on the beach, crowds along La Croisette, and a red carpet leading up to the big cream-coloured Palais de Festivals. They flew over The Carlton Hotel, where most of the international film stars would be staying during the festival, and where Grace Kelly had stayed during the filming of the original To Catch a Thief. The pilot then dropped a little lower and joked about which stars she could spot, just as her phone texted, saying that she had a voicemail. She dialled it, but, one again, it said she had to type her pin in to retrieve messages from abroad. Jemima felt like screaming with frustration that she hadn't thought to set one up before she left the UK. She tried to find deleted text messages but without success. Looking out of the windows at the insanely beautiful scenes below, she suddenly remembered James had made her download Whatsapp – a new app that he had invested in for a client. She wondered if he had sent her anything via that? She hadn't ever used it before or knew anyone who did but he had insisted she download it, so she flicked through the screens until she got to the green app and saw a small red number on the bottom right of it that indicated eight new messages.

Opening the app, Jemima saw that they were all from him and, like the calls, they had all been registered before 2am. The first was at 22.23:

Hope all is going well, my darling? This event is amazing. I wish I was with you and not Petrina who is a bitch personified. You look so beautiful – those jewels suit you… ;-)

She laughed at that with a lump in her throat; he knew how much she loved jewellery, particularly aquamarines and diamonds together.

22.59: No let on anything about a heist. Not seen my doppelganger yet.

23.32: She's on phone to Milos, I guess, as in Montenegrin, or maybe Russian? Can't tell. Just mentioned Evie's name & 'mama'. As well as 'safira', which I bet is sapphire.

23.33: Wasn't Milos – just turned up… said your name and someone called Ivan... hope you're OK.

23.40: He's gone. She just asked who I'm messaging – told her my boss in the US!

Hope you get these x

23.45: Are you ok – haven't seen you for ages. Or Evie. P & I heading to hotel...

00.57: video

01.45: Look at Milos's eyes.

02.01: video

As Jemima read the messages, the Mercedes helicopter came into the Monaco airspace and she briefly looked through the large windows at the Prince's Palace sitting beautifully upon its rock, with the sapphire sea swirling against the cliffs below. How much had that place seen since it was built as a fortress at the end of the 12th century and the first Grimaldis arrived a century later? If only she could work out what had happened and why Fortunata had decided to remake To Catch a Thief and hold the premiere on the Rock. Not for the first time, Jemima thought how it all seemed just too close for comfort: making a movie about a cat burglar, knowing that her father was one, and then screening it near to where her mother committed suicide.

Jemima turned back to her phone and realised that the videos wouldn't open; there was just a never-ending circle as they tried to download. Clearly, she needed Wi-Fi. What the hell did they show? James's innocence, she hoped. As they arrived at the helipad in Fontvieille, Jemima tried to call him again, to no avail.

Jemima thanked Richard as he helped her out of the helicopter and found a car waiting to take her home. She knew the police wanted to talk to her, and although Alexa said they would be at her apartment, she couldn't believe they'd be waiting patiently for her whilst on a manhunt for her future husband. Plus, she had no Wi-

Fi at the apartment, so she decided she'd go to The Fairmont, download the videos, and see if she could find Renault there. After all, if they thought she was an accomplice of her murdering fiancé, surely she'd fare better going to them than waiting patiently at home, as though part of the police manhunt.

# Chapter 31

---

## The Fairmont Hotel, Monaco

The place was buzzing with police as Jemima walked through the automatic doors and down the steps to the large atrium, and she suddenly remembered that she had managed to pinch Petrina's room key card from her bag. It was still in the back of her iPhone case. A policeman asked if she was a guest and she nodded while flashing the card, before being allowed through. She spotted Renault with a bunch of uniformed policemen and official-looking people and sneaked behind a cardboard cut-out advertising Grand Prix deals to the lifts that were on the left. As Jemima took the lift to the top floor, where she knew Petrina's room was, she connected to the hotel's Wi-Fi using her nemesis's room number as a password; she didn't want to use James's, in case it alerted the hotel security.

The videos began to download as she stepped out into the corridor.

The first was really jumpy, taken with his left hand while walking through some gardens. With music in the background, Jemima could just about hear Petrina saying something about her grandmother being murdered and thrown into the sea below. So, she hadn't committed suicide as everyone believed. Jemima could hear Petrina saying, "She is relying on me to tell Lucky where the earrings are, in the hope that he'll come back to get them. And then I guess she'll get him arrested or something. You see, she thinks he murdered my grandmother. She's not very intelligent, my dear mother. She doesn't realise that it is me who is here to get them for my grandfather. He's barely fit enough to get out of bed, let alone climb up this cliff!" Petrina laughed. "I overheard her tell my father that Pierina had left these earrings hidden for her somewhere around here, before her death thirty years ago. With a clue in a book as to where to find them. I mean, how complicated is that? Anyway, now she's gone and given them to Evie Talbot, for goodness' sake. Pyotr wants them or he'll kill my grandfather. Not that I really care about him. I want these earrings as well. He's already given me the necklace."

"What necklace?" Jemima asked aloud as she watched the end of the video that showed them walking towards a cliff and the sound of the sea getting closer.

Jemima suddenly felt uneasy and wondered if James, too, had been murdered – perhaps Petrina had pushed him off the cliffs and that was why no one could find him? No. She firmly pushed these thoughts to the back of her mind: no body had been washed up, and, if James had been pushed do his death, then they would have heard by now, wouldn't there?

Jemima watched the second video that was taken around an hour later in a boat that seemed to be moored and crashing against some rocks. James's voice was fighting over the noise, saying something that she couldn't quite make out. She stood in the corridor to listen again, but now there were chamber maids vacuuming the corridor carpet, so she used Petrina's key card to get into her room. A Do Not Disturb sign hung from the handle and Jemima was safe in the knowledge that Petrina was on Pyotr's boat in St Tropez and not even Spyros's Mystic superboat would have got here faster than by the helicopter that she had come in.

She listened to the video message again.

"My darling, I love you. I think I am going to be killed. Milos is going to kill Evie and frame me. But don't forget – the mark on his eye. They need her earrings for the Russian. They think they're the real ones... They've brought me to his island that Jim told us about... remember the coloboma in Milos's eye..." he said.

There was a thud and the video stopped. The time was 02.01. His last missed call was at exactly 01.59. If only she could listen to her voicemail, but maybe the video relayed the same message from him?

Jemima slumped onto the floor, she was too shocked to scream. They had killed Evie for the wrong earrings, and probably now James. She looked around the room. Petrina clearly hadn't been back since she left to help her mother yesterday where they'd got changed in a palace room. And there were the clothes she'd been wearing at the David Morris party two days ago, strewn over her unmade bed.

A voice called from outside, from the balcony, where the windows were open. "Petrina, darling, are you there?" It was Fortunata's voice. Of course, her suite was next door. As she said in the video, Petrina would have been able to hear everything that her mother had told her father.

Jemima heard Fortunata call to someone who had just knocked on the door. She walked onto the balcony and, straining herself, leaned as far over as she could to the next one. She recognised Renault's voice, and that Fortunata was inviting him inside her suite.

"Assiez-vous, Charles." They spoke in both of their mother tongues...

"Madame Lindberg. I am so sorry about Mademoiselle Talbot. I am sure you were very fond of her."

"Yes, she had become like a second daughter to me."

"I have heard she is – no, was–" he corrected himself "–very good in the movie." Jemima thought it was rather strange to say. "However, it is your daughter Petrina we are looking for."

"Have you found this James Courtney? I have been told he was seen with Petrina walking towards Les Jardins Saint Martin. She wasn't seen again on any of the security cameras. And of course we have him leaving around 2am with Evie."

Jemima knew, once and for all, that it was Milos who had brought Evie here: he had pretended to be James to get a copy of her fiancé's room key card and had then taken Evie to that room and murdered her for the earrings. But why hadn't he just knocked her out, like Ivan had done to Jemima?

Jemima hesitated. Should she run next door and show them the evidence? But how would she explain her presence in Petrina's room? She could explain that she'd seen Petrina at Club 55 with Pyotr and taken her room key. The videos would explain everything. She was about to head for the suite when she remembered the reason why she was in Petrina's room in the first place: the safe.

Jemima went to the cupboard adjacent to the mini bar and found the safe behind the door, exactly where James's was on the floor below. She had absolutely no idea what the code could be, so she checked Petrina's birth year, knowing that it was the same as her brothers': 1978. It didn't work. Of course, James was supposed to have come back with Petrina and found it out, but he'd never made it back to the hotel. Jemima blinked back tears and tried different codes, then looked around the room for anything scribbled on a piece of paper. Jemima then looked back at the clothes discarded on the bed. There was a small black Chanel clutch poking out from under the white palazzo pants Petrina had worn.

Jemima opened it. One of Petrina's Nortaker business cards fell out, and it had her phone number on it. Of course, she'd recognised the sign of the devil in the final digits – 666 – but that only made three out of four. She went back to the safe and tried '6666': it didn't work. Jemima recalled Petrina's tattoo of a leopard on her hand, and wondered how many spots were on a leopard, but realised that even she wouldn't know that. The memory of Petrina's other tattoo came into her head – the infinity sign which so closely resembled the number 8. With a flash she was reminded that '8888' was the sign of wealth. She tapped it in and – hey presto – it worked.

The safe clicked opened, but Jemima's heart sank. Inside there was nothing – absolutely nothing. She wanted to scream again. She had been certain that the diamonds would be here. That was her sole reason for being on the Riviera this summer! Suddenly, Petrina's words from the video came back to her – about Pyotr giving her 'the necklace'. Had he actually given her the Vogel Vanderpless – so that, in fact, the four stolen diamonds were no longer technically stolen and were now rightfully hers, after all?

# Chapter 32

## The Riviera Suite, The Fairmont Hotel

Jemima, almost incandescent with rage and frustration, left Petrina's room and knocked on the suite next door.

"Petrina?" came the response before the door opened and Fortunata's beautiful but worried face appeared from behind it.

"Oh… Jemima. Is everything okay? Have you seen my daughter?"

"Hi, Mrs Lindberg. May I come in?" Fortunata welcomed her in and Jemima said hello to Monsieur Renault. She had managed to calm herself somewhat between leaving the room next door and knew that she had to play this very carefully; she didn't want to implicate herself in this disaster.

"Yes, I have seen Petrina. She was lunching at Club 55 in St Tropez with her boyfriend Milos and, I think, Pyotr Petrovich." She said his name with as good a Russian accent as possible.

Fortunata gasped. "Not Pyotr." She sat down and Jemima followed suit. "I saw his boat out in the ocean but I had hoped he wouldn't involve my daughter."

"Involve your daughter in what, Fortunata?" Renault asked in English.

"The Petroviches have had a hold over my family ever since

my father was caught pinching a ring from Pyotr's great-grandmother back in the fifties. But you know that," she added, looking up directly at the Detective. "I wondered if they would try to get her involved in their quest to retrieve the rest of the Romanov jewels." She paused. "I need a drink."

Fortunata walked towards the mini bar and, opening it, asked if they did too. They both said no simultaneously. Jemima surprised herself – she definitely needed one.

Petrina's mother poured a whole mini bottle of Courvoisier into one of the crystal glasses and walked back to the chairs, took a gulp, and put it down on the low coffee table in front of her as she sat down again.

"When my mother died, I came back and searched their apartment for clues as to why she would kill herself. She had seemed so happy to me whenever we spoke on the phone. Of course, the shame of my father's imprisonment and then his escape was hard to bear, but she was strong. She had been waiting years for him to finally be caught for his decades of thieving. I had just had Petrina, and Mama was going to come and live with us in New York, where no one would have known of her history or humiliation. But then I was called with the devastating news, by your father Charles, that her body had been found washed up on Pointe des Douaniers–" Jemima had run there only a few days earlier after the Casino Square heist "–that she had thrown herself off the Rock. But I know she was murdered." She took another gulp. "For the earrings that she stole before Princess Grace's wedding."

Jemima had to stifle a gasp of surprise. It was Pierina who took the earrings? She decided that she did, in fact, need a drink, and, having pressed record on her phone's memo app, went to the mini bar and poured herself a glass of lemonade, despite wanting something stronger.

"I thought my father was dead, since I never heard from him after his escape," Fortunata continued, "but now I am sure that it was him who killed her. You see, as I said, it was her who stole the earrings from the McCloskey's suite at Hotel de Paris. Not him. He'd been sent to Monaco to get them, and had failed."

"Yes, I remember." said Renault, "My father was very junior at the time, but it was a scandal that he always talked about. His life's mission was to catch the Snow Leopard. Of course, we only found out it was your father after he'd been imprisoned."

"I think he was sent to get them, but my mother had hidden them from him, and, in his anger, he pushed her off the Rock. You see, we had a favourite book…"

"David Dodge's To Catch a Thief?" Jemima asked, remembering that her remake was based more on the original novel than Hitchcock's movie. "You wanted to stick to the original story, not Hitchcock's – so much that she had to have brown hair in the movie, not the beautiful blonde that Grace Kelly's character had?"

"Yes. Darling Evie." She smiled sadly.

"I arrived at the apartment that night after your father had called me," Fortunata said to Renault. "I had caught a plane within a couple of hours from JFK to Nice, leaving Petrina with the nanny. I found a copy of the novel by the side of the bed. I didn't think anything of it, as she loved to dip in and out of it, but there was a red carnation being used as a book mark. She loved red carnations. They are the national flower here," she explained to Jemima, "and the moment she met my father was when Onassis's seaplane dropped hundreds of the flowers on to the water as Grace stepped on to Rainier's Royal Yacht. But the flower was dead and

I thought I'd remove it so it didn't stain Mama's old copy. I opened the book to remove the dead flower and noticed that the word 'palm' was circled in red ink on the same page. I remember sitting on her bed and flicking through the book and finding all the instances of palm – trees, hands, and even a Palm Beach in Cannes – were circled in red. Then my attention was grabbed by a blue circle, so I went through the book again and found, on one of the pages, a whole paragraph circled. It described a pair of blue sapphire earrings that Francie wore and picked out the colour of her eyes. I remembered my father being accused at the time of his imprisonment of stealing a pair of earrings that were to be gifted to Princess Grace by her godmother Pauline McCloskey."

"Yes, that part in the book that you say was circled – in the movie, Evie wore an amazing pair of our Ceylon sapphire earrings, and a similar design is now part of the Royal Riviera Collection. In fact, when we were driving to the premiere last night and Evie was wearing, what we call the Princess Grace earrings, she commented on how she should have worn them for the movie!" said Jemima.

"What do you mean?"

"Those huge sapphire and diamond pendant earrings that Evie wore last night – the ones that have now been stolen – were being donated to the Jewel Museum by my boss, Sidney Vogel. Mr Vogel created them as a replica of the original ones that, I now know, were stolen by your mother before the 1956 wedding. We called them the Princess Grace Sapphires."

Fortunata put her hand to her throat and gasped, "Do you mean the ones Evie was wearing weren't the real ones?"

"No! I mean they're still exquisite; made from Ceylon sapphires and using the same mystery setting, but no, they aren't the originals. How could they be? They were stolen back in 1956."

"Oh my goodness, but then they must still be up on the Rock under the palm tree?" she said.

"Fortunata, carry on with the night you returned to Monaco," Renault instructed kindly, just as Jemima was about to ask what she meant.

"So, I thought it was a message from my mother – that she was telling me where the sapphires that my father had been accused of stealing all those years ago were hidden. Of course, everyone thought that he was dead, having been drowned trying to escape from prison." She finished the rest of her brandy and got up to pour another. "I remembered when I was small, Mama and I would go up to Les Jardins Saint Martins and sit under a palm tree by the edge of the cliffs, looking out to sea. We would plant a red carnation plant there behind the trunk, so only those daring enough to sit close to the edge would ever see it." She came back to sit down with her freshly-poured drink. "I barely slept that night, and, first thing the next morning, I raced up to that tree. Sure enough, there was a freshly planted red carnation plant. I dug it up with my hands. Underneath, in a small leather pouch, was a pair of the most exquisite earrings that I had ever seen. And my husband buys me lots of jewels, so you know I don't say that lightly." She looked at Jemima. "I took them back to the apartment, along with the carnations. And then," Fortunata turned her eyes to Charles, "I came to see your father when the police station opened a few hours later, to identify Mama's body."

"I should have taken the earrings with me. But something kept me back. I guess I'm guilty of hoarding stolen goods?" She looked at Renault who replied with a smile and a shake of his head.

"I have worn them only once, but as a brooch in my hair at an event that my husband's friend, Martha Vanderpless, held at The

Plaza in Manhattan last month."

Jemima thought back to that event; she had gone with James's grandmother, Rosemary. And she realised that it was all very well learning about this dramatic story, but she needed to find her fiancé – hopefully alive, not dead. There was still one question she needed to ask.

"Fortunata, why did you hold the premiere of your movie on the Rock, considering it was the place where your mother was either pushed or committed suicide?" She noticed that Renault was impressed with her question, as a small smile tugged at the corner of his lips.

"I wanted to honour her by remaking her favourite movie, in the original version which was the book we used to read together, and screening it where she died. It probably sounds morbid to you, but to me it doesn't." Fortunata said with what sounded like a lump in her throat.

Jemima wondered why Pierina had buried the earrings up there in the first place, not just leave them hidden in the apartment with a clue? Lucky, who had just escaped gaol, must have followed her up there but not seen where she put them.

"Where are the earrings now?" Renault and Jemima both asked.

"Well, I don't know. I brought them back here to give to the Prince; they were meant for his mother, after all. I was going to do it after the press call this morning. When I arrived here, I placed them to clean in a glass of gin in my bathroom." Renault's eyebrows shot up but Jemima smiled: she knew that trick. "But I didn't feel comfortable leaving them there. Petrina was nosing around my bathroom, according to her father, and she had been asking about the sapphire brooch that I had pinned in my hair ever since she saw my photograph on Page Six in the New York Post. When she asked the day before yesterday – before the David Morris party – I told her that I was going to hide them where her grandmother had left them, buried under a red carnation plant below a palm tree. I thought that she would tell her grandfather, who would come to retrieve them. I would then have him caught and, finally, imprisoned. So, I put the earrings in a bag and buried them up at the Rock. When I saw Evie wearing the replicas, I thought they were the originals and I was shocked. I thought Petrina must have followed me and then given them to the actress. I was going to ask her to get them from Evie after the event. I was surprised – I know that her grandfather still wants them for Pytor Petrovich now."

"They must still be up where you buried them," Jemima said, thinking back to James's video. "That was why Evie was murdered, because the murderer also mistakenly thought she was wearing the original earrings. In fact, Petrina told my fiancé as such," she said, shaking the phone in her hand and standing up. "Actually, I need to go. I really have to find James. He didn't have anything to do with Evie's death," she said to Renault. "In fact, I think you should look at the CCTV more closely. I'd certainly like to." She remembered James's text about Milos's eyes and the video where he said something about Colombia…did he mean drugs? Was something hidden in cocaine? Did Milos's eyes look like he was on cocaine?

"He is your fiancé?" Renault asked her angrily, his attitude towards her suddenly changing. "You should have told me straight away."

"Why? He's done nothing wrong."

"As you know, he is a murder suspect, Miss Fox-Pearl, and you could be an accomplice if you don't tell me where he is. In fact, I told Ms Vogel that the police want to interview you at your apartment. I also seem to remember that you had drugs in your body after the gala?" He stood up and started to pull his phone out of the holder on his belt.

"My drink was spiked, as the doctor said, and someone hit me over the head!" Jemima said in exasperation. "I know you think my fiancé is to blame, but please let me see the CCTV of 'him'–" she made inverted commas in the air "–leading Evie back to his room."

"That is classified police evidence. You can't…"

"Please, Monsieur Renault, please. I need to see something, and, if I am right, I will show you," she pleaded. "This is more than just a murder. This is the planned heist you told us about at the Interpol meeting last week. This was why I was sent down here."

Jemima didn't bother to bring up the other diamonds. She had already started to work out where they were – back with their official owner, Pyotr Petrovich, or with his new girlfriend, Petrina. It seems that the theft of the Vogel Vanderpless necklace back in April at Somerset House was a test for Petrina for far more important pieces. Important to him, anyway. The Romanov Sapphire Earrings that his grandmother had wanted fifty-five years before.

## Chapter 33

## Security Room, The Fairmont Hotel

"**C**ome with me," Renault eventually said to Jemima. Just as Jemima stood up, she looked out of the window and noticed Petrovich's boat coming back to Monaco. Without remarking on it, she left with Renault, leaving Fortunata to freshen up and call her husband who was still out looking for their daughter. Jemima imagined that she was currently on the boat, floating back into the harbour with the murderer, jewel thief boss, and over £100 million worth of diamonds, quite possibly around her neck.

Jemima and the Interpol detective took the lift down to the ground floor, which was still full of police officers, while a crowd of paparazzi and news reporters could be heard shouting from outside. She wondered where they had taken Evie's body and imagined it was the same place Pierina Poparic had been when Fortunata identified her all those years ago. Who would identify Evie, she thought.

Jemima followed Renault into an office where there was a bank of video screens. He spoke in what she recognised as Monegasque to one of the hotel's security guards and motioned for Jemima to sit down in front of one of the screens. She had to admit Milos looked like James, but she wanted to prove it was Milos with Evie. He entered the hotel, walked down the steps to the atrium, and went up to the night concierge, presumably to ask for the room key card. After checking his photograph, the man handed over a card to Milos. Evie didn't look terrified but it was hard to see Milos's face. They entered the lift. The screen changed and they saw Milos grab the actress by the arm, before pulling her out of the lift and down the empty corridor to what she knew was James's room.

"Go back to the elevator." Jemima repeated it in French when she saw the baffled security guard shrug his shoulders. "*Super! Pourriez-vous aller plus proche aux yeux du mec.*" The man did as she asked and zoomed into Milos's eyes and she told him to stop. Right there, in front of her, was a mark on the Serbian's right eye. It looked as though the iris was leaking into the white of the eye. It was called a coloboma – James hadn't said Columbia!

"My fiancé, James Courtney, has no such mark." Jemima pulled out her phone to try and find a photo where they weren't naked together. "There you go." Not only were James's blue-green eyes much bluer than Milos's more yellowy-green ones, there was no mark on either of them. She wanted to cry, but blinked back the tears that stung her eyes. "Do you see what I mean? You can even check the photograph of him that you have on the system. That guy on the CCTV with Evie is not my fiancé."

"I will tell Interpol that we need to search for a different man." Renault said to her and told the security guard to get a picture of the close up that was still in front of them on the screen.

"Wait! He was on trial a few years ago for the robbery of a Damiani boutique in Rome. Petrina got him off!" She Googled it and found a mugshot of him, with the coloboma clearly showing.

"*Merci*, Jemima. I am sorry that we thought it was your fiancé, but you can see why." He made to leave with no further apology of accusing James for murdering the world's most famous film star.

"I understand, but the problem is, he is also missing." And Jemima showed him the last video that James had sent her just after 2am that morning. "If you give me a policeman to help me, I can tell you where I think he is."

Renault looked at her and she knew that she'd have to tell him, even without the bargaining, but he smiled. "That is fine. Go back to your apartment and I will send someone to you. I hope you find him. I am going up to find these jewels that Fortunata hid there yesterday."

* * *

Jemima decided to walk back to her apartment along the promenade. It was 7pm and she was exhausted, but she thought a brisk walk might wake her up before her next mission. She worried about what she would find when – and if – she found James. She was trying so hard not to scream with devastation. She pulled out her phone and called Flora – she missed her friend. She noticed a new missed call from Mr Vogel but this time she couldn't be bothered to call him back. She didn't care about his diamonds anymore; Petrovich had bought them and no doubt organised the theft, but now he had them back, thanks to Petrina. They could be done for wasting police time.

"Jem, how are you? How was the premiere?" Her friend answered straight away.

"It was amazing. I miss you." She blinked back tears. Hearing her best friend's voice made her feel emotional – she had so much to say but couldn't find the words. She hadn't even told her about the engagement; the past few days had been so hectic.

"Are you okay? You sound sad."

"I am just tired: it was a really long night." Jemima didn't want to tell her what was going on, for fear Flora would call her mother.

Her phone was beeping and she recognised Petrina's number. She didn't want to speak to her; she wanted to kill her for all the misery she had set in motion.

"I've got to go, Jem – I am in a cafe and it's really hard to hear. But I wanted to tell you that Granny Tinkerbell died yesterday. I saw her at the weekend and she was so at peace; she was in her nineties and wanted to go. But she gave me something for you – she said she'd forgotten to include it in the envelope she gave you after Christmas."

Jemima hadn't looked properly at the envelope, though she knew that it was all about some tiara and Princess Grace. She thought she was probably done with Monaco jewels for the time being, but thanked Flora, said how sorry and sad she was about her Granny, then said goodbye.

When she hung up, she saw a text message from Petrina's number on her screen.

Jemima. Meet me at the Casino tonight at 10pm and I'll tell you where James is.

What was she playing at now? Why couldn't she just tell her or leave her alone to find him herself? Jemima let herself into the apartment and saw that another note from Henrietta had been pushed under her door. Rushing to sit down on the sofa, she opened the Smythson envelope and read the elegant handwriting on the matching blue card.

My dear Jemima,

Colt called me earlier to ask me to look after you, but I haven't seen you in what feels like days. I do hope that you are alright. I realised that I didn't get your telephone number from him. If you ever need to, please do call me on 06 87 38 25 63. If calling from your mobile phone, I think you must add 00377 and remove the first 0.

Fondly,

Henrietta

How nice, Jemima thought, and when she had retrieved her phone from her bag she added Henrietta's telephone number to her contacts. She then went through to the sitting room and flung open the windows and shutters, before going to the kitchen and filled a glass of water from the bottle that she had put in the fridge a few days earlier. She took a large sip and, going through to her room, put her burner phone inside the bedside table drawer, before taking out her engagement ring and putting it on her finger.

Jemima couldn't believe that Danny Vogel had told his mother that James had "tried to get some of the diamonds from him"; he had paid for them, no doubt. She almost felt like calling Danny to ask what he meant but decided against it and went back through to the sitting room and plonked herself down on the cream coloured sofa, splashing water on to the fabric as she did. She felt so helpless.

Jemima texted Renault to ask what time the policeman was coming over and he replied with a casual

First thing tomorrow morning.

She jumped up, spilling more water, furious that James's life meant so little to them. She called Jim and Spyros, neither of whom answered. She tried Delfine but her phone was off.

Suddenly she got a text from Colt.

All ok? Did you find James? We're back and Delfine told me to tell you both that she's going to Joel Robuchon at the Metropole for dinner with a movie mogul. Come! Oh, and I dropped the Ferrari back at the garage... one less thing for you to do. I am now going to bed. F.

Jemima couldn't help but think that he would have been way

over the limit, but she had far more important things to worry about than Milos's Ferrari.

Although Jemima was exhausted from waking up in the Princess Grace hospital over twelve hours ago and spending the day careering around the coastline, she felt like drowning her sorrows and healing her broken heart with the wine she hadn't spilt on the sofa and floor.

Re-reading Colt's text, Jemima decided on a different course of action. She went into her bedroom and pulled out a gorgeous, black Victoria Beckham catsuit and a pair of black heels. She dressed, quickly did her make up, and left her apartment, but not before pinning a Panetta panther brooch that she had bought yesterday in the boutique that she had passed on Saturday carefully above her left breast. Walking as confidently as she could in heels through the couple of hundred metres to the centre of Monaco and the Hotel Metropole, Jemima thought that she was dressed perfectly to meet Petrina in the Casino and find her boyfriend.

See you there,

she replied to her adversary.

# Chapter 34

---

## The Casino de Monte Carlo

As he was renowned as one of the best chefs in the world, Joel Robuchon's two Michelin starred eponymous Monte Carlo restaurant didn't disappoint. Jemima was famished and rapidly ate everything that the movie mogul had ordered for the table. Mini foie gras burgers to start, followed by red mullet with new potatoes and creamed spinach, were just what she needed if Petrina was going to lead her on a wild goose chase later.

At 9.55pm, she thanked the movie mogul and Spyros for the delicious dinner and, kissing Delfine goodbye, left the hotel in which the restaurant was located. As confidently as possible, despite being full of nerves, she crossed the Casino Square to the beautiful cream-coloured Belle Epoque building that was home to the world's most glamorous casino. She was pleased that she hadn't drowned her nerves in anything stronger than lemonade, and any trace of the earlier rosé had been mopped up with the most delicious food that she'd had since she had arrived in Monaco.

Jemima walked up the steps and the same man, who had previously prevented her entry, looked her up and down with a great deal more attention than simply making sure she was appropriately attired.

Turning left into the Vogel boutique, Jemima walked through several rooms until she saw Pyotr Petrovich and his bodyguard, Ivan, standing behind him. Although Jemima quickly spotted Petrina, too, she was disappointed not to see Milos; she had put Renault on speed dial and wanted to get the murderous jewel thief caught with an appropriately important audience. But, since earlier that evening, his photograph had been circulated around the principality as well as further afield, so she hoped that he'd either been caught or was about to be. Unless, of course, he was wearing another of his latex masks, but at least now the authorities were aware of the birth mark in his eye. She actually wondered what Milos really looked like. Was he a doppelganger of James in real life, or had he been wearing a mask to appear as such. Would she ever know?

Jemima was nervous and exhausted of the whole saga by the time she saw Petrina look up from where they were sitting at the roulette table. She gave Jemima a quick smile and waved her over. This girl probably never worried about anything, Jemima thought, and for a fleeting second wondered if maybe she should finally adhere to Alexa's advice and become Petrina's friend. She definitely had the glamorous life that Jemima wouldn't say no to. But would that mean becoming a jewel thief? Didn't seem much of a hardship, Jemima thought flippantly; at least she'd get to have a share of their spoils. She knew it was ridiculous thinking but she was fed up of the day and endless being on the back burner with this girl. What was that phrase? If you can't beat them, join them. And then she remembered that she still hadn't returned the Vogel jewellery that she'd borrowed the night before. Perhaps she should join the Pink Panthers, after all.

When Jemima got to Petrina, who looked absolutely ravishing

in a scarlet one shoulder dress, she whispered to the man to her right who vacated his red velvet seat. Petrina looked up at Jemima whilst patting the newly-empty chair. Jemima smiled a thanks at the poor man who'd been asked to leave and sat down. She looked at Petrina and almost fainted. The girl had pushed her long pony tail back behind her neck to reveal the Vogel Vanderpless necklace. Sitting heavily on her décolletage, the huge 95.71 pear-shaped diamond rested between the tiny breasts, which were only just covered by the beautiful dress that reflected in the enormous, sparkling, D-Flawless stones. The necklace made Petrina's eyes look violet rather than their natural green. So, Petrovich had given it to her.

Petrina saw the direction of her gaze. "Ha. Bet you didn't expect to see me in these–"

"–Again," Jemima finished for her. "I saw you wearing it at Sass on Saturday night, or at least part of it."

"Bravo," Petrina said and winked at Jemima. "Danny said that you knew a lot more about diamonds than one would think."

"How?" Jemima replied, not really understanding what she meant – she looked like a dumb blonde who knew nothing about diamonds! Ha. She'd been reading about fine gemstones since as long as she could remember.

"How what? How did I get to keep them, or how come I am not in prison?"

"Either. Both," Jemima replied, raising a resigned eyebrow.

"Well, Pyotr decided to gift me the necklace after I found the missing diamonds." She smiled and Jemima tried really hard to keep her cool.

"You stole the diamonds – you definitely didn't find them!"

"Well, some could beg to differ there. After all, that ancient supermodel overdosed on chloroform before the idiot of a thief Paul Pratt took the necklace. I just saved the most important ones from becoming part of an old woman's wardrobe."

"Yes, that was clever of you – poor Danny, being used by you. He was quite smitten."

"I know, and I gather you two had a bit of a fling before I took him from you!"

"Well, I got James." She was bored of playing this game with Petrina. Where was James – that was why she was there.

"So, your boss, Alexa, knows all about it; Pyotr told her after she'd had that meeting with you that he had got the diamonds back. But he didn't let on that he had got them from me, of course."

"Why didn't she tell me?" Jemima said aloud.

She was about to ask how Petrina knew about her meeting with Alexa when she remembered Colt had been told to spy on her. She'd first seen him in Cecconi's just after that meeting. Of course, there was also Ivan the Terrible, who was now standing far too close behind her.

"I've no idea; maybe she thought you needed a holiday down here? Or to stop the Pink Panthers from stealing the sapphire and diamond earrings? But you failed there, didn't you?"

"You killed Evie Talbot, Petrina, and got your hands on more than half a million pounds worth of jewellery. That weren't even the original Romanov sapphires that you and your father have been looking for! Evie was killed for nothing."

"These new ones - they're worth that much?" Petrina said, and Jemima wondered how Petrina knew that Evie wasn't wearing the originals. "Anyway, I did no such thing, and we both know I was with your fiancé all night." She looked at the green felt table in front of her. "That was clever of you. To notice the mark in Milos's eye. Took me a while to work out what it was that made him less good-looking than James. Now that's all cleared up, do you want to know where your boyfriend is?" Looking at Jemima's left hand, she continued, "Nice ring. I don't know why you hid it at the party on Sunday and tried to get your fiancé to flirt with me. I guess it's your fault he's gone missing." Petrina waved at the waiter who refilled her glass of champagne and brought Jemima a fresh one.

Jemima felt like throwing it all over her, or ripping the diamonds from around her neck, but the Russian's bodyguard was still dangerously close and she didn't feel like having her neck broken.

"If you want to redeem yourself, then you'll have to win at this table."

Jemima had never played roulette before. In fact, she'd never even been to a casino before, let alone this one. She looked about her at the room they were in – Le Salle Médécin. It was so elegant, so incredibly sumptuous. She'd read on Wikipedia that the additional room was designed and subsequently built in 1910 by Monegasque architect, François Médecin, fifty years after the original casino, by Charles Garnier, was created and changed Monaco forever, thanks to Princess Caroline. The Princess had been a clever businesswoman who, when her son Charles III became Prince of Monaco in 1856 and 90% of the territory was annexed to France, envisaged how to make monetary matters better and helped her son create the Casino. In 1866, she encouraged the renaming of the central area of the principality after her son: Monte Carlo, in English - Mount Charles.

The walls, which appeared to be painted in gold, thanks to the lighting, had huge paintings of mythological scenes, and large mirrors hung everywhere. The ceiling, from which hung the largest chandeliers Jemima had ever seen, had a celestial mural that might have been more apt for a cathedral. Jemima wondered if it was supposed to make people feel forgiven, should they lose or even win millions from their fellow gamers.

"I have no money to play on a table like this! I want to know where James is – not play a game of roulette. Stop messing me around Petrina. Your nasty game is over. And I have the police out looking for my fiancé and your…" she looked past Petrina to Pyotr, "ex-boyfriend?"

"Oh, Milos was just useful. He's gone now." Petrina didn't react to her outburst or elaborate on where Milos had gone, and Jemima didn't dare ask, but she knew how he'd been useful in framing her fiancé, who might well be alive given that Petrina was willing to wager against it. She knew nothing about gambling, but she was sure there were rules about putting down something that you didn't have.

"Fine, I'll bet against my earrings," Jemima said, touching the family diamonds that her mother had lent her before she had started at Vogel. She had nothing else except the ring and she wasn't about to gamble on that. The ring was worth a great deal more than Petrina would ever know, and she didn't just mean sentimentally. She couldn't believe that the diamonds surrounded the tanzanite – which looked more purple than usual under the lighting – were the same as those which hung around Petrina's neck, even if they were the remnants.

"Fine. Guests first."

Jemima, knowing absolutely nothing about roulette, put down a chip on number 8, knowing it meant wealth and was Petrina's favourite number. Out of the corner of her eye, as the wheel was on the other side of Petrina, she could sense Petrina's surprise. And she was happy that, even if she didn't win, she seemed to have chosen her opposition's spot. Petrina put her chips on the black diamond shape and nodded to the croupier to indicate that they were both ready and the only two playing at this particular game.

The croupier spun the wheel and, after what seemed like forever, the ball landed on the 6.

"I win," said Petrina. "You should never have put your chip on a number. The coloured diamond shapes are best – 50/50 chance."

Jemima couldn't believe it. Petrina hadn't cared so much about the number; it was the colour that would make them win.

"You can keep your sweet little diamonds, though," Petrina said generously, before flashing an enormous yellow diamond ring. "I have my new Graff-coloured diamond one!" she said laughing, before turning to the Russian. "Pyotr, darling, let's go back to yours."

"How did you know that Evie wasn't wearing the original ones – the ones that your mother had all along?"

"Yes, that was clever – I wondered why Danny had the designs in his office. I'd no idea, at the time, that Vogel were into making replicas."

They rose from their chairs and Petrina turned and smiled smugly at Jemima as they walked out. Jemima, her all important question still unanswered, got up as soon as they'd left the room, presuming they were going back to Petrovich's mega-yacht and perhaps to the island – the last place she knew had been James's whereabouts. Jemima followed them out of the private room and through the less well-dressed crowds, to the entrance of the casino, seeing Carly, a Texan girlfriend of hers, playing at another table. She was pleased that she'd worn black but wished her heels weren't so high. She could follow them in the shadows back to his boat and then alert Renault to search it for James.

Petrina and Pyotr got into a red Lamborghini parked outside, so Jemima ran over to Hotel de Paris and jumped into one of the Mercedes minicabs that had just dropped someone off, telling the man to follow the Lamborghini. They eventually caught up to them coming down the hill to the port, but, instead of going to get his tender from the main port to take them out to The Romanov Sapphire, Pyotr Petrovich sped his Lamborghini through the tunnel at the other end of the Port Hercule towards Fontvieille.

# Chapter 35

## Milos od Montenegro, Mediterranean Sea

Jemima's car followed them through the tunnel. She was thankful that her minicab was nicely inconspicuous, being just one of many black cars driving around Monaco at 10pm. The pair parked the sportscar, got out, and walked hand in hand towards where she had first seen Petrina and Milos near his boat in the marina.

The car slowly passed the parked Lamborghini, turning on to Quai Jean-Charles Rey, and stopped outside a restaurant called La Salière. Jemima explained to the driver that she needed him to wait until they had boarded the speed boat, and when they had, she paid him with some of the euros Spyros had given her and got out of the car, thanking him for his cooperation. He didn't look fazed; it was probably not the first time he had been asked to follow a couple by what he presumed was a scorned lover through the streets of Monaco.

Jemima took off her beautiful heels, hid them under a bush on the quay, and clipped her clutch bag to the belt around the waist of the catsuit, before running barefoot along the tarmac to the last jetty until she saw the same Englishman that she had seen before. He was with a group of other English guys, who looked much younger than him, drinking bottles of Pilsners and playing cards.

"Ah, it's you again!" he said to Jemima. "Looks like she's got a new man since when you were last here – haven't seen the Serbian for a day or two. Although, I saw someone who looked very like him in the middle of the night."

"What time?"

"Oh, it was when I got back from Jimmy'z, so around 1am."

"Yes, you bottled early, Pete. Not used to our clients being so abstemious when we're paying!" brayed one of the younger men.

Jemima was worried that Petrina would hear her voice and come out, but the doors to the cabin were closed and the engines had just switched on.

"Have you seen that other guy today – the one you saw last night?" she whispered.

"The South African? No, but I do remember him asking the girl what they were doing – why they weren't going back to the hotel. She said that she wanted to show him something beforehand," he said, laughing, before his guests followed suit. Jemima cringed; she knew what they thought Petrina meant. "I guessed they were going out skinny dipping," the man continued. "I wouldn't mind skinny dipping with her." And they all laughed again.

"Your boat's not big enough," Jemima replied quietly, with a wink – but not joking.

"That's what we're trying to do: get him to buy a bigger one! He'll have more luck with the ladies then," said a different guy, and she realised they probably worked for one of the many yacht brokerages that made millions selling superyachts to the super rich.

"Good luck!" Jemima whispered.

Jemima proceeded to climb onto the low platform at the stern of the Milos od Montenegro, untying the two ropes from the pilings on the jetty, before throwing them back on the wooden platform. She waved to the men, placed a finger to her mouth, then tiptoed up the little steps that lead up on to the deck. The men were now staring at her in disbelief. She just hoped that they didn't rumble her.

As Jemima crawled along the wooden deck, she glimpsed Petrina and her companion through the closed glass door, standing at the controls towards the front of the cabin. She hid under the table, in the enclosed banquette seating. She couldn't have planned a better outfit than the one that she was wearing; she just hoped she was as camouflaged as she thought she was.

The cabin door opened and she heard Petrina telling Pyotr that he must have already untied the boat before the door closed again. The boat moved slowly away from its mooring and was soon picking up speed; the increasing swell caused Jemima to feel queasy, and she started to panic that she'd be sick, despite all the food she'd eaten earlier and having left the champagne Petrina had given her at the Casino.

Sitting under the table, Jemima took the phone out of her bag and went to the map app to locate where they were going, but she guessed that it was to Petrovich's place on Ile Sainte Marguerite – in which case, it would take about an hour. To while away the time, she opened The Daily Mail website to see if there was any further information on Evie's murder:

Milos Poznan, recently revealed as one of notorious Pink Panther jewel thieves, is on the run after murdering American-English actress, Evie Talbot, and stealing over £500,000 of jewellery from the Vogel diamond empire last night in Monaco. A £100,000 reward is being offered for any information on the Serbian man. It is known that he…

Fortunately, they had changed the photograph from James's

company website to a hazy one of Milos, captured from The Fairmont's CCTV. Of course, he was no doubt wearing one of his masks by now, with a fake passport and as far away from Monaco and the Riviera as possible.

* * *

After what seemed like the longest day of her life, Jemima was exhausted but unable to sleep, thanks to the adrenaline and nerves pumping through her body. Being hunched under a table on the wooden deck of a boat that was bumping up and down, and speeding along at around 100mph, was also not exactly comfortable. Not wanting to waste the battery on her phone, she stopped looking at it and, to keep herself as calm as possible, peeked through the gaps in the banquettes and focused on the millions of lights along the coast. Eventually, she felt the boat slow down and the engine quieten, until it was just cruising gently to a stop. Jemima tried to measure her panicked breath; they would be coming out any moment to tie the lines to a jetty or pontoon. Unlike in Fontvieille, there was no lighting, except the moon in the clear sky, and she hid as low as possible, still hoping that her catsuit was camouflaging her against the black leather banquettes. A while later, Jemima heard Petrina and her companion open the cabin door, pad across the wooden deck, and down the steps to the little platform just above the water.

"I'm starving," she heard Petrina say. "Do you think we should get someone to take him some food? I wonder if he's let on where your Romanov sapphires are yet?"

"We'd no by now. No, let us eat first. I have a picnic of sushi from Nobu on the boat. I'll send one of the staff to pick it up and prepare it for us. Come on, let's go up to the villa."

Jemima tried hard not to gasp. James was alive! She felt sure that it was him that Petrina was referring to. She peeked through a gap in the banquettes again and saw that the Russian went first and, chivalrously, held his hand out for Petrina as she climbed down the steps from the deck. When Petrina was standing on the platform, Jemima could see she had changed into a cornflower blue, silk halter-neck dress which perfectly matched the sapphire earrings that hung from the cat burglar's elegant little ears.

Jemima didn't need to be any closer to know that these were the ones Evie was murdered in, created by Vogel in its Hatton Gardens's workshops from the original Van Cleef designs. They now belonged to Pyotr Petrovich with God only knows what other treasures the Panthers had pilfered from boutiques around the world. What was the figure Renault had quoted – almost half a billion euros of fine jewellery stolen in under a decade? And that didn't include the Imperial Romanov heirlooms. So Petrovich, one of the world's biggest oligarchs, was the Pink Panthers' 'big boss', or at least one of them. Then why did he pay over £100 million for the Vogel Vanderpless at the gala back in London in April? He could have employed his newest Pink Panther and girlfriend to steal it all right from the beginning. None of it made much sense.

They must have been in a cove because the water was so still. Jemima decided to wait until she was certain they had stepped off the boat before she moved. She had to get on to the island before the servant came to pick up their delicious food.

She heard Petrovich, in the near distance, say, "Your grandfather is still here. I told him to find out from the South African where my sapphires are. Otherwise, they'd both be dead. You can keep those ones – they suit you – but you must never try to trick me again."

So, the Romanov sapphires were still out there somewhere, but why was James being interrogated over them? Why would he know where they are? But, oh my god – Lucky Poparic, the Snow Leopard, was here. She texted Renault to tell him, attaching a screenshot of where they were – although, surely, he'd know 'Palais Petrovich'? Everyone knew where Pyotr Petrovich lived, it appeared. She wished she knew where on earth James was hidden. She had to get to him first.

After Jemima had heard their voices get so quiet they were no longer audible, she stepped off the speedboat and walked to the end of the little wooden jetty, then hid in the undergrowth at the top of the narrow spread of shingle to wait as one of the Russian's lackeys collected their supper from the cabin of the boat. Crouched under a gorse bush, its thorns sticking into her bare arms and getting tangled in her hair, she saw James's smashed phone on the rocks. Jemima stretched out to get it but couldn't reach, so she quickly withdrew her arm as the man walked back up the jetty, carrying a picnic hamper. As Jemima watched him pass, her eye was caught something glowing in the shallow water under the jetty. She got up to look closer but thought better of it, thinking it was likely just the moon's reflection and that she had no time to waste.

Jemima left the tiny beach and followed the man up towards the villa, maintaining a good distance, before hiding in the shadow of the first building she came to. Once she was sure that the coast was clear, she came out of the shadows and realised that she was standing next to what looked like a medieval keep, like the one on her great aunt's island in Scotland. It seemed like just the place you'd keep a prisoner, particularly as she knew that, in France, this type of building was called a *donjon*, which meant dungeon in English.

In the dim moonlight, Jemima followed the wall to a window which had been left ajar, pushed it open, and climbed through it into a large room. It was dimly lit but she could see that James wasn't there. Instead, there was a large table covered in architectural drawings that she realised were of different jewellery boutiques from around the world: Graff in Dubai, Cartier on Rue de la Paix, Mellerio next door on the same Parisian street, Graff again; this time on Sloane Street in London, David Morris on New Bond Street, London, Van Cleef, and Harry Winston in Paris.

Jemima pulled out her iPhone and, to her dismay, saw that her text to Renault hadn't gone through; how would she get off this island once she had found James? She had virtually no signal. Pushing the dilemma to the back of her mind, she quickly took as many pictures as she could of the drawings and of the room itself with all its computer screens. The walls were papered with newspaper cuttings: the original Daily Mail one which gave the jewel gang their moniker of the Pink Panthers, the Pink Panther article from the New Yorker which had been in the folder that Alexa had given her, and pieces about thefts that had happened at the Cannes Film Festival in previous years. It was like a wall of fame: all the Pinks' proudest moments. On one of the twenty or so screens, she saw an excel spreadsheet and walked over to it. It appeared to be a full list of future heists. Sticking out from the computer was a USB stick so she quickly saved the sheet on to the stick and pulled it out of the computer before putting it in her bag, not knowing what else might be saved.

It dawned on Jemima that this was what Interpol had spent over a decade looking for, and it had been right underneath their noses – only half a kilometre from all the festival heists that the Panthers had orchestrated over the years.

Jemima heard a loo flush. She quickly put her phone away in her clutch. Out walked the infamous Snow Leopard, or rather a much older version than the one she'd seen online...

## Chapter 36

# Ile Sainte Marguerite, Cannes
# Wednesday 11th May 12.30am

Nicolai 'Lucky' Poparic had spent the day lying by the ornate Art Deco swimming pool on the sprawling estate of Le Grand Paradis, Ile Sainte Marguerite, when he wasn't over on the small islet torturing the South African. It was dark now and he had just done his nightly naked swim, and was entering the donjon to shut things up and turn on the alarms. He also wanted to check on the South African's condition via the CCTV. He couldn't have him dying before he revealed where he'd left the earrings, but Petrovich had instructed him to leave the poor man in the cave, where, if he attempted to escape, he would no doubt drown from being unable to swim far with all the injuries that he had sustained by being whipped by Petrovich's cat o'nine tails. That was if the water didn't seep into the cave overnight and drown him anyway. Lucky knew that, at this stage, he wasn't going to divulge where the sapphires were. Maybe he really didn't know, after all, and it was yet another ruse of his granddaughter's – this man's maltreatment – and she had them all along. He wouldn't put it past her.

In the daylight, you could just about see the small islet from where he was lying, but he hadn't been to it in over ten years until that morning. In fact, he'd been nowhere, except in disguise. He couldn't. Avoiding prison came at a high price: a self-imposed confinement. He languished under the protection of Pyotr Petrovich, the Pink Panthers' boss, whose aristocratic grandmother had taught him about more than just jewels; he cringed at the memory of having to have sex with the old lady, when he had beautiful Pierina back in their apartment looking after Fortunata. He often gazed at the beautiful Mediterranean Sea, in which he'd taught Fortunata to swim, and his thoughts turned to his beautiful daughter who he had never heard from or seen again after she left in 1977, until Petrovich had pointed out the photograph of her online a month previously. Her daughter, Petrina, his granddaughter, was as beautiful as both her mother and grandmother. And his guilt struck yet again.

He had killed Pierina. It had been an accident but nevertheless she had died at his hand. She was the one who had stolen the Romanov sapphire earrings that rainy Sunday night back in 1956, when he'd persuaded the then chambermaid to get them for him. He still couldn't work out why she had lied to him for so long. Did she want them for herself? But she had never even wore them. He had thought he would go to his grave not knowing what happened to them. Then, when she wouldn't tell him where she had hidden them that night in the Saint Martin Gardens, after he'd followed her, he had lost his temper and pushed her. Before he could do anything, she had slipped and fallen over the cliff into the sea.

After that, Lucky fled and gave up trying to find the Romanov earrings, hiding out in the mountains above the coast, doing odd jobs for people who wouldn't recognise him from his days of owning his restaurant in Monaco. He did a bit of stealing – nothing of real value – until, one day, twenty years later, he looked in the mirror and realised that his hair had gone white and sparse, his face had aged more quickly than ever in the strong sun, and that he no longer looked like the Lucky Poparic who'd once been one of the most feted and sought after men in Monaco.

In late spring 2001, almost exactly a decade ago, he was working for an American couple as guardien of their substantial property in the Provençal hills when he finally decided that, at almost eighty, he didn't want to be working for other people for the rest of his life. So, he dressed up in some smart clothes that he found in a wardrobe, took the Americans' 1954 prized silver Mercedes that had gullwing doors, and drove to Monaco. Parking the car outside what had once been his restaurant, but was now called Sass Café, he sat at his favourite table and started writing his autobiography. To Catch a Cat, he thought he'd call it, and laughed at how much his wife and daughter had loved the original book of the Hitchcock film, To Catch a Thief. He'd dedicate it to them. He spent several hours sitting there scribbling away on the notepad he'd bought from the tabac in the port, where he used to buy his Gauloises, when a Russian man and his girlfriend sat down next to him for a late lunch. The tables were very close and he couldn't help noticing that the man kept looking over at his notepad. It was written in his native Montenegrin, but the Russian seemed to be reading it. Feeling uncomfortable, he decided to pay his bill and leave but, just as he was getting up, he felt a strong hand on his shoulder. He looked around and into the eyes of Pyotr Petrovich.

"I've got a much better idea," the Russian had said in perfect Montenegrin and, leaving the poor girl to come back from the bathroom to an empty table, he marched Lucky to the very apartment the Snow Leopard had woken up in over fifty years earlier.

Grand Duchess Tatiana's apartment in the Belle Epoque building, Sijean, on Avenue Grand Bretagne was not dissimilar to how it had been all those decades earlier. The colours had not changed much but the wallpapers and paints were new and the antique furniture now had several modern companions. The walls were hung with expensive paintings, both old and new.

The Russian explained what he wanted Lucky to do, how he had been looking for him ever since his grandmother had told him, on her death bed, about all the jewellery there was yet to take back from its unworthy, new owners. Included in this was an incredible pair of sapphire earrings that had disappeared from the McCloskeys as planned, but had never made an appearance in the bundles of jewels that he left with the priest at the Russian Orthodox Church, where the old Grand Duchess was now buried.

The man told Lucky that he also wanted to organise a new band of thieves. Petrovich had become their boss, coordinating their thefts that were ordered and then paid for by men as rich as him from Colombia to Queensland. He wanted someone to run the operation for him, from his private island near Cannes, and this was where Lucky would come in. The arrangement would work well; it was too dangerous for Lucky to stay in Monaco, despite his change in appearance. Gustave Renault's son, Charles, was now Head of Police and part of the local branch of Interpol and would certainly have photographs of Lucky Poparic. Not everyone believed that he had drowned after stealing the old fisherman's boat in 1979 and, like the Lord 'Lucky' Lucan, there had been supposed sightings of the old jewel thief over the years.

So, Lucky had been moved to Ile Sainte Marguerite and told to stay there and plan the international jewel heists – the former Snow

Leopard was now the faceless head honcho.

That was ten years ago and, except for a few excursions off, he had remained happily on the island doing Petrovich's bidding and living in splendour. Despite his huge regret of what he had done that day to his wife, he smiled proudly at all he had achieved since he was a poor bellboy in Budva in the early 1950s.

"Lucky, 'ere you go. Answer it. Will yer!" It wasn't the Russian's housekeeper Milena, but Bambi, his girlfriend, who appeared in a leopard print, silk negligee more suitable to someone a quarter of her age. She was normally passed out in bed by 10 pm from all the alcohol that she drank each evening.

"You're up late."

"This bloody thing woke me. It's been ringin' non-stop. Don't know where that old bat Milena is but she ain't answerin' the blower. Oh, it's stopped again." She dropped the portable device on his lap so it hit one of his swollen arthritic knees. He yelped and knew that she'd done it on purpose, the old hag. He wished he could get rid of her and find a younger model. She was lazy and getting fat, which made the 'exercise' not as fun as it once had been. He was surprised that Petrovich let her stay, since she drank all his expensive liquor. He'd picked up Bambi eight years earlier in Dirty Disney – a London Soho strip joint. Lucky and his gang of thieves had gone there to celebrate his last ever, on-the-job, jewel heist. At 70, Bambi was almost as old as he was, but she had made him laugh and had, in those days, been surprisingly good in the sack for someone of her age – of course, more than half a century of paid work experience had been in her favour. That was the 2003 London heist when his new girlfriend left a Graff diamond ring in a pot of face cream. The press had a field day with the similarities to the famous Peter Sellars's films, and dubbed them The Pink

Panthers.

The phone rang again, bringing him back to the present day.

"Yes," he barked in his broken English.

"Lucky, it's Petrina. We're on our way back. Pyotr wants you to make sure that you alarm the *donjon* properly tonight in case James does manage to get off the islet."

Lucky thought that very unlikely, considering the state he had left him in an hour earlier, and that locking the Pink Panther HQ was what he did every night. So, he got up and walked the few hundred yards to the *donjon* to it lock up before heading to bed with Bambi and her snoring.

Going into the small restroom closet, Lucky took his medication out from behind a false panel at the back of the cabinet above the washbasin; he'd rather no one knew of his increasing health problems, particularly Bambi, who was as sympathetic as a snake. He swallowed the pills while looking in the mirror at the locket around his neck and wondered how long he'd have until he was swallowing the two 150mg pills of potassium cyanide that he kept there, particularly now he hadn't been able to get the location of the sapphire earrings from the South African. One would be enough to do him in, the second was for Bambi – if she wanted it.

Lucky did his final business in the loo, flushed it, and, turning off the light switch, walked back into the planning room while doing up his fly. There, in front of him, was a woman in black standing by the table that was covered with the maps and plans of their future targets and heists. She was unarmed, but he could see her look past him at the gun cabinet, and then notice his old .375 Magnum sitting on a side desk beside one of the twenty odd computer screens, including one that showed the cave to keep an eye on the South African. He saw her look at one of the screens, showing the man lying tied up and beaten in the cave.

The woman suddenly wailed and hurried towards it, then turned and looked at the old man with a look of hatred that he had only seen once before: when he pushed his Pierina to her death.

# Chapter 37

# Îlot de la Tradelière, Cannes

Jemima was shocked by what she saw on the CCTV screen: James was lying tied up in what looked like a cave, with water lapping close by. His body appeared to be badly whipped and cut; his face was also cut and his right eye swollen so badly it barely looked like an eye.

"My boss wants his family's jewels back," was all the little old Snow Leopard said when she turned to look at him, his voice croaky and unmistakeably East European, despite his decades on the French Riviera.

"What has that got to do with my boyfriend?" Jemima spat at him, grabbing the Magnum from under the computer screens before he had the chance. Not that she really knew how to use it, other than pulling the trigger.

"You can use that, but then I won't be able to show you where he is," Lucky said. "Or I could take one of these." And his hand went to a gold locket which hung limply from his neck, mingling with the thin tufts of white chest hair. "I have been thinking about it all day. In between trying to find out where he has hidden those earrings. Pyotr will torture us both, unless we tell him where they are – and perhaps it'd be easier just to take one of these pills. But

I wanted to say goodbye to my granddaughter first…." His voice tailed off and he pointed to another screen, showing Petrina and Pyotr devouring the food they'd brought back from Monaco with them.

Jemima felt surreal, almost as if she was in some sort of Hannibal Lector movie. "You said you would show me where James is. Why would you do that?"

"He might confess to where the earrings are when he sees me holding a gun to your head." She gasped and he laughed. "I am tired of this all. I want to go back to Montenegro and die peacefully. My granddaughter has turned against me; she doesn't care. She has got what she wanted from me. I am no longer of use. If I am honest, I am not sure the South African knows where they are. He would have told me by now – after all that I have had to do to him today."

Jemima almost gagged with disgust. "Where is the Serbian, Milos Poznan?" she asked.

"I have no idea. I have never met him. I suppose he is dead. Russians do that when they have no more use of someone. That is the only reason I am still alive, because he wants the earrings. Your boyfriend too."

"Why are they so important? The Romanovs had hundreds of earrings. Why can't he just buy another pair? And why does James know where they are?"

"You will have to ask Petrovich. It was his grandmother who had wanted them, but she died years ago. Your boyfriend seems to know where they are, according to my granddaughter." The old man shrugged his thin shoulders.

"If I help you get back to Montenegro, will you take me to James?"

Lucky took a few seconds to answer, then nodded and told her to follow him, checking the screen to make sure the pair in the main villa would not interrupt them any time soon.

Jemima followed him out of a side door of the donjon and down a narrow, sandy track that was separated from the beach by gorse bushes. They eventually came to some rocks jutting out into the sea and she could see a tiny wooden boat with two oars pulled up on the shingle beach.

"You will have to go alone. It is a small boat; it will sink with three people in it, and I do not want to be left in the cave when you bring him back."

"We could get the Arno from the jetty just up there," she whispered back.

"Too much noise. We can take it to the mainland when you come back. I will wait for you over there."

"Where am I rowing to? I've never even rowed a boat before!" And she thought of how she'd never complain about the rowing machine in the little gym on Fulham Road again.

"Row towards the moon for ten minutes. It will be easy: the water is very still. There is a small cove this side of the ilot. Go in there and then you will find the cave."

Jemima and the old man pushed the boat down the small slope into the water. When Jemima stepped in the sea, she felt her right foot stinging; she must have cut it on the track. She stepped into the terrifyingly small boat and pushed away from the shore with an oar. She really didn't know if she should believe the old man, but she had her phone and, if need be, she'd just float until she hit the mainland. Jemima realised that she could use her phone to guide her, so she opened Google Maps and propped it between her legs on the little bench as she began to row towards the small landmass,

Ilot de la Tradelière. Ten minutes later, she carefully rowed the tiny boat into the cove and jumped out on to another stony beach, wishing she had some sort of plimsolls on as she felt another sharp stabbing, this time underneath her left foot.

Jemima made sure the boat was secure on the beach and looked around until she saw the cave that the old man had told her about. She crouched down and crawled in. She couldn't see anything but she was sure that she could make out the sounds of ragged breathing coming from the back of the cave. She turned on the phone's torch and immediately saw James, inside where the cave opened out into a larger chamber. A black leather cat o'nine tails propped up against a wall.

When Jemima could stand, she rushed the couple of steps to him and realised that he was almost unconscious and had lost a lot of blood, which was all dried on his torso, soaked in his shirt and trousers and on the sand. She wanted to cry but knew this wasn't the time. Forgetting the old man on the beach, she called Spyros, Jim, and Delfine, but all their phones went straight to voicemail. After all, it was past midnight. Colt had said he was going to bed hours ago. Then she remembered Henrietta de Bourbon's note and the landline number that she had programmed into her phone. She called Henrietta's number and prayed that she wouldn't mind being awoken.

"Hello?" said a worried voice.

"Henrietta, it's Jemima." She took a deep breath. "I am so sorry to bother you, and I won't explain it all now, but – well – I need someone to come and rescue me and my fiancé. We're on a tiny island called Tradelière near Cannes."

"Goodness, my dear, that is near Petrovich's place. Are you in danger?"

"Yes, and James is almost dead. It's Petrovich – I am terrified he'll come and find us and finish us both off."

"No! Oh my goodness," said the old lady, taking down Jemima's number. "I have an old friend in Cannes who will come to get you. But you should call the police and call the air ambulance, my dear. They'll send a helicopter."

"We can't use a helicopter," Jemima said suddenly, fear prickling the back of her neck. "Petrovich will hear a helicopter from miles away."

"Yes, you're right. Okay, I'll rally Pierre-Henri and call you back."

Jemima hung up and stroked James's forehead. The tide was coming higher up the cave and she realised that the old man really had left him here to drown. She wasn't going to go back and rescue him; he could kill himself with his pills for all she cared, or wait for the Russian to do it for him. Why the hell had she got them into this – she stared at her fiancé and tears poured down her cheeks as she leant forward to kiss his bloodied face. She then started talking to him, telling him how much she loved him, and how sorry she was that she asked him to play this silly game in trying to catch Petrina out. She didn't tell him about the diamonds and how Alexa, before she'd even started the job, had conveniently forgotten to tell her that retrieving them had no longer been part of her job description.

Jemima's phone buzzed and she saw it was Henrietta. "My dear, he's coming to get you. I told him that he had to do it as quickly and quietly as possible, and bring you straight to the Princess Grace by helicopter once you arrive back at Cannes. I will meet you there, okay? His wife will be with him – she is a nurse and will bring the necessary medical equipment for your fiancé."

"Thank you so much, Henrietta."

"God speed, my dear."

As Jemima hung up, she saw James's good eye open and look up at her. He smiled as much as his bruised and beaten mouth would allow. He was still wearing his black tie shirt from the gala, but it was more red than white now, with blood seeping into the expensive cotton.

Jemima leant forward and kissed him.

She heard James whisper with difficulty, "I hid the earrings. I found them when Petrina led me through the gardens to bring me here. I remembered what she had said earlier in the evening, when she told me her plans and that she had overheard her mother say to her father where she would bury them, but then she saw the replicas on Evie, so thinking that they were the original ones, she didn't think to look. She thought Fortunata had decided against the ruse to catch her grandfather and instead had given them to Evie for the evening. But obviously I knew the truth and when she was turned around and on the phone to Ivan about where to meet the boat. I picked them up for you from under a red carnation plant."

"James! They're just earrings – it's you I want."

"I know, I know. But I brought them to the island, hidden in a secret pocket in my trousers, and when she said she had given the Russian the earrings, I realised that they must have kidnapped Evie, and taken the ones that she was wearing in error. She then told me Milos had killed her and framed me – that I was on the top of the Interpol hit list."

"Where is Milos?" She didn't think it necessary to ask what he really looked like. Did anyone actually know?

"He came to meet us at the boat and handed over Evie's Vogel earrings. But when he was driving it out here, Ivan shot him in the back of the head, tied a spare anchor to him, and dumped his body out in the water somewhere between here and Monaco."

Jemima gasped.

"When we got to the jetty at Ile Sainte Marguerite, I told Petrina that I had hidden the real ones. That she had given the Russian fakes. She was furious. I thought Ivan was going to shoot me too, but instead he knocked me out. I woke up here. The old man, Lucky, has been torturing me all day to find out where they are."

"My darling, I am so sorry. Why didn't you tell them?" She was weeping.

"I want you to get the earrings and keep them. Sell them when you need to, anonymously. But never tell anyone that you have them. Or they will come after you."

"Where are they?" Jemima said, realising that James was talking as though he wasn't going to be with her much longer.

She started to panic. Where was Henrietta's friend and his wife, the nurse?

"I dropped them, still in the little plastic bag I found them in, over and under the edge of the jetty when we arrived on his island," James said, his voice getting weaker. "I tried to show you and whisper in the video as I followed them to the villa, but then I dropped my phone and it smashed on the rocks without sending."

"It did send, I got it. But I didn't see any sapphires. But I think I know where they will be," she said, remembering the glinting in the water she saw when hiding in the gorse earlier.

"You must get them."

"No, they can wait, we can go and get them together – the rescue team is here." Jemima heard the chugging outside and water lapping against the shingle beach. "And you seem better," she said, with as much encouragement as she could muster, although he didn't seem better at all.

"Yes," he said quietly, as though his energy had seeped away again.

Jemima crawled back out of the cave and hobbled down the shingle to the shore where she saw the fisherman and his wife drop down an anchor. She waved to them and they quickly jumped off the little boat and waded through the water to where she was, before following her into the cave.

Jemima sat down next to James and told him that everything was going to be okay, that they would go to the hospital, and she was going to be right there with him. But his eyes and mouth were closed and she realised there was no sign of breathing. She turned around, screaming silently. The old nurse, soaked by sea water from head to foot, felt his pulse and shook her head sadly.

Jemima screamed, loudly this time. James was dead. It was all her fault. And she knew that her life would never be the same again.

# Chapter 38

## The Days after James's Death

They carefully moved James's body from the cave to the little boat and, with a heavy heart and silent tears streaming down Jemima's face, they chugged back to the mainland – only a kilometre away. She didn't even think to go and get the old man waiting for her at Milos's boat on Ile Saint Marguerite. As the little blue and white fishing boat went past all the superyachts in the harbour, with lights blazing and music streaming from the bars and clubs, she heard in the distance the noise of a helicopter. It was coming from behind them, back out at sea. She looked over the stern and saw lights rising from the little island of Ile Sainte Marguerite. Pyotr and Petrina were obviously leaving their paradisiacal isle. They had probably seen on the screen that James's body was no longer in the cave. Lucky was probably dead by then, having had the sense to pop those pills hidden in the locket.

Jemima knew that the police would have wanted James to have remained in the cave, but there was no way she was going to leave him there. She was shocked, grief-stricken, and appalled with the innate knowledge that his death was, ultimately, down to her. If only she had listened to her heart all the times that those nagging doubts had appeared, she wouldn't be taking her fiancé's lifeless body to an icy slab in a cold hospital morgue.

The fisherman, Pierre-Henri, had called his local policeman friend and she could see an ambulance and a couple of police cars flashing their lights on the harbour side. The fishing boat cruised slowly to its berth in the old part of the port, where its neighbours were fellow fishing vessels that had been there for generations, unlike the multi-million-pound mega-yachts moored up close to the harbour entrance in the deeper waters.

Jemima was numb and grateful for the presence of the fisherman and his wife Agathe who took charge for her. They took James's body to the morgue in Cannes, and, as she wasn't his next of kin, said they would have to inform his brother and grandmother in the morning. Of course, Jemima knew she had to do so beforehand. And she dreaded having to face that almost as much as facing the reality of not having James to wake up to ever again. She was taken back to Monaco, where Henrietta met her outside La Radieuse and gave her a sleeping pill, before putting her to bed in one of her opulent spare rooms.

Jemima woke the next morning and, for one happily ignorant moment, forgot the events of the day before. But then the anguish came crashing in like an iron fist to her stomach and she ran to the bathroom to be violently sick. A few hours later, after painful questioning from the Cannes gendarmes, Charles Renault arrived, bringing Agathe with him, who felt just as protective as Henrietta of l'Anglaise as the old French nurse had taken to calling Jemima.

Charles Renault informed them that Interpol and the local Cannes police had extensively searched the Iles Lérins. The Snow Leopard, Nicolai Poparic, had been found dead by cyanide poisoning on the deck of the Milos od Montenegro, with a priceless emerald and gold locket around his neck open and empty.

In one of the servant's bedrooms of the villa, they had found an old lady lying in a dried pool of blood with a bullet through her head. They hadn't yet found out who it was. Of course, Pyotr and Petrina were nowhere to be found – but Jemima had already told them that she had seen a helicopter take off as they had docked in Cannes. The Detective then said that the donjon, in which she had told them were innumerable papers about the Pink Panthers, had been completely cleared of any evidence; Jemima imagined they took it with them in the helicopter. Pyotr's mega-yacht, The Romanov Sapphire, had been taken control of by Interpol but that, too, had nothing incriminating inside.

"So, you have found absolutely nothing linking Petrovich and Petrina to the Pink Panthers?" Jemima asked as one of the officers took her DNA and fingerprints to eliminate them from their investigations.

*"Rien,"* was the one-word answer and, despite the nausea, Jemima almost smiled to herself, a plan forming in her head.

When the police and Interpol Detective had left, Agathe, who she learnt had actually once been a midwife, sat down next to Jemima on the sofa, looked at her, and suddenly asked in Provencal accented French if Jemima was pregnant.

Jemima looked at her incredulously, *"Enceinte?"* before admitting that she had been feeling sick quite a bit recently but had put it down to motion sickness and not eating enough. She then thought back to her last period; it had been so long ago, but the past months, since she had met James at New Year, had been so very busy that she hadn't really registered when her last one had been. She looked at her tummy and realised that her dress, which she had only bought the week before, was feeling quite snug. Although devastated James wouldn't know his child, she smiled and said that yes, she quite likely was.

This knowledge suddenly empowered Jemima. She remembered the Imperial Romanov earrings – one of the two lots of jewels that had caused all this tragedy – that James had wanted her to have and decided to go and get them as soon as possible. She would decide what to do with them at some point, but, for the time being, they were her secret; well, hers and James's.

That evening, Colt arrived with a huge bouquet of flowers and asked if she'd like to do anything. She knew exactly what she wanted to do and called Renault to ask if she could go to the cave and put some flowers there for James. He reluctantly said yes, then told her not to go on to the main island, Ile Sainte Marguerite, which had now been cordoned off as a crime scene by the police.

* * *

The next morning, Colt and Jemima borrowed a little sailboat from an English friend of Henrietta. With a bouquet of pink King Protea, the South African national flower, that she had bought in a florist on Boulevard des Moulins in Monaco, they sailed along the coast to the tiny Ilot de la Tradelière. As they sailed towards the cove and the scene of James's death, Jemima began to weep. She let the tears run down her cheeks. Colt gave her some privacy and swam to retrieve the little rowing boat which was still where Jemima had left it two nights before. By the time he arrived back alongside the sail boat, Jemima's tears had subsided and she stepped carefully into the rowing boat, clutching the beautiful pink flowers.

Colt cast the boat off and Jemima rowed back to the tiny uninhabited ilot. As she walked up the narrow shingle beach and crawled back into the cave, she began to feel the familiar panicky butterflies, but as she laid the protea at the spot where James had breathed his last breath, she touched the small swell of her tummy. She thought of the hope that the South African national flower represented and how she would do anything to protect James's child. She vowed to teach the little person about their wonderful father who had stolen her heart in only a matter of months. She twisted the tanzanite and diamond ring on her finger and felt a small sense of contentment. And then, turning on her heel, she left the cave forever and swam back to her new friend, Colt, leaving the rowing boat behind.

As they sailed towards the jetty of Villa Petrovich on their way back to Monaco, Jemima told Colt that she wanted to get James's phone that had been left on the shore. She pulled her summer dress over her head, leaving her in the bikini she'd bought at The Fairmont only days earlier, and carefully dived over the side of the sailboat and into the clear blue water. She swam as far as she could underwater, coming up for air just once under the wooden walkway, before diving back down to where she had seen the glinting reflection in the moonlight two nights earlier. After a moment, she found them and swam back up under the jetty. She took a deep breath while tying the plastic bag to the straps of her bikini and tucked it hidden beside her boobs, and then swam over to the shore where she had seen James's smashed phone. She picked it up and waved at Colt with it, before swimming back under the water to the side of Colt's boat. With his help, she clambered on board and they set sail again; she had all she needed from there.

Colt hadn't asked what she was doing under the jetty and the two sailed back, eating their sandwiches on the way while sitting in amiable silence. Later that day, when she was waiting for her friend

Flora and dog Milo to arrive from London for the weekend, on one of Spyros's new planes, she received a call from Alexa.

"Jemima – I am sorry for your loss. However, I would like you to come to the boutique as soon as possible." Not a trace of sympathy emanated down the line. "And please will you bring the jewellery that you borrowed for the gala. You really should have returned it by now." Before Jemima could reply, the line went dead and tears sprung in her eyes – the heartlessness of the woman only reinforced the decision that she had made while sailing back from Ilot de la Tradelière that afternoon.

# Chapter 39

## Vogel Boutique, Casino de Monte Carlo
## Friday 13th May

"Jemima, we are extremely sorry for your loss," said Mr Vogel with real sorrow in his eyes. "And sorry for suspecting your boyfriend, er, fiancé," he corrected himself, looking at her engagement ring, knowing that the diamonds were some of the 'satellites' from the Vogel Vanderpless.

"But we want to know what happened to the sapphire and diamond earrings that were worn by Evie Talbot and are supposed to be displayed in The Jewel Museum," Alexa cut in, straight to the point, again without any remorse for her part in James's death.

"Oh, the Russian has them," Jemima said as casually as she could, still shocked but not surprised by the woman's coldness. "He thinks they are the real Romanov sapphires." She lied and waited a few moments before continuing. "He also has the Vogel Vanderpless necklace now, with all the original stones." And she looked at Alexa glaringly. "But, of course, you knew that. In fact, you have known that since just after you told me you were sending me down here to catch Petrina and retrieve them. Why?"

Alexa looked unusually awkward and glanced over at Renault, who was also in the meeting at the boutique. It was only 9am and the sale staff hadn't yet arrived to put out the fine jewellery which was kept in safes overnight.

"I needed you to get her to lead you to the Snow Leopard, and the headquarters of the Pink Panthers," Renault sighed. "I promised my father that I would one day catch him. When we were alerted to Petrina's connection to the Snow Leopard, and as the investigations progressed, I began to realise that she was our only means of doing so."

"With me, or should I say, my fiancé doing the hard – no, dangerous – work?"

"We never meant for him to be involved," Alexa said, still not sorry.

"So, you thought that if I was in danger, it was okay?" And she thought back to that meeting in Vogel only a week before when she had joked to herself that if she didn't take the job, she might be alive for her next birthday.

"But you are alive and well and, as promised, we will promote you to Director of Communications and you can have a pay rise." Alexa had clearly remembered, too.

"Thank you – by how much?" she knew that Alexa only understood money in the most blunt of terms.

"Well, we can discuss that back in London." Alexa looked around at the Interpol Detective, not wanting to reveal how little her Head of PR was paid.

"No, Alexa, you put my life in danger, indirectly killed my fiancé for absolutely no need whatsoever, and you haven't even caught Petrina."

"You haven't got Petrina?" Alexa asked Renault.

"But we got the Snow Leopard," he replied.

"Dead," she retorted. "Unable to tell you anything about the

Panthers' next moves. She looked at Mr V and saw that he was looking very downcast. Jemima knew how much he liked her.

"Mr V, I don't want to work for Vogel in London anymore." She took a deep breath so she didn't cry. "I am actually expecting my fiancé's baby, later this year, and I want to be near to where he died. Nothing will compensate my fiancé's death, or the fact that our child will grew up having never known his or her father. But I do have some demands, or I will go to the papers. Remember, I am good at getting salacious front page stories, and this is a lot more than the Sahara Scott scandal. I think it is fair that you or Vogel pay Mrs de Bourbon's rent for me to stay in Monaco until a few months after the birth – so, until the end of the year," she continued to stunned silence. "I will, of course, need money to live, so perhaps I can work with la Comtesse here in the boutique on events and local PR. You have a big client event here in early August. Or I could always edit the client magazine that we planned to produce? But I want to be paid a properly salary, finally."

Jemima looked at the Head of Police and Interpol detective, "You could help me get a work visa, couldn't you, Detective Renault?"

He nodded, knowing that his part in the deception would cause his demotion, should Jemima leak it. "*Mais oui bien sur!*" he said, as though it was no problem.

Jemima smiled back, with a new sense of power in herself. "Thank you." She had knowledge about him that would protect her in Monaco, she felt sure.

She looked at the Vogels; Alexa was stirring a spoon noisily around an empty coffee cup.

"I have always wanted to edit a magazine," Jemima said. "And where better to launch a luxury client magazine than in Monaco?"

## Epilogue

---

## La Radieuse
## 12th August 2011

Three months later, Jemima Fox-Pearl heaved herself up on her four-poster bed to lean against the pillows and headboard. Her little dog Milo was lying under the covers; she could hear him panting like crazy, so she knew he was no longer asleep, and almost certainly wanted to go for his morning walk. She looked through the gap in the thin linen curtains and could see the sea already sparkling at 7am. Thanks to the summer heat, she had started to sleep with the shutters and windows open and had only a thin white curtain to stop mosquitoes coming in at night.

Jemima took a long drink of water from the glass beside her, still surprisingly cold from the night before, and lay back against the big white pillows. Just as she knew and was waiting for, she felt the little kicks and movement in her tummy, and looked down at the little bump that was growing bigger every day. She was just over twenty weeks pregnant, and her and James's baby had started its regular morning exercises about a fortnight earlier.

Jemima opened her bedside table drawer and pulled out the letters from Granny Tinkerbell, Flora's grandmother, who was now dead but had given to Jemima at Christmas. In the old Viscountess's will, she had also left Jemima a few other top secret documents about missing jewels, including an inventory catalogue of the Imperial Russian Jewels compiled by someone called Fersman. Jemima had pored through it ever since her friend brought it over from Fairfax Park a month previously. She had searched through every page and couldn't find a Ceylon sapphire brooch belonging to the Tsarina Maria Feodorovna other than one with a large pale blue sapphire, she knew that this was the sapphire that had been set into a sautoir by Cartier for the opera singer, Ganna Waleska . Jemima wondered if, in fact, the McCloskey 'Romanov' sapphire earrings that the Russians had been hunting for fifty-plus years weren't Romanov at all. She couldn't help but smile. Perhaps Barbara Hutton had thought it some sort of ruse – to sell them to the McCloskeys on the pretence that they were special sapphires? Anyway, no one would probably ever know, it was yet another mystery of the jewellery world. There was also a document about a piece of jewellery that had apparently once belonged to Empress Eugenie of France, made for her by the royal jewellers, Mellerio – who had made the floral brooch stolen from Princess Grace's bridesmaid Maree Frisby all those years ago. By coincidence, the Empress had given a priceless tiara to none other than Henrietta de Bourbon's great-great-grandmother, Charlotte Burgoyne, and it had stayed in her family until it was sadly sold after the war. Henrietta wanted to trace it, and the Dowager Viscountess's letters and notes would, hopefully, help.

At the back of the drawer, next to the black USB stick which she had taken from the *donjon*, was a nondescript cardboard box. Hidden in cotton wool under her Panetta panther brooch were the enormous Romanov – or rather McCloskey – sapphire and diamond pendant earrings. They were James's legacy for her and their unborn baby. She held the cool stones in her hand and smiled. They really were incredibly beautiful. Maybe, if she was having a girl, they would be hers one day. Or maybe she would sell them if she ever needed to, like their original owner, Tsarina Maria Feodorovna, had with most of her jewels when she'd escaped Russia after the Revolution so she too could provide for her family. Jemima knew that she already had a buyer, but he could wait. He had decided the fate of her and her unborn baby, so she would do the same with his precious sapphires. For the time being, she was staying safely in Henrietta's apartment, until the baby was born. And the Vogels were paying the bill.

Jemima got up and went through to the sitting room, where her friend Flora, who seemed to be coming out most weekends to look after Jemima – or rather, enjoy the Riviera – was still fast asleep on the sofa bed with a copy of *The Vogel Review* open next to her. Jemima tiptoed over and pulled the duvet over her best friend while retrieving the glossy magazine to close and put neatly aside. It was the first issue which had come out at the client gala only a few days earlier. She was so proud of it.

Jemima went back into the bedroom, took off her nightdress, and put on a bikini and a white Zara sundress over the top. Her tummy had suddenly popped out at five months pregnant, but her boobs were massive and she didn't particularly like her newly-acquired frumpy maternity bikini. She called for Milo, who hopped off the four-poster bed and followed her out of the apartment and down the path to Larvotto Beach where they did their daily swim and walk. On her way back, she waved at Henrietta and went to join her at the café Note Bleue. Every morning, the elegant old lady took her two Jack Russell terriers, Tipple and Cocktail, for a walk, before stopping for a coffee while reading *The Daily Mail* that she bought from the kiosk on the promenade one level up from the beach.

"Have you thought about what I said about my mother's tiara?"

"Yes. And I am excited to start looking into it."

"Well, don't do anything until after the baby is born."

"I've little else to do. And I've become rather obsessed with the Empress in the last few months. When can we go and explore Eugenie's Villa Cyrnos in Cap Roquebrune."

"I thought we could go next week?"

"How exciting!"

"And, you know, my dear, you can stay here as long as you like. Even after the Vogels have stopped paying! Your friend Flora does remind me of her grandmother. I remembered after you left last evening, that back in the fifties, Viscount Fairfax and his wife Sarah, or Tinkerbell as her family called her, came over to Princess Grace and Prince Rainier's Royal Wedding. They stayed in the apartment which you are in."

"Wow, I can't wait to tell Flora. She's still fast asleep from all that Pol Roger you gave us last night."

"You only had a glass. In my day, everyone drank champagne when they were pregnant. Of course, I never needed to worry about abstention."

Jemima leant over to kiss the old lady's soft powdered cheek. She wondered if she had wanted children or not; maybe it just didn't happen? But the old lady had become like a grandmother to her these past few months. She got up, said goodbye, and, calling Milo, passed the newspaper kiosk on her way back to the apartment. She smiled with a funny satisfaction as she saw a headline from *Monaco Life*.

After a break of three months, the Pink Panthers target one of Paris's most iconic and oldest jewellery boutiques.

Petrina was now doing her grandfather's work and, after taking three months off, she clearly had a lot planned for her feline friends over the next few years. Interpol and Renault were now after her. But Jemima knew her every move. She had all the details of every single heist and more on the black USB stick, and backed up on her new Apple MacBook Air.

Jemima knew everything that Petrina had planned, and, when she was ready, she would start her revenge.

# The End

# Notes

I was first 'introduced' to Monaco in 2008 when I was Head of PR at Graff Diamonds in London, the fine jewellery brand had a boutique in the Hotel de Paris, run by the wonderful Nicole Rey.

Of course I had heard of the principality before, but knew very little about it other than its Grand Prix and of course, the beautiful Princess Grace. I knew about her a very long time before I did Monaco.

One of my first favourite films as a child was High Society. I think it was this that made me dream of living the high life, it definitely made me want to be an actress like Grace Kelly, and a princess too no doubt! To Catch a Thief and Rear Window are two more favourites.

I only learned about the jewellery heists, at the Hotel de Paris in the days leading up to Grace Kelly's wedding to Prince Rainier, on reading a piece by the journalist John Seabrook, entitled Wedding of The Century. It had been his mother, the journalist Elizabeth Toomey, who had broken the story in the States. She was sent over on the SS Constitution with the wedding party, to cover the week for UP's news service. There is very little online or indeed anywhere, about the thefts – so I used my artistic licence to create the story of the sapphire and diamond earrings being stolen, and the Mellerio brooch from Maree Frisby Pamp. The oldest jeweller in the world, Mellerio, returns in The Paris Connection. The two diamond and gemstone necklaces stolen from the McCloskeys and their value, are described correctly in the storyline.

The sapphire and diamond pendant earrings that I have created, and called the Princess Grace earrings, are very similar designs to a pair of Van Cleef pendant earrings belonging to Elizabeth Taylor. They were sold by Christies in December 2011 in their famous 'The Collection of Elizabeth Taylor: The Legendary Jewels, Evening Sale'. What I have called the Romanov Sapphires, that Pyotr Petrovich is hunting for, are based on a large pale blue sapphire, which really was set in a sautoir for the opera singer, Ganna Waleska and which did once belong to Tsarina Maria Feodorovna, set as a brooch. It became part of Cartier's 2015 Etourdissant High Jewellery Collection and reset as an exquisite cuff bracelet. You can read about it online at The Jewellery Editor by Maria Doulton. However, there was only one Romanov sapphire set in a brooch – not three. These two in the story, I have invented.

The boutique in which Vogel is located in the novel, at the Casino de Monte Carlo, is now Graff Diamonds, however in 2011, this particular space was full of slot machines! Graff's boutique was then in the Hotel de Paris – where it returns this summer 2019, with the Casino boutique still being run by Nicole Rey.

Tetou Restaurant in Golfe Juan, was sadly demolished last year, 2018, but it was absolutely one of the top places to be seen, and its bouillabaisse was renowned as being the best on the Riviera. I went there when I lived in Monaco in 2011 during the Cannes Film Festival, and still remember literally bumping into Brad Pitt who was leaving the restaurant with Angelina Jolie. I still think it was one of the highlights of my year in Monaco, if not my life!!

La Radieuse, where Jemima stays, was indeed the beautiful building that I lived in whilst I was living in Monaco in 2011. I cannot tell you how beautiful the apartment was – it was a dream when I moved in. I still wish that I had never left! I took my little Jack Russell/ Dachsund (Jacksund) terrier Milo out with me and we'd run along the coast almost every day – either East to Cap Martin and Roquebrune, or West through Monaco to Cap d'Ail and beyond. It was just above Larvotto Beach and I remember being able to swim as late as November.

Monaco is a very special place for me and I hope one day, to take my children there and show them all the places I loved visiting. It is so much more than the rich person's paradise that people think – it is hugely rich with over a thousand years of fascinating history, as is the whole of the French Riviera. My heart is still very much there.

# Acknowledgements

Again this book couldn't have been written without an enormous amount of help from various people in various guises.

Firstly I read so many books about jewellery collections of the era and of the history of Monaco. They will be listed on my website www.josiegoodbody.com. As are the articles that enabled my research. Vincent Meylan's book on Van Cleef, was of particular help.

Steven Saltzman, is mine and many other people's, man of Monaco. He saved me at a sticky point in my time there and has remained a brilliant friend and sounding board ever since. I am sure you can tell who he is in the book! My friend Josefine Kristiensen has reminded me of where places are and what they're called, when I can't bear to use Google again! She was the first person to have me to stay there, and we did watch the 2009 Grand Prix together with Ivana Trump from the Hotel de Paris, who told us how hard it is to drive a Ferrari GP car in high heels – thanks to the "annoying paddles" instead of peddles! My friend Anna Rockall saved me once when my drink had been spiked and I ended up in the Princess Grace Hospital – just like Jemima, although I think the bang to my head was because I'd fallen over. I must also thank Carly Sutton for telling me how super yachts are configured. And lastly Stelios Haji-Ioannou who welcomed me to Monaco in April 2011, with a trip around the principality in his classic turquoise Bentley and hosted my 33rd birthday in his insanely amazing apartment overlooking Port Hercule.

I'd like to thank Xavier Rugeroni and Camille Trenda for seamlessly organising, what I know will be the most wonderful launch party at The Fairmont Hotel in June. Richard Livingstone for allowing me to hold it at his hotel. And Jeremy Morris for his generosity in hosting my London launch in his beautiful New Bond Street boutique, David Morris – The London Jeweller.

My great friends Victoria Baring and Wiggy Bamforth both painstakingly read through the book, each at different stages and helped so much with the syntax and facts. Victoria particularly helped me write the roulette scene, without her amendments – Jemima could have ended up losing everything she owned! Wiggy helped me rewrite much of the third draft, whilst starting a new job too! My wonder women!

My godmother Ann Page, who lives in Perth, WA, and generously paid for the publishing of the copies of the book that you have, hopefully, now read!

I have dedicated this to my father, Mark Goodbody, who since my mother died in 2011 - whilst I was living in Monaco, has lovingly looked after my brother and I in every way possible. Daddy came to stay in Monaco with me for New Year 2012, and had a ball looking at all the immense yachts in Port Hercule and laughing at some of their names. He still talks about one called 'Nag Nag'! I think it was just what he needed after the trauma of mum's death, six weeks earlier.

I found an incredible cover designer, Luisa Berta, and the beautiful gouache on the cover is by a Korean jewellery artist called Ayoung Nam. Thank you to both of them! And my brilliant brother Alastair for creating the actual print version of the cover for me.

I would like to thank the Neish family, from whom my husband and rent a cottage on their huge Wiltshire farm. It has been the most heavenly peaceful and perfect place to write, and bring up our son Arthur. We can't wait to bring his sister back here in August!

Although I started writing this particular story in 2011, I have since published two others which come before this one in the series. However, I dipped in and out of this in 2017 whilst pregnant with my first child Arthur, who arrived at the end of that year. He has been the most joyful part of my life so far. And has kept me laughing and smiling while agonising over the story. It was however when I found out that I was pregnant again at the beginning of 2019, that I got stuck in and actually rewrote and finished the majority of the novel, while he was at childcare with his amazing 'nanny' Kirsty, to whom I must give lots of thanks too. I can't wait for his sister to arrive in August, when I'll be back at book four – The Paris Connection.

Lastly, I must thank my amazing husband, Ben, who has enabled me to finish what I started way back in 2011 after Mummy died and I was sitting in La Radieuse, not really knowing what to do. He has taken days off work to look after our son Arthur, so that I can get on with it all, as well as encourage me to keep going when I have been exhausted, pregnant, and despondent. I can't wait to spend a romantic weekend away with him at The Fairmont Monte Carlo one day!

And then of course – thank you to you for buying and reading my third novel – I do hope that you have enjoyed it.

Josie
April 2019

#montecarloconnection

# About the Author

Josie Goodbody worked in PR and Marketing in London for several of the world's top fine jewellery houses. After a year living in Monaco, followed by three in Argentina and Uruguay, Josie now lives on the Dorset/ Wiltshire borders with her husband, their son and little dog Milo. They are expecting a daughter in Summer 2019. This is her third book in the Jemima Fox series. The first and second, The Diamond Connection and The Christmas Connection, are both available on Amazon.

9 781916 146709